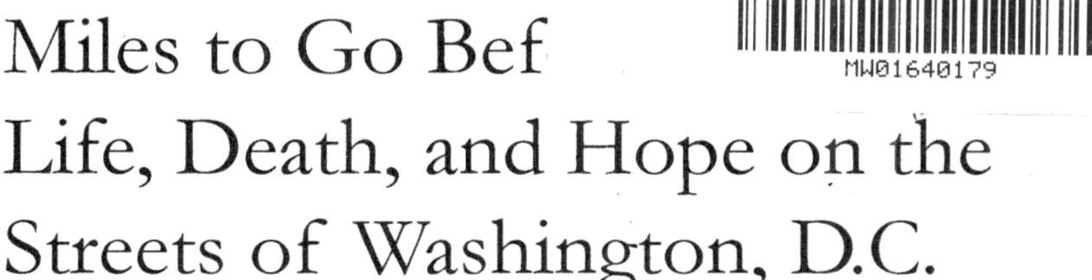

Miles to Go Bef
Life, Death, and Hope on the Streets of Washington, D.C.

By Christopher M. Archer

America Star Books
Frederick, Maryland

Second printing

Hardcover 9781456022181
Softcover 9781424173860
Paperback 9781604414226
PUBLISHED BY AMERICA STAR BOOKS, LLLP
www.americastarbooks.pub
Frederick, Maryland

DEDICATION

This book is dedicated to my brother Bruce, who never had a chance in this life. You have been my inspiration for as long as I can remember. I hope I have lived my life as I know you would have lived yours, and that it has been enough for the both of us.

ACKNOWLEDGEMENTS

I would like to thank those people who made this book possible. First and foremost my undying love and thanks to my mother Linda and step-father Robert, who are not only my parents, but my best friends as well. Thank you for everything. Also, thanks to Patrick, Dayve, and Sonja for the friendship and all the support through the years. You always listened to my stories, read my drafts and gave me the insight, energy, and perseverance to believe I was doing the right thing and this book might one day be possible. Thanks to Spencer for all the conversations and the faith and the wonderful times scuba diving in the Florida Keys and Bahamas. A special thanks to the men and woman of the Metropolitan Police Department and the Metro Transit Police Department, Washington D.C., for doing such an incredible job and under such difficult circumstances. Too few people appreciate what you do each and every day and I hope this book opens a few eyes and sheds some light on the difficult job you have. To the members of the Third District Tactical Unit 1991-1996, you are the most dedicated and courageous people I have ever worked with, and you were, are and always will be my heroes! I will never forget the special times we shared, the education you taught me, and the faith you brought into my life. Finally, thank you to my wife Poppy, for giving so much of yourself and always being there for me. Your unconditional love, support and guidance has, and always will be an amazing gift and inspiration to me and without you, I am lost again.

This book is a work of non-fiction, and the stories contained are true. They are written as I experienced them through my eyes, for better or for worse. In most cases, I've changed names to protect those that do not wish to be known, especially those who are still working as police officers. In other cases, as is the case in law-enforcement every day, I simply did not, or could not get the names of all the people whom I came in contact with and decided to write about, so I have given or changed their names as well. I apologize for this. I was extremely careful and conscious of the fact I'm not only writing about factual events, but also my interpretations of these events as they transpired before me. The difficulty in writing a book about these events, and interjecting my feelings being a part of them, is trying to maintain the careful balance between fact and interpretation. As is the case with many things, we all see things a little differently. I hope I have done this well.

INTRODUCTION

My fifteen-year old brother Bruce, babysitting me one night, quietly stepped into the kitchen and carefully placed one end of a rope around a cabinet handle, then the other end tightly around his neck. Leaning forward to hyperventilate, he quickly lost consciousness and strangled himself to death. He died alone late that night while I slept soundly in my bed, dreaming of my upcoming tenth birthday and all the presents I would receive. My life, and the life of my mother and stepfather would never be the same. In an instant, a piece of me was lost too, and emptiness entered deep into my soul.

Until then, death had no real meaning to me. I was, like most kids, invincible, and so was my family. Suddenly, death became very real, and I quickly wove a protective shell around myself that few people would penetrate. On the outside, I remained the outgoing and energetic kid I had always been. But on the inside, I struggled deeply to understand the meaning behind my brother's death. Eventually, as time wore on and I grew older, I would gradually forget the pain and anger and learn to push these feelings deep within the safe confines of my distant memory. But the emptiness would remain the same, and I would always wonder why it was him that died and not me.

People are often shaped and molded by tragic experiences. I know I'm no different. I slowly began to accept I've spent a large part of my life blaming myself for my brother's death, for being so close and not being there to help him. Sometimes, I felt like I was alternating between wanting to live my own life as well as my brothers. Ultimately, the guilt of having been home, sleeping in my bed while he died in the next room had become almost overwhelming. As I grew older, I cultivated these feelings as an excuse not to care, about myself, or really anyone else. To be honest, sometimes I really didn't care whether I lived or whether I died.

Finally, one day late in the fall of 1988, tired of just going through the motions of my life and feeling sorry for myself, I decided it was time to seek out my own existence, my own place in the world. I wanted my life to have meaning, to justify my existence. But mostly, I wanted to make a difference.

Some people believe that life is a journey. If that is true, then my real journey began in the fall of 1989, on an unseasonably balmy, dark

September morning as I stood awkwardly in front of the Washington D.C. Metropolitan Police Department's Third District Headquarters, in a city I had lived near my whole adult life but knew nothing about. Next to me, at my feet, lay a large plastic trash bag filled with uniforms and equipment. I knew once I opened these doors and stepped inside, there was no turning back, and like the death of my brother, my life would again be changed forever. Something had compelled me to this point in my life and to this strange, alien place. As I quietly passed through the steel doors of the police station, I had more than just the burning desire to serve and protect. I had questions about my life that needed to be answered.

FOREWORD

I hovered motionless; my body submerged twenty feet below the Atlantic Ocean's surface, gently swaying back and forth in the soft current. I was as far removed from the violent streets of the city as one could be. Forty feet below me, through the crystal clear water, a nurse shark quietly skimmed across the top of the reef, searching for food. Hundreds of other fish, each displaying a different color of the rainbow, scurried about paying no particular attention to the shark, or me for that matter. I didn't feel in the least bit threatened. Everything at this particular moment seemed exactly as it was meant to be. I was in awe of such a beautiful sight. I knew the world was sometimes a violent, painful place, of which I had seen more than my share. But it was moments like this that made me realize it was all worth it. I had come a long way from the confusion and anger that dotted my adolescence. For one of the rare times in my life, I was completely at peace with myself and the rest of the world.

Just minutes before, I too had been swimming on the reef below, gliding alongside the shark and other fish. For whatever reason, they didn't seem to take much notice of this strange, large intruder and seemed to treat me as if I belonged here with them. Maybe a curious glance here or there or perhaps a gentle movement away if I ventured too close; but mostly, I was accepted as one of them. I couldn't think of any other place where life was so simple, so easily defined. And I couldn't think of any other place I would rather be. I glanced over at my friend, Spencer, and I could tell he was sharing similar thoughts. He gave me quick thumbs up, signaling it was time for us to return to the surface and reality. I sighed, and reluctantly eased myself up the last twenty feet of water.

As my head popped above the water's surface, I was met by an almost perfect blue sky, dotted periodically with small, white fluffy clouds. The late April sun glistened directly over my head, warming the calm turquoise water that surrounded me. With the exception of our dive boat floating peacefully over the horizon, there wasn't another soul to be found. Spencer, whom I was visiting for the weekend, was floating on his back about twenty feet away, taking in the late afternoon sun. Earlier in the day, over lunch in Key West, he had confided in me, telling me this was often one of his favorite parts of scuba diving—the gentle surface float back to the boat. I had promised him I would try it, but for now, I was content to just stare over the horizon, enjoying the amazing sense of peace and harmony encompassing my body with each passing wave.

Scuba diving has always been my one true love. In my world, all too often cascaded with violence and insanity, slipping away below the ocean's surface and into the deep blue depths provides the perfect escape. An escape into a world where man is not really meant to be, yet for just a few brief moments, is welcomed almost as if he has been there forever. Here, there is no trying to piece together murders, shootings and robberies, or understanding senseless death. No searching for answers to questions that can't be answered. Here, it's just a simple state of existence, in perhaps its truest and purest form.

I had traveled to Key West to visit Spencer, taking a few days off from work to visit my childhood and high-school friend. It was amazing that no matter how much time passed between us, in this case several years, we still seemed to maintain a friendship and an uncommon sense of communion. It's funny, because since our days after high school, our lives had taken such very different paths. Spencer traveled to Wisconsin to study biology at the University of Wisconsin-Stevens Point. From there, he entered into the Peace Corps and traveled to Niger, Africa, where he spent the next two years of his life putting his biology degree and survival skills to the test. I, on the other hand, stayed local and attended Montgomery College. After several years pursuing my associate's degree and a sputtering basketball career, I joined the Metropolitan Police Department in Washington D.C. Yet despite these differences, there was a belief we were both searchers, searching for similar things, and to an extent, had at this point in our lives reached a common point of understanding. Spencer, who is of Sudanese descent, was raised from early childhood by several relatives following the death of his mother. Although not altogether the same as mine, we had both grown up in tumultuous environments that would later test our ability to maintain an even keel. As was the case on my previous visits, much of our time was spent under water, sharing in our mutual love of scuba diving. I think, though, perhaps what I liked most about spending time with Spencer was the time we spent out of the water, either hanging out in the dive boat, driving around Florida, or just sipping a few beers in any one of Key West's bars. It was in one of these bars, Barefoot Bob's, where we had one of our best conversations, and I first explained to him why I wanted to write about my experiences as a police officer.

After sharing with each other the latest of our life's twists and turns, our conversation turned to our career choices, and the effects they've had on our lives—mine as a police officer, and Spencer's as a biologist with the fish and wildlife service. Both of us, for whatever reason, and by distinctly different paths, chose a life of public service. I think this might be typical of persons raised under difficult circumstances, as both of us were

After a few rounds of cold Bass Ale and a heavy dose of The Grateful Dead, our conversation took an interesting turn. Several hours earlier, we had passed by an old house that once belonged to Ernest Hemingway. As we stood in front of his house, Spencer reflected on how Hemingway was one of his favorite authors. I asked him why, and he answered that Hemingway wrote about real people with real problems in a language that was both beautiful yet gritty, and these were things he could relate too. I agreed. I was not exactly an expert on Hemingway's works, but I had read enough to understand what he was saying. We both agreed that we appreciated the way Hemingway mirrored his life through external characters and how he used simple, short sentences to build complex dialogues. For me, just the mere fact of being here, standing in front of this house had a very surreal, moving effect. Not in an egotistical, comparative sense, for I certainly would never be so arrogant as to think I could ever write as eloquently and passionately as Hemingway, but more in the sense of understanding and appreciating the desire to write stories about real life and real people, in simplistic terms. And it was here, standing on this dark street at one o'clock in the morning that I realized a little bit more about why I had decided to write about my experiences with the police department. It's funny how these revelations come to us, sometimes when we least expect it and quite often in the strangest of places. I realized I was not just searching for personal answers about my life, and the death of my brother, as was my original intent, but I also wanted to tell stories about other people's lives, and how they had influenced and affected me and helped me to develop an understanding about the events of my own life.

I had just finished my third Bass Ale when Spencer turned his gaze away from a group of topless women riding Harley-Davidson motorcycles cruising down the street, the effects of a motorcycle celebration being held over the weekend. He had a look of deep contemplation covering his face, and for a moment, I think I was a bit afraid of what he was about to say.

"Do you know what I sometimes wish?" he asked, wiping the back of his hand across the base of his mouth. I briefly held my breath.

"No. What?" I responded curiously. My head moved with the beat of Jimi Hendrix's "Land of the New Rising Sun" playing in the background.

"I wish when I was younger, I would have tried to pursue something more artistic," he said. "Like music or art." I knew the direction he was going, and the exact meaning of his words.

"Me too," I answered. "I've always had this great admiration for people with artistic talent, especially writers. I just think it would be such an amazing thing to be able to create something, something from inside of me that could have a lasting effect on someone else."

"That's it exactly. That's what being an artist is about," Spencer agreed, a smile covering his face. "It's about being able to express an idea or a belief, and then sharing it with someone else." Unlike Spencer, who played guitar, I'd never really taken to any artistic activities, at least not until the last few years, when I took to dabbling with writing short stories. But up until this point, I'd never really thought of my writing as anything other than a way for me to understand my inner feelings. For me, writing had simply been a means of trying to understand the elements of my life, the death of my brother and the course my life had taken.

"You know, maybe that's what your book is really going to be about," Spencer said, referring to earlier discussions about my writing. "Maybe it's your way of reaching out to someone else. Showing them a small part of the world they haven't experienced." I listened to each word intently. He was right. Maybe I hadn't really thought much about it, but I did want it to touch other people. Just in the way he and I talked about our jobs, our lives, and our goals and ambitions, I also wanted to talk to people about being a police officer. And coming from Spencer, who knew me about as well as anyone, this was not just a passing statement. He had endured many long hours listening to my stories, not so much as they appear in my book but more as good friends spending an evening together catching up with the latest events. He had as good an idea as to what my book would shape into as I did. I took a small sip from a fresh glass of beer. The cool liquid soothed my parched throat, still salty from our earlier dives.

"Maybe you're right," I answered. "I think I've spent so much time searching for answers to my own personal questions, I've forgotten that maybe it's just as important to tell these stories in the hopes of getting other people to understand a piece of the world that's too often ignored." I knew Spencer could relate to this. In some ways, he and I were in identical situations. His job with the Fish and Wildlife Service had recently taken its toll on him, just as my job had done with me. Trying to protect the natural environment of the Florida Keys from over-development, as he did each and every day, certainly had to be a most formidable, depressing task. I know we had spent many hours sharing with each other the sometimes hopelessness of our careers. Certainly, our jobs lent themselves to a side of the human race at its worst, and provided a true test to our abilities to motivate ourselves to continue pushing forward. It was in this thought that I realized I wasn't really writing a book, per se, as one would define the term book. What I was doing was simply sharing a piece of myself transcended through my experiences.

"I remember when I went on that ride-along several years ago. When we went the wrong way on that one way street, and this kid on a bike yelled to your partner, "Hey, you're going the wrong way," and your partner yelled back, ""Fuck you, I'm the police, I'll go anyway I want to. Mind your own fucking business," I couldn't believe he said that." Spencer acknowledged after taking a sip of beer.

"Yeah, I guess that's all too often the perception people get when they think of police officers," I answered. "Just like the perceptions we all get about drug dealers, prostitutes and shooting victims. But perception is not necessarily reality. I think maybe that's why it's important for me to try and paint a different picture."

"I agree," Spencer said.

I took a moment to reflect on my own life. I have to admit, I have a hard time finding any memories from my childhood, or at least from the time before I was a teenager. I'm sure this has a lot to do with my brother's death, and that I've pushed many of them deep into my subconscious. Yet images still came to me in brief pictures. Not haunting images, as they had once been. I had long since dispelled most of these. Rather, they were quick, hazy, flashes. The one's that seem to keep creeping up when you least expect them. I thought about the devastation my brother's death had on my family for so long. It's amazing it didn't destroy us. I thought about my mom's fight with depression. I thought about my high school friend Don, who took so much time out of his life to be there for me, but who ultimately died of cancer while I was still in high school. I thought about my biological father, who was an abusive alcoholic and who skipped out on my family when I was five years old. I thought about my step dad, who unselfishly stepped in after my brother's death to guide my mom and me in a positive direction. I guess mostly, I thought about the questions surrounding my life, and how long I had been searching for this mythical sense of purpose. I could see why these seemed to be the motivating issues behind my desire to write. Deep down inside, I wanted someone to jump out and say, "Hey, everything's going to be all right. You're not the only one with these types of problems." But as I began to write, I realized I also wanted to show others what my life is about, and how my experiences with the police department affected me as a person and as a human being.

I remember an article I wrote for the *Washington Post* several years ago, and it appears in this book. It was about a woman on the street, who saved a man's life with a piece of dirty newspaper and a shirt after he had been shot in the chest. For me, sharing this experience with this woman was a moment of complete awe, another turning point in my life. I was permanently touched by how this woman had affected me, and how she had touched my life in such an amazing and positive way. And I thought she deserved to be recognized for this. So I wrote about the incident in the paper. Several weeks after the article ran, I received a small handwritten note from a woman who had read the article. She told me it had made her cry. I was shocked. I couldn't believe that something I wrote could have such an effect on someone else. I felt a strong sense of pride, not so much for myself, for I had really hadn't done anything at all. Instead, I felt this pride for the woman who was the inspiration for my story. I realized not only was I writing in search of my own existence, but also to place a face—and a story—behind the people with whom I came in contact with on the streets as a police officer, and who had such an amazing effect on my life. Perhaps if they had such an effect on me, then maybe they might have similar effects on others.

I have come to understand both what my book, and what my life, is really about. It is about making a difference. I know that sounds silly, but sometimes, I just want to scream out for the people I meet who don't have a voice to scream out for themselves. For me, this has been a subtle, surreal fight. I choose to scream through writing. To scream out for the everyday people who make up the world of a police officer. The people we read about every day, but never really know much about.

I've decided I want to give something back. So bad, I can taste its sweetness on my lips, like a soft, ripe peach on a blistering hot summer day. I want people to cry, just as I have cried many, many times. I want people to be afraid, just as I've been afraid many, many times. And I want people to feel the pain of someone's death, just as I have many, many times. Finally, I want people to feel the tingle in the spine that I feel when I realize how much people can overcome and endure, and still strive to change our world for the better.

Mostly, I wish I could just take everyone's hand, and show you the world I've seen for the past few years. I wish you could see and experience the people I've met. And if these stories affect you, and give you a better understanding of a piece of the world you haven't experienced, then I will have succeeded in a way I could never have imagined. So do me the smallest of favors. Take a hold of my hand for just a few, brief moments and come with me on my journey. Perhaps it might inspire you to do the same.

PART ONE

DEATH

"The lack of existence; the state of being dead."—Webster's New American Dictionary

What if I told you there was no place
You could run to
To hide from your fears
Where good is bad, and bad is good
And all the cries you cry
No one can hear

Is it heaven, is it hell
Life is what you make it only time will tell
Is it heaven, is it hell

-24-7 Spyz

CHAPTER ONE

Officer Lyons never said much, either to me or anyone else. I guess this was somewhat comforting knowing it wasn't just me, and I knew he had the heavy burden of teaching me how to be an effective police officer, or as I would learn later, how not to be a major fuck-up. I was, and always will be a product of the District Of Columbia Metropolitan Police Departments infamous classes of 1989-90, a time period the United States Congress mandated the District of Columbia to hire a ridiculous amount of new police recruits, and gave them little more than a few years to do so. It was through this experience I came to learn that, although given more than adequate academy training, many new hires slipped through the cracks and the city was soon inundated with officers with criminal records, or who were simply just not qualified. Thus, during my initial field training period, a time in which we worked with veteran officers assigned to teach us the practicalities of our academy training, I quickly learned aspirations leaned more towards keeping us out of trouble and weeding out the fuck-ups than actually providing us with real, tangible on the job training. Don't get me wrong; I had some amazing training officers, who served the city with diligence and dedication and taught me many of the things I needed to become a good police officer. But, like so many other things in life, I knew this was more my chance to gain some confidence, garner some kind of working knowledge of the basic, everyday routine and prepare myself for the utter chaos that would soon serve as my career. Truly learning how to become a cop would come much later.

Anyway, back to Lyons. Aside from his quiet, shy demeanor, I knew nothing about him other than he had served over ten years with the department and was known for having a laid back personality. For me, it didn't really matter who I was working with. I was scared shitless, pure and simple. I knew I had about two weeks to ride with him and I only hoped I would carry my weight and keep from making a fool of myself.

"All right" was Lyons's answer to everything, regardless if it was a question, comment, or statement. Sometimes, as we rode together, I would purposely wait until a dead silence filled the air and I was sure he wasn't paying attention. Then, I would say something completely fucked up or ask some crazy question that had no answer. Regardless of what I said, like clockwork, he would just glance my way with a smile and simply answer "All right." I would sit back and laugh, but I sometimes I wondered if this was just his way of making fun of me. Either way, it was still quite hilarious. I really enjoyed working with Lyons. He knew the so-called "ropes," of the job and I knew I would learn a lot from him. I think he liked me as well, and I stress the word think, because I also suspected that deep down inside, he sometimes wished I would just shut the hell up and stop bothering him with my constant barrage of questions.

Lyons had two very noticeable physical traits; his walk, which was more of an up and down bobbing motion, like a buoy in the ocean, and his ever present smile. Not a full, Cheshire cat smile, but a slight, sneaky smirk, which always seemed to give the appearance of someone who had just been caught snatching cookies from mom's cookie jar. His looks, coupled with his quietness, really complemented his laid-back style of police work. This I admired greatly. I had never seen Lyons lose his cool, which was a rare quality, especially in a major city police department and I knew in the face of pressure, he would always conduct himself professionally.

It was a chilly Tuesday morning, the kind where you can't quite figure out whether to roll down the car window a notch and freeze to death, or turn on the heat and sweat like a waterfall. Ultimately, you just crack the window a bit, crank the heat and hope for some kind of symbiotic balance. It must have been somewhere around 11:00 a.m. I hated Tuesdays, especially working the dayshift, which was from seven in the morning until three in the afternoon. I was never much of a morning person, and while most of the world was settling down enjoying lunch, I was still trying to exercise the sleep demons from my body. Dayshift was usually very slow, even in a city like Washington, D.C., which was fine by me. I was still learning and could always use the spare time to engage in

Lyons' vast, and as I kidded him, untapped police knowledge. A steady flow of mid-day traffic filled 16th Street in the Northwest quadrant on one of the city's busiest roads.

"We can eat at Trio's up on the "Hill." That is, if this traffic ever lets up," Lyons blurted, probably in response to my now grumbling stomach.

"All right," I answered, trying my best to mimic him. He glanced at me and smiled and we both shared a quick laugh. Trio's meant pizza, the best in the area, and the "Hill" meant Adams Morgan, an ethnically wonderful and diverse neighborhood with some of the best restaurants around. Perhaps the only thing about Lyons that really unnerved me, and today was no exception was his preference to wearing his uniform hat while driving a car. I thought this was silly, but with discretion being the better part of valor, I decided to keep this little nuisance to myself and save it for a later day.

"Scout car eighty-five," sounded a low monotone voice coming from the car radio.

"Shit. Not now," Lyons shouted. "It never fails. As soon as you try to eat, that stupid, godforsaken piece of electronics wants to pay a social visit. There's just no such thing as eating in police work."

"Scout car eighty-five...ten four," I answered sarcastically into the radio microphone, hoping the dispatcher would detect my distinct tone of displeasure. The code of ten four signaled my acknowledgement of the transmission and alerted the dispatcher we were a two-man car.

"Scout car eighty-five, respond to 2420 16th St. and check on the welfare in apartment 107. The complainant states the occupant of this apartment has not left for several days, and family members are concerned with his whereabouts," explained the dispatcher.

"Scout car eighty-five, responding ten-four," I sighed, unable to think of anything other than my grumbling stomach. My thoughts played back the dispatcher's voice as I tried to anticipate purpose of our assignment. If the family was so concerned about his welfare, why didn't they just check on the resident themselves? Why did they need the police to respond? This didn't really seem to be what I considered a police related function. Oh well, I was just a rookie, and I had been forewarned many times that a cop's job was both diverse and endless. I quickly crammed several sticks of chewing gum into my eager mouth, hoping to subdue my hunger pains just a little while longer. Thankfully, 2420 16th St. was only a few blocks away, northbound, which was the direction we were traveling anyway.

Within five minutes we were on the scene of the assignment. Lyons slowly eased our car into the semi-circular driveway, pulling to the front of the building. He was out of the car first, slamming the driver's side door with vengeance. He was holding his uniform hat in one hand and his portable radio in the other. Seeing him reminded me of being taught to always keep our hands free. If one of my supervisors ever saw me with both my hands full, which meant I couldn't reach my gun, they'd have a fit. I can still hear Sgt. Yancy, one of my favorite supervisors, and her screeching voice, "Archer, how the hell are you going to grab your gun if you have your hands full!" I would immediately drop whatever I was holding in a frantic attempt to free up my strong hand. I grabbed my notebook and baton, disregarding my hat, which I had long ago stuffed under my car seat earlier in the morning. I hated them with a passion. They made us look like bus drivers (no offense intended). Slowly I opened my door and stepped out into the chilly autumn air. We both began the short walk to the front door, neither of us saying a word.

The Dorchester House is a massive apartment complex taking up the entire corner of 16th street and Kalorama Road and one of the largest for several blocks. Not only was it tall, at least six stories, but also had two wings expanding both east and west, making it appear much more like a hotel than an apartment building. I was sure there must be hundreds of apartments inside. The first think I noticed as Lyons pulled open the huge glass front door was how neat and orderly everything seemed. The entrance lobby was huge with dark green plush carpeting and light colored walls.

"Shit, one hell of a place," I said to myself, but loud enough for Lyons to hear.

"It's all right," Lyons answered as he scanned the lobby. I was busy taking in my surroundings, briefly imagining we were in the 1920's and awaiting some swing band to start playing.

"Officers! Officers! I'm glad you're here," came an excited voice from off in the distance. From around the corner scurried a small, short man wearing glasses and a dark blue suit. He was quickly making his way towards Lyons, his hand extended forward. Lyons accepted his handshake and waved me over. "I'm the manager. I was the one who called."

"What's the problem, sir?" Lyons asked calmly.

"There's this man who lives in apartment 107. He's a teacher, and well, someone from his school called my office this morning and asked why he hadn't shown up for work the last few days," he said. "This is very unlike him, you know. Well, I told them I hadn't seen him for several days, but I would check on him. When I knocked on his door, no one would answer. I'm very concerned. There's this horrible odor coming from his room. God, it's just terrible. I can't imagine what's going on."

"What kind of smell?" Lyons asked hesitantly. I could sense some apprehension coming from Lyons's voice.

"It's a horrible, rotten smell."

"It's OK, sir. We'll check on it. Do you have a master key for this apartment?" Lyons asked with a slight grimace on his lips. I could tell he had something on his mind.

"Yes, I do. Shall I go fetch it?"

"Please. And then we'll need you to show us exactly where apartment 107 is?" I chimed in, feeling silly standing around not saying anything. Lyons quickly glanced at me with an expression basically advising me to shut my rookie ass up.

"Have you talked with anyone else, someone who knows this man?" Lyons asked. "You know, maybe someone who could give us some information?"

"No, I haven't. You know, it's not unusual for him to stay in for a few days. He kind of keeps to himself a lot," the manager answered as we followed him into a long and dimly lit hallway with apartment doors evenly spaced on each side. We turned a corner and walked into an office. Lyons and I waited outside, neither one of us saying a word. After a few moments, the manager returned with a set of keys in his hand.

"I have it. Are you ready to go?" he said with a tone of excitement in his voice.

"Yeah, let's go" answered Lyons. We followed him around another corner and down a hallway that was exactly the same as the one we had just traveled.

"Are all of the hallways exactly the same?" I asked.

"Yes, basically," the manager answered. I wondered how anyone could find his way around. I was glad we were with someone who knew the building, or else I would've been lost some time ago.

"It's right around the next corner," the manager shouted over his shoulder. Lyons was directly behind him, and I was slowly bringing up the rear.

Suddenly, Lyons stopped in his tracks and turned his face back towards me. A look of utter disgust enveloped his usually cheerful face. I stopped immediately, startled and confused. I looked ahead towards the manager, who had stopped as well. He too had the same look of disgust on his face. What was going on? Suddenly, my nose was assaulted by the foulest smell I had ever experienced. Only this was no ordinary smell. This smell traveled through the air in a thick cloud, grasping my face and body like a vice. I became lightheaded, swaying softly in my tracks. With each breath, I could feel this strange scent entering my body, invading my lungs. I began to choke. I looked over at Lyons and saw he was having similar difficulties. The corners of his mouth were curled up to his ears like a clown sucking on a lemon.

"Shit, shit, shit!" Lyons repeated over and over in a low grumbling voice.

"What? What the fuck is that smell?" I yelled back.

"That's the smell of death, man, a stinker." As I listened to the word "stinker" roll from Lyons's mouth, I wasn't quite sure exactly what he meant. The word, so easily defined, just wouldn't register in my head. Although I had absolutely no idea what awaited us in apartment 107, what I did know was I was no longer hungry, and I didn't think I would ever eat again.

The manager led us slowly around the corner. My mind kept repeating the words "death" and "stinker". I knew we were close because the smell was now everywhere, in the air, on the walls, even on my uniform. It was getting thicker and thicker, like a sticky humid summer day. I couldn't talk, I couldn't think, and save for a few short gasps, I couldn't even breathe.

"Right here, officers," the manager said in a shallow, frightened voice pointing to a door in front of us. With a loud thud, Lyons rapped on the door several times with his baton. We waited a few moments. There was no response. Again Lyons rapped on the door, only this time a little harder. A few moments passed and there was still no answer.

"Open the door!" Lyons shouted as he turned to face the manager. He had the key ready and gently slid it into the top lock and turned it slowly. I instinctively stepped back and slipped safely behind Lyons's body. This seemed to be a comfortable place to be for the time being. An eternity must have passed before I heard the lock catch and turn. Lyons reached out with his baton and slowly pushed open the door. Both of us had our guns drawn as the three of us eased forward into apartment 107.

"Get off of me!" I said nervously as the manager clung to my back like a backpack. He was pushing me into Lyons, which I am sure was really pissing him off since I was already pretty much climbing his back as well.

"I'm sorry," he answered softly.

My eyes immediately fixed on the far end of the room and began to scan first left and then right. The apartment was very small and neat, probably an efficiency. There wasn't a foyer and I didn't immediately see any hallways. Just one big room divided into two smaller sections. As Lyons and I continued in, I could see a living room, then a small kitchen, which was separated from the rest of the apartment by a large curtain that was pulled open. Next to the kitchen was a small hallway, maybe five to ten feet long, leading back to a small bathroom. The bathroom light was on. In the living room was a couch, a small wooden chair and matching coffee table. Across the room, directly in front of me were a window with shades pulled down and a table with a metal lamp sitting on top. My eyes continued to scan to my right where there was a metal frame bed with a night stand on the left. And it was at this exact moment that I saw my first dead body.

Tingling chills crawled up my spine as I noticed the body lying face up on top of the bed. A slight trickle of dried fluid flowed from the side of his mouth to the mattress, where it formed a small dried stain on otherwise clean white sheets. His head and stomach were extremely bloated and both his arms were protruding out from beneath the sides of the sheets. Both legs were extended straight, his feet dangling over the bottom part of the mattress. I heard Lyons grumble something as he slowly walked towards the bed. I think he said, "Meet Mr. Smell."

"Get on the radio and advise the dispatcher we need an ambulance here. Advise we have an unconscious man, and we also need a Homicide Detective," Lyons said calmly. I barely heard him, my eyes still transfixed on the body in the bed. Not even the horrible smell could distract my curiosity and shock at seeing death so up close and personal.

"Come on Archer, we need that fucking ambulance!" Lyons shouted, smacking me hard on the shoulders.

I quickly scurried out of the apartment and headed down the hallway. I needed to find a location that would provide a clear radio transmission. About halfway down the hallway, I lifted my portable radio to my mouth and called the dispatcher. Surprisingly, she answered clearly, and I was quickly able to advise her of our situation and what we needed. Soon, I realized my new vantage point had placed me safely out of reach of the horrible smell, and I took advantage of this with several deep breaths of fresh, clean air. Feeling slightly refreshed, I made my way back and when I arrived, Lyons was waiting for me at the door.

"Take a look around and see if you see anything suspicious. But don't touch anything!" He said. We can't really start with anything until Homicide gets here. I'm going back with the manager to his office and check to see if they have any family members on file and their phone numbers. I'll be back in a minute. Don't let anyone in this room without my permission, unless it's a Detective, OK." I could tell he was trying not to sound too bossy, but I understood. I was still a rookie, and even though I felt confident in how to handle this situation, I knew Lyons still felt a little uncomfortable with my abilities.

"No problem Lyons. I'll get on it right away and start taking some notes," I answered confidently. As I was talking, my eyes kept glancing over towards the body. Lyons and the manager left. I was on my own.

It took several minutes for me to gather the courage to walk back into the apartment alone.

"Hello?" I asked myself as I eased into the living room. I knew no one was around to answer, and if someone had, I'm sure I would have had a heart attack right then and there. My breathing was in short, carefully selected bursts. I thought of this as "stink breathing". It became an art to suck in just enough air to breathe yet not enough to let too much stench in. Despite this new technique, every few seconds I still gagged on the odor still hovering around me. How could anything smell so freaking bad? I made my way into the living room and began looking around. For the next few minutes, I carefully looked for anything out of the ordinary; Nothing. No signs of struggle. No furniture knocked over and no bloody weapon lying on the floor. Finally, after feeling confident scanning the apartment, I took a seat at the opposite end of the room and waited for Lyons to return. I was mentally drained, and there was nothing else I could do. The smell was beginning to overwhelm me. I closed my eyes and tried to think of anything other than the man lying on the bed across the room from me. I became very, very tired.

For a moment, I remembered back when I was a child, maybe seven or eight years old. I was walking home from school, carrying my books in a bag over my shoulder and a football under my arm. The sun was shining brightly in the sky and the warm spring air reminded me of the upcoming summer vacation. I couldn't wait. As I rounded the corner of an apartment building and started across the grassy courtyard towards my home, I caught a glimpse of an older kid standing on the sidewalk just in front of my door. He was holding a long tree branch he had pulled off of a tree.

"Hey kid. Where do you think you're going?" He said smiling. I froze in my tracks, now only a few feet away. I didn't say a word.

"I guess you didn't hear me punk. I asked you where you're going," he said again, standing with his arms crossed. He looked at least twelve or thirteen years old, and I certainly didn't recognize him from the neighborhood. My knees began to shake.

"I'm going home," I answered.

"Not until you give me that football!" he said as he dropped his right arm, extending the tree branch to the ground. "And everything else you have!" My gaze dropped to the ground. I didn't want him to see how afraid I was. Slowly, I dropped my book bag to the ground, letting it come to rest along-side my feet. My only hope was to run. I was fast, very fast, and had never been caught or beaten in any race. But this was different. He was blocking the only path to my house and safety. Even if I got past him, I would still have to make it to my door.

"Give up the football and empty your pockets!" He shouted. He was losing his patience. "Or else!" He began whipping the tree branch through the air. It made snapping sounds as it whizzed across the front of my face. I had to do something fast. Gathering all the courage I could muster, I threw the football with all of my force into his stomach and sprinted past him. He buckled over and dropped to his knees.

"I'll get you punk. I'm going to beat the shit out of you!" He screamed as he scrambled back to his feet. But it was too late. I was at my door turning the key and a second later I was safe inside.

"What's wrong with you pea brain?" My brother Bruce asked as I ran across the living room floor. He was watching cartoons on television.

"Some big kid took my books and my football," I answered. I was beginning to calm down.

"Who took your books? Who was he?" he asked.

"I don't know. I've never seen him before," I answered. "But I think he's still outside." My brother was walking towards the kitchen window, which faced the courtyard.

"Is that him standing with the tree branch?"

"Yes. That's him," I answered. My stomach felt sick.

"Stay here."

"What are you going to do?" I asked.

"I'm going to get that stuff back."

"What if he's stronger than you?" I asked as he opened the door and walked out. It shut behind him.

My brother Bruce was five years older than me. For most of my life he had been the soft-spoken, introverted one. I was the carefree, outgoing one. Until now, I had never really needed his help. Instead, I tried to avoid his constant picking. It wasn't that we didn't get along. We did. It was just we were such different people. While he would remain in the house reading books, working on models or playing board games, I was always outside playing football or running around with my friends. But we always found a few moments to roll around our bedroom, playing make believe and tag.

I scrambled over to the kitchen window and pulled open one of the blinds. I was holding my breath. Bruce was standing next to the big kid, who stood at least two inches taller and weighed at least twenty pounds heavier. I couldn't hear what they were saying, but I knew they weren't making friends. Suddenly, the big kid started swinging the tree branch at Bruce, hitting him squarely on the shoulder and arms. Then, without any forewarning, Bruce coiled back and then sprang forward with both arms extended. His body crashed against the big kid at full force, his forearm cutting across the bridge of his nose and knocking him to the ground. There he remained, a steady stream of blood dripping out of both nostrils. Bruce walked over, picked up my football and book bag and carried it back to the house. For the first time in as long as I could remember, I realized the strong bond my brother and I had formed, even if for just a short time and the deep admiration I carried for him. It's strange, because up until now, these distant memories seemed so few and far between. I never really realized how much I missed having him around. But I would never get the chance to tell him. I wouldn't even get the chance to say good-bye.

Suddenly, I was back to reality and the present day. It was almost as if I was waking from some horrible dream. My forehead was covered in sweat. I was still alone inside the apartment. I glanced over at the bed and again saw the lifeless body, his head propped up against a pillow. He looked so peaceful. I wondered if this was how my brother had looked the night he died. His body had been taken away before I woke up and I was forever left with this image of him hanging from a rope, not a peaceful body lying in bed. I wished I could have told him I missed him and said goodbye.

It was several minutes before I heard the first sound. Snapping my head up, I again glanced towards the bed. My arms and face were still covered in a thin coat of sweat. I heard the noise again. It was a slow, barely audible groaning noise, almost like breathing. Never once taking my eyes off the body, I leaned forward and listened carefully. The only sound now was the steady beat of my heart. Then, suddenly, I heard it again. It definitely sounded like breathing and it was coming from somewhere near the body on the bed. I shook my head several times. Something wasn't quite right. Then, ever so slightly, his hand moved. If I hadn't been staring right at him, I would have never noticed. But I was. And I did. And I was now scared shitless. I glanced over towards the kitchen. On a counter was a half-eaten plate of food. Next to it was a half-empty glass of water. Next to the bed, lying on the floor was a small pile of crumpled clothes. It was as if everything had just stopped, frozen in time. One minute you're alive, and then without warning, you're dead. But you're not really dead because you're freaking lying on the bed and breathing! My head started spinning around and around.

"Snap out of it," Lyons said, his voice thankfully bringing me back to the world of the living. He was standing over top of me.

"I swear I think the body moved," I said, standing up. "And it also sounded like he was breathing."

"I doubt it. It was probably just your imagination," he answered. "Sometimes bodies go through a settling process. They're filled with gas and the muscles tend to spasm. Besides, you looked kind of out of it when I came in. Maybe you were just daydreaming."

"I guess so. This is the first time I've been this close to a dead person. I can't wait until we can get the hell out of here. This room, this place gives me the fucking creeps." As I was talking with Lyons, several men walked into the room. They were wearing blue nylon jackets with the words "D.C. Medical Examiner" written across the back. Another man, looking very much like Dick Tracy, sporting a hideously loud purple colored suit with a blue tie and carrying a hand held radio, followed closely behind. He was a Detective from Homicide Division. One of the medical examiners knelt down besides the body.

"Yeah, he's dead all right," he said with little emotion.

"What's up Lyons? Training again?" asked the Homicide Detective with the suit and the radio as he pushed past me.

"You know it," Lyons answered. He said nothing to me, and walked up to the body and pulled out a notepad.

"I can't take this smell too much longer. I'm going to puke," I blurted to Lyons.

"Just a few more minutes, relax." I heard someone again mutter the words "He's dead." Then, as quickly as he had come, the Homicide Detective walked past us and headed for the door.

"It's going to be a Natural Death report for now," he said. "Put me down as notified and on the scene. The family's out in the hall. I'll get a positive identification and then interview them in the manager's office." Then he was gone.

"Hey, can we get some help over here?" One of the medical examiners shouted.

"All right, all right," Lyons answered. "Come on, let's get this over with." We walked over to the bed. Two women suddenly entered into the apartment. Both of them were crying hysterically and I immediately knew they were family members. I felt horrible. I knew exactly how they were feeling. I wanted to tell them it was going to be OK, but I wasn't so sure it would be and I was suddenly thankful I never had to see my brother like this. After few seconds, they were gone, and my chance had passed. I was glad. In the end, I didn't really have much to say, and I don't think I was ready to watch them suffer any more.

"After we get done here, you'll need to get their names and information for the report. They'll be in the manager's office," Lyons said.

"Ok," I answered. One of the people from the coroner's office pulled out a large plastic bag with a long zipper on the front. He unzipped it and pulled it open.

"Ok, let's go. We'll lift him on the count of three," he said, situating himself on the opposite side of the bed. "One, two, three!" On the third count, we each grabbed a body part and lifted the dead man from the bed. I had hold of both his feet. They were cold and clammy, and I was afraid I might pull them off. Immediately as we lifted, a cloud of stench escaped from his open mouth. I could hear the stale, dead air as it flowed from deep within his lungs and slowly out from between his lips. My eyes rolled back in my head. I was sure I was finally going to pass out. The smell was finally going to win. Quickly, the coroner turned and pushed the body bag on the bed.

"Ok, let him down nice and easy." This is exactly what we did. The body fit inside the bag perfectly. He zipped it shut, and we lifted the bag off the bed and placed it on a stretcher in the hallway.

"Thank you very much gentlemen," the coroner said as he pushed the stretcher down the hallway, rounded a corner and was gone.

It would be more than an hour before we were finally finished. People needed to be interviewed and reports had to be taken. But for me, the worst was over. For all intents and purposes, this was just a routine assignment. Little did I know this would be the first of many I would see in my police career. If I had known then what I know now, maybe I might have just said forget it and chosen something else to do for a living. But I didn't. I was seeing life and death, and though I didn't necessarily like all of it, I was slowly beginning to understand the reality of it. So for the moment, I was content to finish the day, go home and to try to forget about it. But death would not leave me so easily. I would carry the smell with me for the rest of the day, and week and I would secretly wonder if others could smell it as well.

"So, how about that pizza?" Lyons said as we pulled out of the driveway and headed towards Columbia Road. It was two o'clock in the afternoon. I didn't even bother to answer. I just stared at him like he was fucking crazy.

CHAPTER TWO

It was an unseasonably cool, crisp fall Wednesday afternoon in the city. It was around 5 o'clock and bright red and pale yellow leaves slipped quietly to the ground from the scarce few trees scattered amongst the drab apartment buildings along the upper Northwest 14th street corridor. Dilapidated warehouses, boarded up businesses and older brick row houses formed most of the landscape of 14th Street. Empty lots dotted seemingly every corner, and I wondered how an area boarding the famous Shaw District, with so much history could have slipped so far down. I was riding with Officer Miller, who was my new training officer. We were in his assigned car, scout eighty-six. Miller was a prototypical cop, with a confidence that carefully straddled the always-thin line between earned arrogance and skillful ability. I could see this in his walk and in the way he wore his uniform freshly pressed and crisp. The way he spoke to people both on the street and within the department and the way he carried himself around others showed me he enjoyed his job and took a great deal of pride in working in the city. I could definitely relate and wanted to emulate this. Prior to joining the DC Police, I had applied for and been offered jobs with several other police departments in the area, which is no small feat given the last count stood well over forty. But I had chosen Washington, DC as the place where I knew I would see and experience the most and which certainly needed people who relied on this inner desire to serve the profession. Growing up in the DC Metropolitan area and listening to the constant media barrage of steadily rising violent crime statistics and murder rates that would later propel the capital city being dubbed the "Homicide Capital" of the states didn't hurt either. The District of Columbia was where it was at, and if you wanted to be a cop, this would be the place to be.

Our assigned area for today covered some of the more crime-infested areas in the Third District. DC is divided into seven police districts, which are then sub-divided into patrol sectors, with certain cars assigned to certain areas. The Third District covered both residential and business areas and was known for such notable areas as Howard University, Dupont Circle, Adams Morgan, Columbia Heights and parts of the National Zoo. Although some areas were still well established, such as Dupont Circle and Adams Morgan, other areas were just beginning the slow process of redeveloping and revitalizing, especially around 7th, 9th and U streets in the historical Shaw/Howard neighborhoods. These areas had certainly seen their share of economic hard times and turmoil in the late sixties, seventies and early eighties. Localized drug dealers and criminals now mingled hand-in-hand with people working for revitalization. Nowhere was this more prevalent than in the 1300 block of Clifton Street, where three low-income high-rise apartment buildings towered above the local architecture. To speak about these apartments in the context of poverty would be an understatement, as nothing can quite explain what it's like to walk through piss, shit, used syringes, and condoms as was the daily routine passing through the halls of these buildings.

I really liked Miller, who had already taught me many of the skills necessary to work in such intense area. Miller was considerably shorter than me, but carried a solid, muscular frame. A single gold tooth shined from his mouth. Our assigned area was drug central, and the streets were routinely filled with street level trafficking. During the past week, we had already made a couple of narcotics arrests and found a couple of people who were wanted on warrants. I was slowly becoming more and more comfortable with my own abilities and was really starting to feel like an actual partner instead of a training rookie. I felt like I could hold my own.

Miller and I were just getting ready to check out an area noted for its open-air marijuana market in the 1400 block of Clifton Street when the call came over the radio. "Scout car eight-six?"

"Eight-six go ahead," I answered, preparing to write the address of the assignment on our activity sheet. It was pretty early in the evening and I wasn't expecting anything too serious, maybe a drug complaint or some disorderly kids on the corner.

"Eight-six, we have a report of a 10-33 at 1371 Fairmount Street." 10-33 meant an officer was in need of immediate assistance and was the mother of all calls. In fact, these were probably the most important words a police officer could ever hear. I wasn't at all surprised when

Miller floored the gas pedal and quickly weaved us onto 12th Street and briefly into oncoming traffic for the quick three-block ride to Fairmount Street.

"Scout eight-six, I copy, ten four," I screamed into the radio, trying to shout over the wail of our siren.

"Scout eight-six, we have a report of the board on the scene with an MO suspect. They're fighting and need assistance," replied the dispatcher.

"Eight-six, copy," I answered. I was still shouting. The board was short for ambulance crew, and MO meant a mental patient, usually one who was acting extremely bizarre or dangerous. I was actually glad I was not yet certified to ride alone as although I was definitely confident in my abilities, I had yet to face this type of call.

Our police car skidded to a halt behind a large red fire truck, missing the rear bumper by inches. In front of the truck was an ambulance with its lights on and still spinning. Seeing a fire truck on the scene was not out of the ordinary in DC since these trucks were often dispatched as the primary unit if an ambulance wasn't immediately available. Fire Truck crews were trained first responders and could provide initial medical assistance and assessment until a medical unit could respond. Miller and I quickly jumped out of the car and jogged to the front of the building.

Building 1371 was an old, decrepit apartment style row house connected to houses on both sides. At one time it was probably someone's private home, but had since been converted into a small three-story apartment building. Miller threw open the wood and glass front door and carefully stepped inside. Slipping in behind him, I realized both of us left our batons in the car. This thought quickly escaped my mind as I had more pressing issues to think of, such as what lie ahead. I followed closely behind Miller, my eyes scanning up the three flights of stairs for signs of trouble.

"Up here officers. We're on the top floor!" A voice shouted from the top-floor landing. I saw the bright red, flushed face of a medic as he peered down over the edge motioning desperately for us to come up.

"Okay, we're on our way," Miller answered as he raced up the stairs two at a time. I was still right behind him, my adrenaline pumping sky high. In a matter of seconds, we were at the last staircase leading up to the third floor landing. As I made my way up the last few stairs, I began to see what was happening. On the far left of the landing in front of a closed apartment door were three medics sitting on top of a large man.

A fourth medic was standing on the far right side of the landing, directly in front of the top of the staircase. I recognized him as the one who had motioned us up. His face was scratched and bloody and he was sweating like a pig. I glanced back to the other three men, and noticed they too were sweating and bleeding.

"What the fuck is going on?" Miller asked as he cautiously stepped onto the landing. I bumped into him in my hurry to get to the top.

"Sorry, I didn't see you stop," I said sheepishly, realizing my rookieness was again starting to show. I scurried several steps to the side.

"We got a call for a sick MO at this address," the medic by the stairs said pointing to a closed apartment door. "When we got to the third floor, the man over there was just coming out of his apartment," he added pointing to the man on the floor. "As soon as he saw us, he just went berserk and started fighting us. He jumped on Jackson and threw him to the floor like he was a rag doll. Let me tell you, he's strong as hell." He sounded winded and his voice was raspy as he sucked in gulps of air while talking. He took a moment to collect himself and continued. "We all just piled on top of him. That's all we could do. While we were trying to get him under control, I put in a call through our dispatcher for some police assistance. But I think we're all right now."

"I didn't do anything wrong," the MO said in a garbled, barely audible voice. "I can't breathe. Please let me up." I could barely make out the outline of his face from underneath the bodies still squatting on top of him. They had him pinned down pretty good, and I don't think they were in any hurry to let him back up.

"You guys can let him up now," Miller said, slowly walking across the landing toward them. "I'd like to have a few words with him."

"Are you sure? This guys really a nut," one of the medics said.

"Yeah, I'm sure. We can handle this," Miller answered, a slight smile covering his face. "Can we, Archer?"

"Yeah, I guess so," I answered nervously. To be honest, I trusted Miller with just about anything. But I wasn't so sure about this.

"You guess so? Can I get a little more confidence than that?"

"Okay, sure, we can handle this," I answered with a little more authority in my voice. "Was that better?"

"Much better rookie," he answered, still smiling. I was sure Miller had nerves of steel and ice water running through his veins. But right now, my nerves were made of wood and my blood was boiling hot.

"Okay, but don't you dare say we didn't warn you," blurted one of the other medics still sitting on the MO. "Okay, on the count of three. Ready, one, two, three, now!" Suddenly, all three men scrambled to their feet and in perfect unison raced to the far side of the landing, knocking each other against several apartment doors in the process. I had never seen three men move so fast. I couldn't help but laugh. The MO remained on the floor, his face turned towards us. He slowly sat up and wiped his sweaty brow with his shirt sleeve.

"Thank you, officers. That's much better," he said in the same garbled voice as before. He appeared to be pretty big, maybe six foot two or three and about two hundred and fifty or sixty pounds. I could see where he could be a handful if he was violent. "I'm okay now, really."

"Sure you are. No doubt in my mind. Now, how about telling me what the problem is?" Miller asked, approaching him cautiously. I pulled out my notebook and started getting ready to jot some notes.

"I'm fine, sir, really. I just forgot to take my medication is all. I guess I just kind of flipped out," he answered. He was still sitting on the floor.

"Just kind of flipped out? Man, it took three of us to get you down to the ground!" I heard one of the medics shout from safely behind my back.

"Take it easy," I said over my shoulder. "We'll take care of this from here." I didn't want to sound rude, but I also didn't want anyone setting this man off again, either.

"What's your name?" Miller asked. He moved a little bit closer to the MO, and was now only a couple feet away.

"I'm not sure," he answered. "Can I stand up please, please? I need some air."

"Yeah, sure," Miller answered. The MO slowly stood up. I realized that my earlier estimates on his size were a little inaccurate. He was much bigger. "Why can't you remember your name?"

"I need my medicine. If I don't take it, it's hard for me to concentrate." Aside from his memory lapse, he now seemed pretty calm and normal. I turned my attention to the medic crew.

"Tell me exactly what happened?" I asked turning to one of the medics. All four of them were standing on the staircase behind me. I couldn't help but get the feeling they were positioning themselves to run.

"It's like I told you before, we got a call for the sick MO. When we got up to the apartment, this guy was on his way out. He seemed really normal at first, but then, for no reason, he just flipped out and started fighting us. We rolled around for a few minutes before we were able to get him under control."

"Do you want us to press charges against him for assault?" I asked.

"Fuck that. I just want to get the hell out of here. Just handle it any way you want, and we'll go ahead and clear the assignment," he answered.

"Sure. No problem." I turned my attention back to Miller, who was still standing next to the MO and laughing. I assumed everything was going fine.

"Miller, I'm going to clear the board okay. They don't want to press charges, so I don't think we'll need them anymore."

"Okay," he answered. Before I could even finish my next sentence, I heard loud footsteps racing down the stairs. I turned just in time to see the last of ambulance crew turning the corner on the second floor. I laughed to myself. I guess they had gotten just a little more than they had bargained for. I turned my attention back to Miller. He was still questioning the MO.

"I think everything's fine here," Miller said as I eased over to his side. "He's going to go back inside his apartment and take his medicine." Working my eyes around the landing area, I started noticing the difficulties the ambulance crew had trying to subdue the MO. The landing area was only about the size of a small kitchen, maybe 10 feet across in width and 10 feet in depth. There was a flimsy, wooden guardrail leading up the stairway and along the ledge. I pressed my hand against it and it gave sufficiently. I was certain it could not support any weight. I glanced over the edge and to the bottom floor, three long levels below. That was a fall I didn't want to take.

"Uh, Miller," I said, motioning towards the guardrail. He looked at me, and nodded his head in acknowledgement. Then he slowly maneuvered his body away from the ledge where he was now standing and over towards the front of the apartment door.

"Thanks," he mumbled slightly, still keeping his eyes on the MO.

"It's like I said, I just kind of lost myself for a minute. I'm fine now. I really didn't mean to hurt anyone," the MO said softly. His hands were cupped in front of him and he was rocking back and forth on his heels. This looked very odd to me.

"Sure, but you understand you have to keep taking your medicine. If a doctor prescribes medicine for you, you have to take it," Miller said. "Do you understand?"

"I know, I know. It's just that, I wanted to go to the store. And when those guys jumped on me, I kind of panicked. Like I said, I really didn't mean to hurt anyone."

"I believe you. By the way, just what do you take medication for, anyway?"

"I'm schizophrenic," he answered matter-of-factly. Miller casually took a couple of steps backwards. "But it's not what you think. I'm fine. That's why I can stay at home. I have a great doctor, and as long as I take my medication, then you'd never even know."

"I see. Well, as long as you're okay now, we're going to leave," Miller said, turning his back away from him and facing me. I closed my notebook and started shoving it in my back pocket. For exactly three seconds, both Miller and I had taken our eyes off him. Which was a mistake, for it took him only about two seconds to get his hands on Miller.

"Mother fucker!" Miller yelled as he crashed face first to the floor, his body taking the full brunt of the MO who was now behind him trying to get on top of him.

"Shit!" I yelled out loud. I grabbed my portable radio and screamed for assistance. "10-33! Scout eighty-six!" I pushed the radio into my belt and reached for my baton but it wasn't there. I had left it in the car. Having little other choice, I jumped on top of the MO's back and grabbed for his head.

"Get this asshole off of me!" Miller was yelling. The MO was clawing at his face and kneeing him in the stomach.

"I'm trying!" I screamed. I was pounding the MO in the back with my fists as hard as I could. He was fat, and my punches hit his soft, blubbery flesh like it was a huge loaf of bread. I desperately tried grabbing hold of one of his wrists.

"Get the fuck off!" I screamed at him, hoping to divert his attention away from Miller, who was taking the brunt of the assault. It worked. Straddling Miller's body, the MO turned towards me, reached out a hand and grabbed me by the collar of my uniform shirt. With his other hand, he simultaneously scratched across the base of my chin, ripping the flesh with a poorly trimmed fingernail, and with the other hand, ripped down the length of my shirt, tearing out the buttons. I pushed my body backwards, falling against the far side of the landing with a loud crash. My body slid across the floor and came to rest at the edge of the landing. My head went over the edge, giving me one hell of a good view of the first floor three stories below. This was definitely too close. I quickly scrambled back to my feet and reluctantly jumped back into the fray. Miller and I were getting our asses kicked, and I didn't like it one bit.

Miller had seized the momentary distraction I had provided and regained his balance. Lifting his body off the ground, he was now on his knees and landing solid punches into the MO's upper body. The MO was covering his face and trying to move in closer to Miller. I grabbed both his legs with my arms and locked on hard. For the next a few seconds, my body mopped the floor as he kicked me and swung his legs from one side of the landing to the next. Finally, Miller landed several punches to his head, and the MO fell to his side. Miller quickly scrambled to his feet and sprang on top of him. I let go of his legs, grabbed one of his arms and locked it behind his back. Using the combined full force of our weight, Miller and I leveraged him to the ground and on his stomach. We had finally gained control.

"Jesus Christ, that was fucked up!" I said between short gasps for air. "They never explained this shit to me in the Academy!"

"Yeah, you're not kidding. That was close," Miller answered. He was also breathing hard. "Just whatever you do, don't let go."

"I wasn't planning on it. I'm not going anywhere until we get some backup," I answered. I heard sirens coming from outside the building. In a few seconds, the Calvary would arrive.

"You managed to get on the radio?" Miller asked, his face turning flushed from the pressure of trying to hold the MO down. His feet were still kicking wildly, but we were maintaining control.

"Yeah, it was the first thing I did," I answered. Both of my arms were numb from the exertion of trying to maintain a grip on his arms.

"Well, remind me to put in a good word on your performance evaluation sheet for that one, okay?"

"Uh, yeah, sure. Whatever you say," I answered. I could hear footsteps as other officers raced up the stairs to assist us.

"Up here, on the third floor!" I screamed. I turned just in time to see several officers climbing the last flight of stairs.

Looking over at Miller, whose face was scratched and covered with blood, I couldn't help the feeling of déjà vu. I think..., no, I'm sure we must have looked to these officers exactly like the ambulance crew had looked to Miller and me just a few minutes ago, which seemed altogether an eternity. Who would have thought it?

"Are you guys all right?" One of the officers asked as he raced over to assist.

"What the hell do you think?" Miller answered sarcastically. Once the other officers grabbed the MO, I stood up to survey the damage. All things considered, I was pretty lucky. I had a pretty good scratch on my chin, a few scratches on my arms and a torn shirt. I now understood all too well what the ambulance crew had gone through just a few minutes earlier. I had never seen a man go from one extreme to the other so quickly. It was a frightening thought. It was a thought I mulled over quite often as I spent the next two weeks on injured leave, contemplating what the rest of my career might hold.

CHAPTER THREE

The radio was uncommonly quiet on this, one of my first nights riding alone. Up until now, I had spent my days, and nights, riding around with various training officers. Now, after a rigorous ten-week field training program, I was working on my own, for better or for worse. I glanced at my watch. Ten o' clock. What a job, I thought, driving around the city waiting for a crime to be committed, like some starving vulture. I should be home in bed with a good Stephen King novel, or sleeping like the rest of the normal world. But mine was no ordinary job, and as I would soon learn, this would be no ordinary night.

"Scout car eighty-eight?" came a soft female voice over the radio.

"Ten ninety-nine," answered the voice of Sanchez, signaling his availability. Ten ninety-nine meant he was a single man car.

"Scout car eighty-eight and a unit to assist for the sound of gunshots in the eleven hundred block of Harvard Street," the dispatcher responded.

The sound of the radio startled me, as it always seemed to do. No matter how much I tried to predict it, radio assignments always seemed to follow agonizing moments of utter silence, and came just when you least expected it. I recognized Sanchez's voice as a cop who had assisted me on a few earlier assignments. Since coming to the Third District, I had viewed him as a pretty good role model. He had been on the department for about five years, so he was old enough to know his shit, but still young enough that he hadn't yet burned out.

"Scout car eighty-nine," I screamed into my radio as a strange mixture of anticipation and anxiety swept over me. I cursed myself for screaming, which was rapidly becoming a bad habit.

"Go ahead scout car eighty-nine," the dispatcher answered.

"I'm ten ninety nine also. I'll assist eighty-eight with his assignment." My voice was a lot calmer now.

"Both units use extreme caution and advise when you're on the scene." Her voice was very soothing, like a disc jockey for a late night jazz station. This somewhat betrayed the seriousness of our assignment, and lent an eerie sense of calm to an otherwise stressful situation. I activated my car's emergency equipment and began the short ride to Harvard Street.

As my car raced down the rain-slicked street, a million thoughts filtered through my mind. Was I really prepared for what I might encounter? I had yet to experience firsthand anything serious, let alone a possible shooting. I mean I had made a few arrests and investigated robberies and drug violations. I had even seen a few deaths, but they had been from natural causes. I knew this type of call could be anything from a car backfiring to what I feared most, an actual shooting. That possibility seemed quite real in a city with one of the highest homicide rates in the country. Gently, I applied my car's brakes, realizing only now that I had been traveling at an insane speed of sixty miles per hour. The worn out brakes squealed and hissed as I rounded the corner onto Harvard Street—so much for the element of surprise.

I strained my eyes to see through the film of dirt and water still covering my windshield. On each side of the street were several abandoned houses, some with boarded up windows and doors. I envisioned a family of rats within, dancing amongst syringes, used condoms and empty liquor bottles. I'd been told this was an area well known for drug trafficking. But tonight, the street was empty.

Directly up ahead I saw a bold, bright light. It was an Amoco sign. A crowd was gathered at the far end of the gas station's parking lot, and I pulled up to see what had caught their attention. I brought my car to a cautious stop. I sensed something was wrong, and that it was waiting just beyond the perimeter of the people who had gathered to watch.

"Scout car eighty-nine, I'm on the scene," I voiced to the dispatcher.

"Advise what you have as soon as possible," she answered back. I took a deep breath and slowly opened my car door. As I wandered into the crowd, I noticed a look of disbelieving numbness on their faces. I was afraid they would sense how nervous I was, but no one seemed to notice. It didn't take long before I saw what they did: a car idling on the side of the street with blood streaming down the opened passenger side door. My eyes slowly followed the stream of blood as it cascaded on to the street and flowed downhill into a gutter. Then I saw the body.

"Scout car eighty-nine. I have a priority. Get me an ambulance at my location now!" I screamed into my portable radio.

"Scout car eighty-nine, an ambulance is on the way. Advise what you have," the dispatcher answered.

"I have a shooting, one man down. Stand by for further!" I yelled as I raced towards the victim. At this moment, I was acting on sheer instinct and training alone, nervous and unsure what to do. I knelt down beside the body, but I knew it was too late. He was just a kid, maybe twenty years old. Though he was almost dead, his eyes continued to stare through me, into my soul, asking me to explain what happened.

"I'm sorry," I whispered softly. "I tried to get here as fast as I could...I promise." I was quickly overcome by the realization that there was nothing I could do to help him. A steady pool of blood and gray-colored fluid seeped from the back of his skull, and I knew immediately that he had taken a head shot.

His body began to shake violently and a small trickle of blood escaped from his lips. His hand clenched mine tightly, and then relaxed. That was it. No last words, no speech, just death. In a matter of seconds, he died in my arms. I wondered what his last thoughts were before the bullets penetrated his body, splattering his brains across the street. I remember what my thoughts were at his age; school, girls, and making the varsity basketball team. Not bullets. Not death. Not of being a cold body on a cold night on a cold street.

When I finally gathered the strength to stand up, I felt immense anger. I was angry for losing control, for suddenly feeling more like a person than a police officer. I knew that I was supposed to hide my emotions and fears. I knew that people in the crowd would expect me to be strong. I remember once asking a veteran officer how he felt about constantly being confronted with violence and death, and how he responded flatly that after a while you simply become inured to it. I prayed that would never happen to me.

I could see other officers scrambling around the area, rushing to assist what appeared to be a second victim whose body had been hidden from my vision. Sanchez was standing on my right, talking with someone from the ambulance crew. Two medics rushed by, knocking me to the side as they knelt down beside the victim I had discovered. Another group of medics gathered around the second victim. My legs were trembling uncontrollably. I walked closer, trying to see what was happening, but everything was moving in slow motion. As I moved closer, I could see this man was still alive. Whoever had shot him had first handcuffed his hands behind his back. So this is what Washington, D.C.'s escalating violence looked like close up. What I had often read about, wondered about, but never seen. What I wanted so badly to be a part of, but could never quite fathom its intensity.

Standing upright, as if at attention, I could see a small group of people gathered around the sidewalk. I focused in on an older black woman, with gray hair and small framed reading glasses that encased her gentle eyes. She was wearing a brightly colored dress. She was standing on the edge of the crowd, closest to me, yet she stood alone. Her hands were clenched tightly in fists, and a steady stream of tears rolled down her cheeks. I stepped aside slightly and watched as her gaze followed my movement. Again I stepped slightly to the side, and again her eyes followed me. A nervous panic flowed into my veins. I felt that she was looking at me for some explanation. I searched my heart for something to say to her. I looked at my uniform, my badge, and my gun—capable of taking a human life. But I had nothing capable of bringing back life. Supposedly, I was trained to handle any circumstance, to be compassionate and to help guide people through stressful situations. That's not what this woman wanted. She wanted an answer for why this violence had to happen. And I had none. In the end, I looked at her, as anyone else would have, with confusion and sadness. Ashamed, I lowered my gaze to the ground, staring at my blood-soaked shoes, feeling very much like a coward.

A small group of about five kids had gathered across the street, on the corner, and were snickering among themselves.

"Why are you laughing?" I asked angrily. No answer.

"I asked you a question," I repeated. Again, there was no answer.

"Go home. Everything is over," I said. They had stopped laughing, and now were looking at me with a youthful combination of curiosity and arrogance. For some of these kids, I suppose death means very little. Maybe it's just expected, something they become socialized to as a simple fact of life. For some though, perhaps it's expected too early. In a world of inequality, violence and poverty, maybe death can be a welcome escape. A game of suicide, only daring someone else to take your life instead of taking your own.

A slight tap on my back brought me back to reality. It was a soft, innocent tap. Lazily, I spun on my heels and came face to face with the culprit. He was a young boy, perhaps just a few weeks shy of his tenth birthday.

"Officer, what happened up there? Why are all those police here?" He asked in a slow deliberate voice. I couldn't help but think of my brother's death many years ago.

"Someone died last night," was my only response as I fought back the tears.

I walked slowly back to my scout car, taking one final look at the Amoco station and the remaining crowd. Other officers were walking around tying up loose ends. I felt a small sense of understanding. Not much, but just a little. As I stared at the street, I could have sworn the dark, nighttime clouds overhead opened ever so slightly. From within this opening came a small beam of moonlight, slowly pushing its way down to earth, finally coming to rest on the bloodstained street below, illuminating it for all to see, perhaps a gentle reminder of our ignorance.

I gazed up into the now open hole in the sky. I could see many stars: bright, beautiful stars. Then, as suddenly as it had come, the clouds closed up and all was dark again. It all seemed so simple, and for the moment, I thought maybe I felt just the smallest sense of relief.

CHAPTER FOUR

Escaped zoo animal, I was sure that was what the voice on the radio had said. I tossed this thought around in my head, over and over. Just what the hell did she mean by escaped zoo animal? I was certain I had heard the dispatcher correctly. But I couldn't believe it. Zoo animals just didn't escape, did they, at least not in Washington, D.C. It wasn't as if they were serving time in prison, desperately plotting for the big escape. I mean, this was a zoo, with animals not people, most of who were probably quite happy and content. My imagination was working overtime. Given my close proximity to the National Zoo, anything seemed possible. I briefly visualized lions and tigers stalking Columbia Rd, or perhaps giraffes blocking traffic on Eighteenth Street. The possibilities seemed at least endless, if not believable. Needless to say, I was certainly in no rush to get there.

"Scout car eighty-five. I copy the assignment. That was for an escaped zoo animal, correct?" I asked, knowing I had just misunderstood the dispatcher's original transmission, and fully expecting a good round of kidding from my co-workers for my brief lapse.

"That is correct Scout eighty-five. The complainant will be standing by for you in front of the address." I was certain I heard laughter coming from the radio. Maybe the dispatcher was joking. No, that couldn't be it. Dispatcher's weren't allowed to have a sense of humor. I was scheduled to pick up a ride-along at five o' clock, which was only an hour away. Ride-along was citizens from the community who rode with police officers to observe police work. I was glad I could clear this particular assignment alone. The last thing I needed was some citizen ridiculing me in my time of confusion. The address was for the rear alley in the 2600 block of Ontario Rd., in the northwest quadrant of the city. I knew this area all too well. It was a residential area, a few short blocks from the hustle and bustle of Columbia Rd. in Adams Morgan. Mostly, this street consisted of row houses and some larger apartment buildings. Unfortunately, I also knew this area was but a few blocks away from The National Zoo. Even worse, The National Zoo has a service way entrance only three or four blocks away on Adams Mill Rd. This fact lent frightening credibility to this unbelievable assignment, and again visions of various animals from the wild kingdom danced in my head. I wondered if Marlon Perkins might be available for emergency advice.

I must have driven past the actual location at least three times. I probably would have continued on my quest up and down the block had I not finally noticed a woman standing a few feet off of the street just inside the opening to an alley. She was jumping up and down and waving her arms back and forth. She appeared to be smiling. I threw my scout car into reverse, backed up a few feet and pulled into the remarkably long alley. Save for a few scattered trash containers here and there, it was relatively empty.

"Officer, Officer," shouted the woman standing in the alley. I slowly exited my car, trying to keep my wits about me. I was still a little spooked and unsure, afraid that at any moment some crazed beast might leap from nowhere and rip me to pieces.

"It's about time. I've been waiting for almost an hour," she said, standing in front of me and staring into my face.

"Calm down ma'am. I just got the assignment a few minutes ago and I got here as fast as I could. We've been very busy today," I answered back, lying through my teeth. This was the first call I had received today. But I couldn't let her know that. "So what's the problem? And please tell me this has nothing to do with an escaped zoo animal."

"Escaped zoo animal? Good heavens no. You're kidding, right?" She answered in a slightly confused tone. I contemplated trying to explain, but thought better of it.

"Don't worry, it's an inside joke. I was just kidding. Now, please, tell me why you called," I asked, breaking a few moments of awkward silence.

"Actually, I'm not the one who called. A lady inside the building called. We're neighbors. Anyway, the problem is right over there, near those parked cars." She was pointing to several parked vehicles on the north side of the alley, about a hundred feet away. Next to these cars, there was an indentation where a walkway led towards what figured to be some sort of backyard or courtyard.

"The only things I see are some cars and an alley. Maybe you could be a bit more specific?" I asked.

"Of course you don't see anything. That's because it's just around the corner, beyond where those cars are parked. You'll have to go take a look for yourself to find out. I'm staying right here," she responded with a smile.

"Can you at least give me a hint?" I pleaded.

"I think the lady upstairs thought she saw a strange animal moving around back there. And when I came down, I heard some strange growling noises," she answered. I sensed a slight bit of sarcasm in her voice. Yet, she also seemed a little frightened as well.

Strange growling noises? What did she mean by that? This was getting really strange, really fast. Forget it, I thought. Like the Nike commercial says, just do it. I needed to get it over with so I could go back to the station and pick up my ride-along. Taking one more glimpse over my shoulder, I caught a glimpse of the woman in full. She couldn't have been more than twenty-one or twenty two years old. I was surprised. At first, I had envisioned her as much older. She had long blonde hair with a slight wave in front and deep bronze colored skin. What a break. I was in the midst of a beautiful woman at a time when I was sure I was on the verge of making a complete fool of myself.

"What did you say your name was?" She yelled from behind me.

"I didn't, but its Christopher," I responded back.

"Christopher, huh?" She stated with a smile.

"Yeah, why?" I asked

"Just curious," she replied, still smiling. I wondered what she found so amusing.

By now, most of my initial fears were gone, replaced by a burning curiosity. I had convinced myself that this was simply some kind of joke. Somewhere beyond the parked cars ahead was an innocent stray cat, and my new female friend was just enjoying my confusion. She probably enjoyed seeing a D.C. cop in a state of disarray. Not too hard to accomplish, unfortunately. Oh well, good community relations. My curiosity was now at its peak, for the first car now were only a few precious steps away.

The closer I came to the first parked car, the more my ears seemed to pick up a low, steady hissing noise. It was coming from around the corner. At first, I tried to dismiss it, blaming it on my overactive imagination. Maybe it was coming from my portable radio. No such luck. Upon review, I could clearly see that I had turned my radio off long ago. The woman from the alley was now quiet as a mouse, and when I glanced over my shoulder to see if she was still there, I could see her staring at me intensely. Both her hands were on her chin and her mouth seemed to be hanging wide open. I chuckled to myself. She was really enjoying this, which did not surprise me one bit.

When I finally reached the front bumper of the first car, I could again hear the steady hissing noise coming from around the corner to my left. Only now it was much louder and had metamorphosed into a full-blown growl. What the hell was it? It definitely sounded alive, like an animal. Only not like any animal I had ever heard before. It must be a wounded cat. That was it. I was suddenly very proud of myself for this brilliant revelation. My mind tossed a few ideas around, and then suddenly, I knew what I would do. Bracing myself against the side of the third and final parked car and within but a couple of feet from the corner wall, I prepared to act.

"Ah ha!" I screamed as loud as I could as I launched myself around the corner and into a concrete side area. I was sure I had scared the living hell out of this cat and that at any moment it would be flying off into the alley in a frightened furry flash. I couldn't wait to see the look on the woman's face as this lovable little feline careened through the alley.

Bad move. Coming to rest on the concrete ground I could barely make out the depth of the cut I was in. Despite being light outside, the recesses of the alley seemed uncannily dark and morbid. Gradually, I could somewhat focus on the far corners. I scanned around quickly straining to see. There was a lot of scattered trash lying around, but other than that, it was empty. As I looked closer, I noticed every few seconds, something would move. Then it would stop. It was dark in color, and furry; my cat. I had located my cat. As I took a few slow steps forward, that's when I noticed the eyes. They were as red as the sun, pure fire, as if belonging to Satan himself. Whatever it was, it had spotted me, and was much larger than any ordinary cat. Trying to suck down the lump that now occupied my throat, I decided to retreat a few steps. The growling noise was now much louder and the entire alley seemed to echo its sound. Whatever this thing was, it was pissed off. Then suddenly it moved again, slowly at first, as if trying to decide exactly what to do. Then it moved a little faster and with more deliberation, and still even a little faster. It was now charging me one foot at a time and with seemingly no fear in its heart.

For the next few seconds, Carl Lewis had nothing on me. I had magically transformed myself into the fastest white man on Earth as I raised my knees to my chest and dug each shiny leather shoe into the hard ground. My scout car seemed an eternity away. My strides had now become somewhat uniformed and even and I was secure in the fact that I was hauling some serious ass. No sir, nothing would catch me today. Not the demon from the alley. Not even a cold.

A sharp blast of intense pain shot up my right leg as I felt my right foot give out beneath me. I had stepped into a pothole. My hat did Olympic somersaults through the blue sky as my body rose into the air and then began its descent back down to Earth. My face was the first to hit the ground, with a resounding thud, followed quickly by the rest of my body. As I lay on the ground gathering my thoughts, a voice inside of my head told me to look back. No, don't look back. That's what victims did in horror movies. That's how you get caught. Just get up and run, baby, run. I couldn't resist. As I scrambled back onto my feet, I shot a quick glimpse over my left shoulder and finally recognized the horrible truth. Cujo, the mixed something mutt, some kind of stocky, fat pooch weighing in at least fifteen pounds and displaying razor sharp teeth was bearing down for the kill. He wants me, I thought. He wants me real bad.

Not today, I thought, ignoring the look of sheer determination emulating from Cujo's fiery eyes. For a short, pudgy animal with minimal to no ground clearance, he was moving with remarkable agility and speed. I, however, was carrying at least thirty pounds of police equipment and starting to get winded. I shifted into fourth gear and bolted towards home base, my scout car. Twenty feet, fifteen feet, ten feet, nine feet, eight feet, seven feet, six feet, five feet, four feet, three feet, two feet, one, airborne. With athletic grace, I propelled my body through time and space, landing on the hood of my car with a loud crunch. I quickly scrambled to the rooftop, which was a level higher, and safer. Sitting gingerly on the roof, straddling the light bar and siren housing with both legs, I looked towards Cujo. He was beginning to labor and seemed to have slowed a bit. Yet he was still motoring towards my car, determined to catch his prey. A ghastly thought then entered my mind. What if Cujo can jump?

Please, please have remembered to wear your baton, I thought as I reached towards my belt. Usually I would leave the cursed thing in the car. I hated the way it would hang from my belt and thump against my leg when I walked. As luck would have it, today I had instinctively thrust it onto my belt, and I sighed with relief as my sweaty hand now clutched the cold smoothness of its handle. Should this animal decide to become a hanging curveball, I was prepared to send it deep over the left field fence. What was it thinking? Could it possibly be serious, or was it trying to intimidate me. Either way, if war was what this wretched animal wanted, war it would get. Planting one foot on the siren bar and the other on the hood, I dug in at the plate and waited for my pitch.

I would never get my chance. The dog suddenly came to a screeching halt, kicking up dirt and gravel as it came to rest about twenty feet from my car. There it sat, sitting up on its hind legs sizing me up. Great, here I am a crusader of truth and justice, trapped on the hood of my police car by some crazed version of a Steven King character. There was no dignity in this. What was worse was that now I could hear wave after wave of laughter coming from my female friend who had since retreated to the mouth of the alley on Ontario Road.

"Unbelievable. This is just simply unbelievable. No one will ever believe this really happened. This is like…like…something straight out of *Saturday Night Live*," she screamed, choking on her words between bursts of laughter.

"I don't really need to hear your comparisons right now ma'am," I said, not really expecting an answer. "This is a bit embarrassing."

"I'm really sorry, Chris. I just meant to tease you a little," she answered, sounding genuinely concerned. I glanced around looking for Cujo. He was still sitting motionless in the same place as before. "Listen, I really hate to leave you in this predicament, but I have to go."

"OK, I see how it is. Just have your little laugh, and then split. No problem. I think I can handle everything from here. I must admit though, this has easily been one of the highlights—or lowlights, depending on how you look at it—of my brief career," I answered back as my friend waved good-bye and escaped out of view onto Ontario Rd.

"Officer, Officer!" came a loud voice from above. I craned my neck into the sky searching for its origin.

"Up here in the window. Is everything all right?" I could see the face of an older woman peering out from an open window three stories above.

"Everything's fine. I'm just collecting my thoughts and enjoying the view from the top of my car," I yelled up to her. "It's quite peaceful."

"I'm the one who called the police, about the animal. Did you find him?" She asked.

"Uh, yeah, sort of, actually, I think he kind of found me," I shouted back, feeling very, very silly. I finally realized that my options were running out. Rabies was definitely a possibility, and I could not leave this animal in the alley wandering freely around and terrorizing the local neighborhood. I had been desperately hoping I would not have to call my supervisor for advice, but now understood that this was my only course of action. My career was now officially screwed.

"What are you going to do?" the woman yelled from the third floor.

"I'm not exactly sure yet," I answered. "Do you have any suggestions?" I reached for my portable radio and called for my supervisor. A few seconds later, Sgt. Cumberland acknowledged. I explained to her my situation as best I could. After a few seconds of confused silence, she said to call the dispatcher and notify the animal control board. "And whatever you do, do not shoot him!" She yelled before signing off. Great, shooting this animal was the last thing I was thinking about. But as I sat and weighed my options, I realized maybe shooting him was going to be a necessity. I glanced at my holstered gun, unable to fully comprehend that my first-ever police shooting might involve shooting a rabid dog. It would definitely have been justified, and I cringed at the thought of what would happen if Cujo were to take off running. I knew I couldn't let him go. I'd have to pursue him through the alleys of the city, gun drawn and yelling "Freeze or I'll shoot!" I had just finished telling the dispatcher to notify someone from the Animal Control Board when I heard the footsteps behind me.

"I have an idea!" A woman blurted standing behind my scout car. I recognized her as the woman from the upstairs window. She was a smaller, older lady, and she was holding a small wire cage in her left hand. In her right hand she held a package of hot-dogs. "If we can somehow coax him into this cage, it will close behind him automatically."

"You sound like you've done this before," I answered.

"I did, once before, same kind of situation. The man from Animal Control left this cage behind, so I kept it." I glanced over towards Cujo who was now moving slowly towards several trash containers leaning next to a garage door. He appeared to be having major difficulties moving. Within a matter of seconds he had disappeared behind one of the plastic cans.

"It will never work," I stated as I turned back towards her. "He's too smart. I can't really explain it, but there's something very different and strange about this particular dog.

"You've been watching too many movies. I'll give him ten minutes and either his curiosity or his appetite will get the better of him," replied the woman. She carefully placed the cage to the side of the alley. She then opened the package of hot dogs and tossed several into the back of the cage. Finally, leaning over, she opened the cage door and returned to the side of my car. Never in a million years did I ever expect my police career to encompass this. Rescuing cats from a tree, maybe, but trying to outsmart a rabid dog in downtown Washington, D.C.? No way. Now we began the waiting game.

"Good luck, Officer. I'll be upstairs if you need me. Just yell, my window's open," she said as she headed back towards the front of the building.

"You mean you're not going to stay and see if it really works?" I asked sheepishly.

"No, I can't. I have to go pick up a friend. Besides, I love animals and I don't really care to see one I know will eventually be killed. Just give the cage back to Animal Control when they arrive. Good luck!"

I was now alone. Well, sort of alone. Every few moments I could hear the distinctive sound of Cujo shuffling around behind the garbage cans and was reminded that my friend still wanted to play. I must have counted at least ten minutes before he finally took notice of the bait. Cautiously sticking his nose out from behind a trash can, he caught a scent of the hot dogs. To be honest, I really had no idea whether or not rabid dogs would even eat them. Whatever the case, he definitely seemed somewhat interested in what waited inside the metal cage. Taking little notice of me, he slowly waddled towards the cage, stopping every few feet to take in a few sniffs. Stretching his neck out and squinting first left and then right, I figured he was trying to decide whether it was safe to continue. Perhaps he was slightly confused by the empty scout car roof. I had since escaped into the safe confines of the driver's seat, and was now slumped down and peering ever so slightly over the edge of the door. I held my breath, knowing that any sudden noise would scare him back behind the garbage cans. I couldn't believe this was going to work. Of all the luck, most of which had been bad, this incident seemed to finally be nearing its completion. One caged dog, several happy citizens, and a tired police officer back in service. Unfortunately, this was not to be the case.

"Easy does it." The sound of a voice startled me. I jumped out of my seat, banging my head against the scout car's roof. Sticking my head out the window, I saw a white D.C. government Animal Control truck parked at the mouth of the alley. Walking past me was the driver. He was holding a long metal pole with a circular rope dangling from the end.

"I didn't mean to startle you Officer," he said, keeping his attention on the dog.

"No problem. You didn't startle me, I just had a muscle spasm," I answered as I opened the door of my car and got out. "What are you going to do?"

"Catch him with this pole if he'll just stay still a few more moments."

"No way. He's pretty clever. Mean, too."

"Son, I've been up against the meanest of the mean. One more rabid dog isn't going to put no chill in my spine!"

"This isn't any ordinary dog."

"Just stand back, and take notes." I moved in behind him and watched intently over his shoulder. My feet readied themselves to take action. I had been caught off guard once already. Fool me once, shame on you. Fool me twice, shame on me.

"Just a little closer," the man was mumbling to himself. The noose was now only a few feet above Cujo's head. Realizing he was now being stalked, the dog turned his attention away from the hotdogs and now towards us. Hunching back slightly, he sat motionless staring into our faces. He didn't seem to notice the rope that was only several inches above his head.

"Just a little bit closer, come on...steady, steady!" With a simultaneous snapping motion, both rope and dog leapt into the air.

"Shit!" I yelled as I turned and raced back to my car. Once safely on the opposite side, I turned back, fully expecting to see one D.C. government employee rolling on the ground clutching at the furry animal gnawing at his throat. I was wrong.

"Goddamn. You scared the shit out of me!" the man yelled as he carried the dog back towards his truck. Cujo was hanging from the end of the pole, his seemingly lifeless body suspended in the air.

"Sorry. I guess I overreacted a bit," I answered sheepishly.

"Man, you seen too many movies," he answered.

"Yea, I've been told that before."

In a few moments, he was gone. Off to take Cujo to Animal Control Headquarters, or wherever they would dispose of the body. And, I was off to pick up my ride-along, and fully deny any involvement I had in this crazy situation.

CHAPTER FIVE

After rounding the corner of Columbia and Ontario Road, I began slowly making my way towards a Safeway supermarket half a block away, my stomach growling terribly, eagerly anticipating the dinner I had put off for the last couple of hours. So far, January had been an exceptionally cold month, and I was looking forward to the warmth of being inside almost as much as eating. My four-block foot beat, which consisted of walking around and trying not to freeze to death didn't have much in the way of places to keep warm, so my body had literally frozen solid long ago. I've heard that a good officer never gets cold, hungry or wet. I guess I just really sucked, because I was cold as shit, starving, and had been soaked many, many times before.

"What's up fellas?" I waved as I passed several street vendors camped out on the sidewalk parallel to Columbia Road.

"Nothing much, Officer," one of the men answered back in a thick Jamaican accent. He was standing in front of a large wooden stand covered with wool and knit skullcaps. Man, they looked so warm. Reggae music blasted from a boom box sitting next to the curb. "How's about a hat to keep the head warm Officer?"

"No thanks, I've already got one," I replied, pointing to the ridiculous uniform hat sitting on top of my head. I looked like a bus driver.

"You must be crazy, man. That hat isn't going to do nothing but freeze to the top of your head," he said, laughing out loud. Several of the other vendors joined in on the laughter.

"I know, I know. But I don't have much of a choice," I answered sheepishly. "Rules are rules!" He was right. My hat had frozen to the top of my head. What was worse was not only had it frozen, it was also stuck at a sideways angle, making my head look lopsided.

"You need to be a little rebellious, man. They can't be paying you enough to freeze." Another man shouted.

"You got that right. That's why I'm heading indoors for a while," I said. I reached my arm out and gently pushed open the glass door, contemplating what I was going to eat. Maybe some fried chicken, or maybe some hot soup, or maybe just a huge chocolate bar. I was so hungry just about anything would suffice. I hadn't even made it two steps inside when my radio crackled with life.

"Foot beat five...priority...I need backup...right away!" The voice was male, but I had no idea who it was. He was screaming.

"Foot beat five, what's your location?" The dispatcher asked. The radio was silent for a few seconds.

"Foot beat five, I repeat, what is your location?" The dispatcher asked again. Still there was no answer.

"Cruiser two-forty-two," a voice responded, breaking several seconds of silence. I held my radio up to my ear, my heart pounding with every breath.

"Go ahead, two-forty-two," the dispatcher answered.

"Foot beat five is detailed to Howard University for the basketball game. Try raising any unit on that detail and find out what's going on and who's in need of assistance."

"Foot beat four!" shouted another voice on the radio.

"Go ahead foot beat four," answered the dispatcher.

"I'm with foot beat five. We need as many units as you can send. Send them to Burr Gymnasium, immediately!"

"What do you have, foot beat four?" The dispatcher asked. I couldn't believe the dispatcher was wasting so much time.

"Dispatcher, just start sending the damn units!" Cruiser Two-forty-two interrupted. Thank you, I said to myself. Finally, someone had the guts to make a decision.

"Be advised, all units. We have a priority at Howard University. All units, respond code one," the dispatcher said. Within seconds, every available unit in service was answering to respond. I counted ten cars before foot beat four returned to the radio.

"Foot beat four!"

"Go ahead foot beat four," answered the dispatcher.

"Keep sending units. We've got a riot. Keep' em coming."

My adrenaline immediately shot to the ceiling. I had to get there. But, I was stuck without a car. I ran out into Columbia Road, hoping to spot a scout car heading to the call. I didn't have to wait long. Within seconds, scout car eighty-eight was bearing down Columbia Road at about seventy miles per hour. Without thinking, I bolted into the middle of the road and began waving my arms back and forth above my head. The scout car skidded to a halt several feet in front of me.

"Hurry up!" the officer inside shouted as he flung open the passenger door.

"I'm in!" I screamed as I jumped into the seat. Within seconds we were racing across 16th Street. The radio was alive with the voice of officers, who were still screaming for more units to assist.

By the time we arrived on the scene, the dispatcher had already started requesting units from across the city. Every officer in the Third District had already responded, and scattered officers were still calling for more assistance. I couldn't believe it. All hell must be breaking loose. Our car skidded to a halt on Georgia Avenue, right at Howard University's main entrance. I tossed my frozen hat in the backseat, grabbed my baton and followed several other officers towards Burr gymnasium. As we rounded the corner and came within sight of the gym, I suddenly found myself in the middle of a crowd of at least a thousand people. Officers were scattered here and there, making their way through the crowd and towards the gym's front doors. I grabbed the butt of my pistol, not wanting anyone to pull it out as I tunneled through the crowd.

"What the hell is going on?" A lieutenant yelled as we pushed to the front doors. Broken glass was scattered across the concrete.

"They oversold the game. All these people have tickets, but can't get in," answered an officer, who had scratches on his face and a torn shirt. "All of a sudden, they just started pushing forward. We couldn't stop them." I looked around and saw about ten of our officers, and about ten Howard University Police Officers as well. They all had terrified looks on their faces. I could just imagine the feeling of having a thousand people trying to push through you to get inside of a building. No wonder they had been screaming for as many units as they could get.

By now, there were at least fifty officers lined up across the front of the gym. We had formed a line, and the crowd had retreated slightly. Shouts came from the crowd about police brutality and several pleas to storm the doors again. Thankfully, no one acted on these requests. It had become a standoff.

"Listen up everyone!" The lieutenant, whom I hadn't ever seen before, shouted into a megaphone. "You are not going to be allowed in to see the game." A sudden burst of angry shouts came from the crowd. Several items were tossed in our direction, only to fall harmlessly to the ground just short of us. Tensions were mounting rapidly. There were more pleas to storm the doors. I braced my legs and prepared for the charge.

"I know that most of you have tickets. There's been a mistake, and you will be reimbursed for the price of the ticket. But for now, we have no choice but to deny anyone else access to the game. It's completely full," the lieutenant shouted. More shouts came from the unsettled, angry crowd. I was sure they were going to storm at any moment.

"What about those of us who traveled here to see this game?" A lady asked. She had pushed to the front of the crowd. "We came all the way from Virginia. It's not right."

"I understand," the lieutenant answered. He was now perched on top of a scout car's roof, as if he were preparing to order a charge. "I sympathize with you. But there's nothing we can do. There's been a terrible mix-up. What's been done is done. Right now, the gym is completely full and we can't let in anyone else."

"So what are we supposed to do? We've got friends inside who we rode here with." The same lady asked.

"You can wait here until the game is over." The lady shook her head and vanished back into the crowd.

"Listen. If you are waiting for someone inside, you can wait here until the game is over," the lieutenant repeated, shouting into the crowd. Slowly, people started to disperse back into the campus. For the next twenty minutes, we held our line until the crowd had diminished to a respectable, but still formidable 500.

It was at this time that the first poor command decision was made, which would ultimately predicate the insanity which would soon follow. With the exception of ten of us, every other officer was sent back into service. A sergeant pleaded with the lieutenant to keep more officers on hand, but the lieutenant swore he knew what he was doing and everything was now under control. I just prayed I wasn't going to be one of the officers asked to stay. I suppose, in hindsight, and if I wasn't still a clueless rookie, I would have already made my way back to a car and returned to my comfortable, albeit cold, foot beat. But, what can I say. I was a rookie, and instead I just stood there, with the words "pick me" blazoned across my forehead.

"Archer. You, Dunn, and Nelson stay here in front of the door," the lieutenant said as I quietly tried to sneak away.

"Yes, sir," I answered, cursing under my breath. I knew this was going to be bad.

For the next hour, the ten of us held fast, pacing back and forth over the broken glass, scanning the crowd for any signs of discontent or impending violence. An uneasy quietness had developed within the crowd. Every few minutes, shouts of storming the doors erupted from pockets in the crowd, causing us all to clench our teeth. If they stormed the doors now, we would be crushed like bugs. Fortunately, cooler heads prevailed, and we were able to make it to the end of the game without incident.

"Just a little more, and we're out of here," I thought to myself as the game finally ended and people slowly exited the gym and met with friends outside. The conclusion of the game, coupled with the reunion of friends seemed to have an eerie calming effect. For the first time, I honestly thought the worst was over, but I couldn't have been more mistaken. As if on cue, the University Marching Band came storming out of the gym, blasting the campus fight song loudly into the night sky. People began crowding around, forming an impromptu celebration in front of the gym. Everyone was happy, and content to celebrate with song and dance. Personally, I could have cared less what was happening. As long as we weren't being trampled, I was considering it a good night. However, the sound of the blaring music seemed to rub our lieutenant the wrong way, and within seconds, he was back on the hood of the scout car, commanding the band to cease playing. This, in case you're keeping count, would be the second major command mistake. Slowly, the crowd started getting riled up, and the band continued to play louder and louder. I gritted my teeth, knowing all too well we were only one small moment away from all hell breaking loose again, this time with me stuck right in the middle.

"You must stop playing immediately!" The lieutenant shouted again through the megaphone. I could tell he was getting angrier and angrier. I just stood motionless, praying to myself. Unfortunately, I must not have prayed hard enough, or to the right god, for when I glanced up at the lieutenant, he was frantically waving for me to come over. No, no, no. Not me. I'm not ready for this! Slowly and reluctantly I made my way to his car.

"Yes, sir," I said, standing stoically, like Custer at his last stand. I was prepared to take my beating.

"I want you and a couple of other officers to go into the crowd and tell the band to stop playing. It's too late at night for this to be going on," he said sternly. I knew that resistance was futile.

"OK let me get this right, sir. You want us to go into that crowd of about 500 people and stop the band from playing?" another officer standing next to me asked.

"Yeah!" I chimed in, echoing his sentiments. "Is that really wise?"

"That's correct," the lieutenant answered, crushing me and my rebellion with his best and most authoritative stare. "That is a direct order, Officer!"

So there it was. The dreaded direct order, which no matter how embedded in insanity, or lack of just plain basic common sense, had to be followed, lest we be charged with the most absurd and overused disciplinary charge in the history of law-enforcement: insubordination. There was no reasoning our way out of this, since intelligent minds had been made up, and even more intelligent orders had been given. So, there was nothing left but to embark on the unthinkable. Clutching my baton at my side, and out of view, I pushed behind several other officers and waded into the mass of people. It was bad enough we had kept the crowd from storming the gymnasium a second time, but now we were going to force the school band from playing their fight song, which I later learned was a time-honored tradition. I guess it didn't take a rocket scientist to realize this was going to be, as they say on the streets, all bad.

My initial trip through the crowd was volatile, to say the least. Shouts of "fuck the police" echoed through the air, which was fine, because, well, sticks and stones may break my bones, and so forth. However, what did get on my nerves was every few seconds, I felt a hand squeeze my ass, or tug on my belt. Had they been female, I might not have minded, in fact, I might have even enjoyed it, in some sick, strange, police sort of way. But I was surrounded by mostly males, whom I knew were the culprits, and whom were not displaying even an ounce of brotherly affection, and I really didn't appreciate them grasping my ass. The crowd of people was so tightly pushed together that I could barely stand up straight, sometimes finding it difficult to even keep both feet planted on the ground. For the most part, most of the people were good-natured, and probably had no desire to hurt any of us. But I knew there were instigators around, who probably wanted nothing better than to start a full-fledged riot. So I withstood the jeers and taunting, and shrugged off the physical jolts and grabs. Soon, I would be back on my beat, stuffing my stomach with piping hot food.

I'm not exactly sure what exactly set off the next chain of events. I know I was wedged in between several people, my feet barely touching the ground and unable to move. Two officers several feet ahead of me were approaching a drummer, who was beating away in the back of the band. Then, in a flash, the proverbial shit hit the fan. Bodies began flying all around me. Fists, arms and feet flailed through the air, and I was lifted off the ground, almost like a slam dancer lifted in a mosh pit. I quickly lost sight of the other officers, and my view of the world became a spinning circle. The only thing I could think of was protecting my gun. I knew I wasn't going to pull it out, but I didn't want anyone else getting their hands on it either.

I quickly turned back in the direction I had come, and took two steps forward. Suddenly, from my left, I barely caught sight of a dark object out of the corner of my left eye heading right at my head. I turned partially away, and within seconds a sharp pain exploded on the bridge of my nose. My eyesight went blank and I fell to my knees. Salty fluid ran down my nose and into my mouth. It was blood. I spit a mouthful onto the ground. People were running all around me, kicking and punching me in my ribs and torso. I rolled onto my stomach and pushed myself to my knees. Shielding my face with my hands, I clutched my baton in my right hand and scrambled to my feet. I wanted so badly to just start swinging away, taking out my fear and anger on anyone who passed too close, but something inside of me wouldn't let me do it. Instead, I lumbered towards the gym, where I knew other officers would be. Every few seconds, looking around, I saw other officers battling with people in the crowd. Batons were swinging wildly back and forth. Using my baton as a shield, I nudged people out of my way as I picked up my pace. The blood continued to flow down the front of my face, making it difficult for me to see clearly. A huge man with a skullcap on his head pushed in front of me, cocked his right arm and prepared to strike. I shifted my weight to my rear and prepared to block, when out of nowhere, another officer swung his baton and struck the man across the back of his head.

The baton broke in two, with the end piece still in the officer's hand, while the tip flew towards the sky. Amazingly, the man just shook it off, turned away and took off in the opposite direction. Suddenly, I felt something hard connect on the back of my head, causing me to lose my balance and stumble again to my knees. I immediately sprang back to my feet, grasped my baton in both hands like a baseball bat, turned and prepared to swing. I came face to face with a frightened old lady, who screamed and threw her hands up to protect her face.

"I'm not going to hit you!" I shouted, feeling like an idiot. I dropped my stick to my side. "Get out of here!" She turned and ran away. I cursed myself for losing my cool. I turned back towards the gym and continued to push forward.

Once I reached the entrance to Burr Gymnasium, I located several other officers. They looked almost as bad as I did. A crowd of at least fifty or more officers were running up the street, a little late, but, better late than never. My head ached and my knees were wobbly. I gave myself about another minute before I was going to collapse. Thankfully, I saw an ambulance parked near the entrance to the university and without hesitation I sprinted back through a smaller group of rioters and ran right up into the back of the ambulance.

"Man, I guess you got it pretty bad!" One of the ambulance medics said as I stumbled in. There were two other officers already being treated.

"Does it really look that bad?" I asked, spitting another mouthful of blood onto the floor. With the exception of the blood in my mouth, my splitting headache and my dizziness, I actually felt pretty good.

"Well...uh...have you actually taken a look at yourself?" He answered hesitantly.

"No," I replied, getting a little frightened. I glanced at my legs and noticed baseball-sized holes in the pants of both knees. Bloody bare skin was exposed through the tattered fabric. As I scanned upwards to my lower torso, I could actually make out footprints from where feet had stepped on me. It was a miracle I was still standing.

"I guess I do look pretty ragged," I said. I plopped onto a bench, closed my eyes and waited my turn to be treated.

"We'll just clean you up a bit," the medic said as he stood over me. "This laceration above your eye isn't that serious. It won't need stitches.

And the cuts to your knees are just superficial. What's got me concerned, however, is your headache. There's a slight chance you might have a concussion. Maybe you should come with us to the hospital and get checked out." My dizziness had subsided, and the only thing I could think of was getting back into the crowd and helping out the other officers. "There's also some bleeding coming from the back of your head. Were you hit there?"

"I need to get back out to help," I said as I stood up and opened the back of the ambulance. My legs were still wobbly. "If my headache doesn't go away before I check off tonight, I'll drive myself in." I didn't wait for a response. Looking like a homeless person whom had lived on the streets for the past year, I jumped out of the ambulance and headed back in the direction of the gymnasium.

"Everything's pretty quiet now," an officer said to me as I walked next to him. "By the way, you look like shit."

"Thanks asshole. I feel like shit," I answered smiling. Most of the crowd was still milling about, but the confrontations seemed to have stopped. The same lieutenant from earlier was back on the hood of his scout car and blaring out commands to the crowd and other officers. He was still trying to tell the crowd to go home. I turned away, not wanting to get volunteered for another fucked-up assignment.

After several minutes of arguing and resisting, a man emerged from the center of the crowd and announced himself as president of the student government association. He began pleading with the crowd to disperse and go home. Finally, the crowd began to listen.

Again, I was just starting to think the worst was over when I caught site of a huge rock sailing for my head. I ducked at the last minute, and it crashed to the ground not more than two feet away. I turned to the direction from which it had come. Another rock, this one even bigger, flew through the air, heading directly for the lieutenants head. At the last instant, he ducked, and it crashed against the hood of his car, leaving behind a good-sized dent. Several other rocks hummed through the air, sending officers running for cover. I advanced to the side of a scout car and ducked behind. This was insane, I thought to myself.

"Get them! Somebody get them!" the lieutenant shouted to no one in particular. He was pointing to a group of about ten kids who had positioned themselves on the opposite side of an adjacent fence and were standing on top of some football bleachers. Beside them were piles of large of rocks. Then they unloaded on the lieutenants scout car. Rocks flew through the air like rain. I jumped to my feet, and along with several other officers took off towards the bleachers. In my present condition, I had absolutely no business engaging in any foot pursuits, but I was still pretty much running on adrenaline, and I can assure you, adrenaline can be a bitch to contain.

Within seconds, I was on the football field, running in full stride across the artificial turf. The kids had a good-sized lead, but I was slowly gaining ground. J.U.N.O, our police helicopter, came zooming out of the dark night sky, aiming a high intensity spotlight on the kids as they ran across the field, making their way for a fence on the other side. Hovering only about ten or twenty feet above the ground, the helicopter slowly followed their path. I ran directly underneath, taking a moment to glance at the metallic bottom. I picked up my speed and pressed forward.

Once I hit the far sideline of the field, I realized I was not going to catch them. The other officers were still running behind me. Most of the kids had by now scaled to the top of the fence, which stood about ten or twelve feet high, and were jumping to safety on the other side. I was pissed.

Then, just ahead of me, I saw two fat kids still laboring for the fence. They were only a few feet away, but if I picked up my pace just a little bit, maybe I could pull them down. I gritted my teeth and sprinted with every ounce of energy my body still had. As I got just a few feet from the base of the fence, one of the fat kids had reached the top, and was straddling the fence, and the other was just reaching the top rung. I had only one chance. Thrusting my body forward, I flung myself into the base of the fence. I bounced off like a trampoline, my body flying backwards onto my side. But more importantly, I had sent a massive vibration up the height of the fence. To my surprise, it worked. The fat kid on top flew off, executing a perfect swan dive, and landing on the hard ground on the other side with a painful thud. He screamed in pain as his body bounced on the dirt. Amazingly, he sprang to his feet and ran off. The other fat kid was not so lucky. He fell backwards, landing on his side with a jolting crash. Before he had the time to think about getting up and running, several officers converged on him and placed him under arrest. I lay on the ground smiling, content that despite the beating I had taken, I was still able to catch one of the rock throwers.

After two or three minutes of just sitting on the ground, watching the eerie image of the helicopter hovering above the football field, I finally got to my feet and headed back towards the campus. My night was over.

PART TWO

LIFE

"To continue to live." Webster's New American Dictionary

Don't be tempted by the shiny apple
Don't you eat of a bitter fruit
Hunger only for a taste of justice
Hunger only for a world of truth
'Cause all that you have is your soul

-Tracy Chapman

CHAPTER SIX

How in the world did I ever get myself into this situation? Here I was, hanging upside down from the top of an eight-foot chain link fence, my waist and pants entangled on the barbed wiring on top. All of the blood in my body was now rushing to my head and my equipment belt was slowly sliding down my torso, pulling the crotch of my pants up the crack of my ass. My radio, which was in its case on my belt, was filled with the sounds of other officers who were now trying desperately to locate me. To think, only a few minutes ago, I had been safely in the confines of my scout car, enjoying a warm cup of coffee and reading the newspaper. And to make matters worse, I could now make out the shadowy dark silhouette of the man I had been chasing, now kneeling on the opposite side of the yard and staring right at me. His arm was extended forward and he was pointing a gun right at my head.

The night had started on the calm side. This was my second month working with the Rapid Deployment Unit, a specialized unit that patrolled some of the most dangerous areas in the city. After a year of working with field training officers and walking a foot beat, I was definitely ready to try something new. So, when an opening came up for an experimental unit designed to concentrate on high drug areas, it didn't take much convincing for me to sign up. In fact, I can still remember the exact conversation with Sgt. Sartor, one of the primary recruiters for this unit, as he tracked me down at my locker one day. It was short and sweet, and went something like this:

"Archer, your new assignment starts Saturday night at eleven p.m." That was it. In one sentence, I was recruited.

Our job was to infiltrate high crime neighborhoods, especially where homicides had occurred, and to aggressively patrol for any and all violations we could see. Having only a little more than a year on the department, I considered myself fortunate to be assigned to such a specialized unit. Our headquarters was based out of an old warehouse located near the Anacostia River. No desks, no lockers. Just a large dusty, filthy room with a few broken down tables, a chalkboard and a lot of young, aggressive officers, who wanted nothing else in life but to lock people up. Our cars, if you could call them that, were all recycled and out of service junkers that barely ran. But, such was life in D.C., and the work made all the inconveniences seem mild in comparison.

On this particular night, it was decided we would work in the Fifth District, an area in the Northeast quadrant of the city. Our focus was the Montana Terrace neighborhood, a compact apartment complex that sits atop a hill off of Montana Street. This neighborhood had long ago carved itself out as one of the worst, and most dangerous, areas in the city, and open-air crack cocaine markets flourished within the shielded confines of the walkways and parking lots. Once roll call was over, I grabbed my map, checked out a portable radio and headed for my car.

My regular partner, Tim Jackson, had taken leave for the night, so I was forced to make my way around scenic Montana Terrace alone, a thought I was not the least bit comfortable with. Tim was a great guy, and above all else, he had this amazing calming effect over those people with whom he came in contact. I always felt at ease around him, and enjoyed his company immensely. But as luck would have it, tonight I was alone, and had it not been for my poorly photocopied street map, I'm certain I would have wandered around the city for hours trying to find our assigned area.

"Hey scrub! What's up?" I said to Officer Quientero as I grabbed a courtesy cup from behind the counter and made my way to the coffee machine in the back. The 7-11 was empty, save for the gentleman working behind the counter. He flashed me a smile as I passed by, and I casually tipped my hat in return. I'm certain he was more than happy to see several police officers in his store, especially considering it was well past midnight.

"Nada, Arch. What's up with you?" Quientero answered back. He had a cup of coffee in his hand as well.

"Aside from being lost, tired as shit and hungry, I'm fine," I said as I poured piping hot coffee into my cup. It was probably only thirty degrees outside, and every bone and joint in my body was frozen solid.

"Where's Jackson?" Quientero asked, referring to Tim.

"That bum took leave. I think he's going fishing in the morning."

"It figures. They got you riding alone?"

"Yeah, I don't mind, except I don't have a clue where anything is. My street map really sucks." I finished putting my customary ten packets of sugar in my coffee, and after stirring up the sugary, black muck I took a long sip. My throat and stomach burned as the hot liquid entered my system.

"I know what you mean. Ace and I have been trying to find our way around, too. It's like a maze around here. None of the streets make any sense," Quientero answered.

"Where's Ace?" I asked, scanning the store for Acevedo. He was Quientero's assigned partner.

"He's doing some paperwork back at the station. I'm getting ready to go pick him up as soon as I finish my coffee."

"OK dude. I'm going to grab a paper and hit an alley somewhere. I don't really feel like doing much tonight, especially since Tim's off. I've been in court all week and I'm tired as shit. Raise me on the radio if you and Ace decide to do something later on," I said making my way towards the cash register. The prior day's *Washington Post* was stuffed under my left arm.

"No problem. Give us about an hour and I'll give you a call. And be safe, OK?" He answered as he eased past me and out the front door.

"You bet." I shouted behind him. "You do the same."

"Twenty-seven cents, please," the man behind the counter said in a deep voice.

"Sure," I answered as I stuffed my hand deep into my pocket and searched for some change. "Been pretty quiet tonight?"

"Yeah, there's not much business after midnight. How about you?" He asked. He took the thirty cents from me and dropped the coins into the cash register.

"I'm just coming on, midnights. I'll come back in a couple of hours and let you know," I answered smiling.

"That's OK if it's that busy; don't bring the bad guys in here with you."

"Now do I look like the type of person who would do that to you, and jeopardize my free coffee for the rest of my career? Can you imagine what the police would do without free coffee? We would probably all melt, like the witch in the *Wizard of Oz*," I said, laughing out loud. My friend behind the counter laughed, as well. I pushed open the front door and jogged to my scout car.

I decided to put off reading the paper until later. I was determined to learn my way around the neighborhood if it took me the whole night. I slowly made my way up Rhode Island Avenue, glancing at my map every few seconds to check the cross streets. Bingo. Montana Street was only a few blocks ahead. I eased down the gas pedal and accelerated forward.

"Cruiser four-seventy-four with a priority," yelled the dispatcher over the radio. I jumped in my seat, nearly spilling my coffee. Four-seventy-four was one of our cars, although I couldn't immediately make out the voice.

"Go ahead four-seventy-four. All other units restrict transmission," answered the dispatcher. A lump formed in my throat. Since it was one of our units, they had to be somewhat close.

"Four-seventy-four, we're behind a tan-colored, four-door Chevy with D.C. registration seven, nine, seven...two, four, six. Attempting to initiate a traffic stop but they are refusing to pull over. Get me some assistance," stated the voice from cruiser four-seventy-four. I still couldn't make out who it was.

"What is your exact location four-seventy-four?" The dispatcher asked.

"We're going eastbound on Montana Street, I think towards Rhode Island Avenue! We're traveling at a high rate of speed."

Shit! They were coming right towards me. I threw down my map and floored the gas pedal. My back slammed against the seat as my car accelerated several gears.

"OK we're now turning onto...onto...dispatcher, be advised we've turned off of Montana Street, but I'm not sure what street we're on. Stand by for further."

"Four-seventy-four, advise your location. All other units, be on the lookout for cruiser four-seventy-four, somewhere off of Montana Street," answered the dispatcher.

My car skidded across the intersection of Rhode Island Avenue and Montana Street, going into a slight fishtail as I turned on to Montana. I could hear the sounds of sirens all around, but I couldn't decipher which one's were four-seventy-fours and which were those of the cars racing in to assist. I slammed my brakes and came to a jarring stop. I hit the power windows and slid them open. I tried desperately to make out the location of the sirens. They were getting louder and louder, and coming at me from my right side. I jammed my car into drive and made a right turn onto Saratoga Street. I was halfway down the block when I realized how narrow this street was. On each side of me were parked cars, barely making enough room for two lanes of traffic. And the sounds of the sirens were getting closer and closer, coming right at me. Damn. I had to get off of this street. I slammed the gas pedal and raced for the next intersection, which was only a couple of hundred feet away. The sirens were right on me now, and I turned my head in every direction trying to see from where they were coming.

Suddenly, in the blink of an eye, high beam lights from a car directly ahead blinded me. A split second later, a scout car raced around the corner directly behind. They were heading right toward me.

"Cruiser four-seventy-four, we're heading west bound on Saratoga Street. Still at a very high rate of speed," yelled the officer. In a matter of seconds, I was going to nail this car head on. It made no attempt to slow down. I grabbed the steering wheel and whipped it to the right, pulling the passenger side of my car to within inches of the parked cars. I quickly ripped the wheel back to the left and straightened her out. My speed was about forty miles per hour, which was about half the speed of the cars racing at me. The car heading towards me picked up speed and pulled to their far right. I knew they would not try and stop. They were going to try and squeeze by.

"You're not going to make it, asshole! Stop the fucking car!" I shouted out loud. I couldn't believe they weren't going to stop. There was no way they had enough clearance to get by me. I grasped the steering wheel with both of my hands as hard as I could and prepared for impact. Please, please, please let there be enough room!

I whipped my head to the left, my mouth hanging wide open as a tan colored Chevy pulled directly next to me, only heading in the opposite direction. Even though we were traveling different ways, and at a high rate of speed, I could still clearly make out the expression of the man driving the car as he and his passenger flew past. It was a look of inhumanity and complete disregard. It was a look I would never forget. With maybe two inches to spare, the car cleared past me, and I was left to stare into the darkness.

I checked my rearview mirror and caught a glimpse of the Chevy's rear as it began to fishtail in the back. The effort in passing me had caused the driver to begin losing control of his vehicle. Then I caught the rear of the pursuing scout car still directly behind, which must have just barely missed me as well, only to be honest, I never even saw it. They had not even flinched. Turning my attention back to my front, I saw the upcoming intersection closing in from about twenty-five feet away.

"Cruiser four-seventy-four, they're losing control. They're losing control!" Someone shouted over the radio. I slammed on my brakes and ripped the wheel all the way to the left, causing my car to viciously skid across the intersection almost out of control. Turning 180 degrees, I cut the wheel back to the right and pulled my car in the direction from which they had been traveling. I turned just in time to see the Chevy skid uncontrollably to its right and suddenly flip onto its side. It skidded several feet on its side before smashing into the side of a telephone pole. The sound of the crash filled the once-quiet night air, and a steady stream of smoke poured out from its engine. I hit the gas and raced towards the wreck.

"Cruiser four-seventy-four, we have a crack up. Get me an ambulance."

"An ambulance is on the way four-seventy-four. Is everything under control at this time?" The dispatcher asked. I was now only a few hundred feet away, and my adrenaline was racing through my veins like water. The officers in cruiser four-seventy-four had jumped out of their scout car and were running towards the accident. I pulled in behind them and jumped out of my car. As I was racing towards the wreck, my eyes caught some motion coming from the driver's side door, which was facing straight up into the night sky. Someone was pulling himself out of the window, onto the door, and then he jumped to the ground and began running across the street towards a residential neighborhood.

"Cruiser four-sixty-five with a priority!" I screamed into my portable hand held radio.

"Go ahead with your priority four-sixty-five," answered the dispatcher.

"I've got one suspect running on foot from four-seventy-four's location. He's a black male wearing blue jeans and black shirt. Dark colored ski jacket. He's heading south on..." I yelled into the radio. My voice came in short bursts as I tried to run and talk at the same time. I had no idea what street the suspect was running on, and he had at least a twenty-five yard lead on me.

"Four-sixty-five, give me further information. What is your location?" the dispatcher shouted. I looked to my right and left for a street sign, but there was none—only a long street and row after row of small, brick single-family homes. I shoved my radio into its case on my belt and picked up my pace.

"I repeat, four-sixty-five, give me your location...four-sixty-five, do you copy?" The dispatcher asked again. I ignored the transmission. My suspect was directly ahead of me, and I was slowly gaining ground. I had no idea where I was, and there was no way I was going to let him get away.

"All units, be on the lookout for an officer engaged in a foot pursuit somewhere near the 1400 Block of Saratoga Street," yelled the dispatcher, her voice coming in short, nervous bursts. I wanted to let her know where I was, but I didn't have a clue. This could have been any street in the world, and it would have made no difference. I was lost. And I wasn't stopping.

I could see the icy cold breaths of air coming from my mouth. The burning in my lungs was almost unbearable. My pace was well above what I was used to, and I knew I was only good for a couple of blocks. Unfortunately, the suspect ahead of me didn't seem to be tiring at all. My lungs felt like a long knife had been thrust deep inside them.

Suddenly, the suspect turned sharply to his left and cut across the front lawn of a house. I turned right behind him. He ran to the side of the house and headed towards the back. I still followed directly behind. Once at the back of the house, he took two long steps and scaled a five-foot-high chain fence. His feet landed on the other side in full stride. I hit the fence with my left hand on top and threw my legs over the right. I stumbled slightly as my feet landed on the frozen ground with a thud. I quickly regained my balance and continued in pursuit. Up ahead, the suspect was slowing down. I knew my chance was coming. I bit into my lower lip and picked up my speed. For the next few moments, we continued through a series of back yards and over fence after fence after fence. I had long ago lost track of how far we had traveled.

Now we were running through the grassy back yard of a house. He was still about fifty feet in front of me, but he was gradually slowing down. It was pitch black, and the only thing I could see were my breath and his shadowy outline darting ahead. He hit the fence of another yard and scaled it in one swift motion. I couldn't believe he was still running so fast. I knew I couldn't continue much longer, and I had little to no chance of getting any assistance. Even though I could hear sirens off in the distance coming from scout cars searching for me, only luck would put them in my exact location.

I grasped the top of the fence, wincing in pain as one of the barbs penetrated my glove and pierced my skin. I quickly hoisted myself up and over, landing on the other side. My knees buckled under the strain of my weight. I could feel my heart beating at the base of my neck, and the pressure was becoming almost unbearable. My only condolence was in knowing he was still only a few feet ahead, and he was steadily losing his pace. His jogging was now labored, and he kept glancing over his shoulder to see where I was. Cutting to his right, he grasped the top of another fence, this one wooden, and lifted himself up. Straddling the top, he thrust himself over. I heard a loud crash from the other side as he landed on the ground. Then I heard him wince in pain. Judging by the sound, I was certain he had landed in an awkward position and twisted a knee or ankle. I had finally caught a break.

I raced to the base of the wooden fence and pulled myself to the top. Then I glanced through the yard and saw him limping across towards the opposite side. There was another fence, but this one was steel. His limp was profound, and I was certain he had severely sprained one of his ankles or knees. I jumped down and raced after him. He had pulled himself over the steel fence and was heading along the side of a house. I could see the outer glow of streetlights coming from the direction he was running, and could barely make out what appeared to be a street. Instead of climbing the fence, I turned to my left and started running parallel to him on the opposite side of the fence. If he continued towards the street, I could cut him off on the other side of the houses. Besides, I really didn't think I could make it up another fence, especially this one, which was about eight-feet high. Then, without warning, he hooked to his right and started walking away from me and into the darkness of another yard. I stopped and strained to see as his outline vanished from my sight. I eased myself forward, my hand on the butt of my holstered pistol. My other hand turned off my radio. I wanted to hear if anything moved, which is exactly what I heard. The only problem was the movement wasn't coming from his direction. It was coming from directly behind me.

I quickly spun on my heels and scanned the yard searching for the source of the sound. Coming from the rear of the house was a large, dark object moving with graceful speed and swiftness. I took a few steps back, my hand still clenched to the butt of my pistol. What the hell was it? I knew it wasn't possible for my suspect to have doubled back behind me so quickly. However, my questions were very quickly answered. Breaking into full stride, with white sharp teeth protruding from a wide snarl, was a huge Rottweiler bearing down on me.

In a flash I was sprinting in the opposite direction, my hands reaching for the cold, wiry strands of the chain fence. Mustering all of my strength, I hoisted myself up several rungs, my leather Reebok tennis shoes digging into the small spaces between the metal strands. Thank God I had ditched my old patent leather dress shoes several years ago. Although many a supervisor had threatened to discipline me for wearing unauthorized shoes, it was at this time I knew I had done the right thing in ignoring them. Using short, quick hand over hand grabs, I quickly climbed to the top. The Rottweiler reached the base of the fence and made a final leap for my legs, missing by a mere foot, no pun intended.

For the next few seconds, I watched as the frustrated canine below paced back and forth waiting for me to fall. I grasped the sharp barbs on the top rung of the fence, clenching my teeth as they ripped through my gloves and again shredded the palms of my hands. I could feel the blood dripping down my fingers. Finally, I was able to pull my torso over the top. As I brought my right leg up to my chest and prepared to swing it over, I abruptly felt the balance in my body make a sudden shift. Instantly, I found myself falling forward over the other side of the fence, head first. I clenched my legs together and dug my fingers deep into the metal fence. I was now almost completely parallel to the ground, but at least I had momentarily stopped my falling. The only thing preventing this was my equipment belt and pants, which had somehow become entangled on the top barbs of the fence. My stomach and face were facing the fence, and my back was to the area where I last saw the suspect, about whom I had now completely forgotten. On the other side of the fence, the Rottweiler had now retreated a few steps, but was still barking uncontrollably. I tried to pull my upper body up toward the top of the fence to untangle my uniform, but the angle I was hanging at left me unable to do so. I was stuck. I twisted my body slightly around and searched the far yard for signs of my suspect.

Out of the corner of my eye, I saw another slight movement. My eyes began to focus through the darkness, and I could just make out the distinctive shape of a man facing me. As my eyes began to focus even more, I could see him more clearly. I recognized his face. He was the same man I saw earlier driving the car past me during the chase. He had the exact same cold, blank expression on his face. I estimated his distance at about twenty feet, and he was crouched down on one knee. I could hear his labored breathing in between growls coming from the frustrated dog behind me. Slowly, ever so slowly, he raised his right arm and extended it in my direction. He was holding something dark, and I am sure it was a gun. I panicked.

Desperately, I wiggled my body up towards the top of the fence and reached for my holster. I was disoriented, and my hands moved around the outline of my equipment belt, feeling for the familiar handle of my gun. My mind kept repeating, "It's on the right side. It's on the right side!" My stomach muscles burned with fire as I tried to keep my chest up at my waist and parallel to the ground. The only way to describe the way I looked and felt was to think of a worm squirming at the end of a fishing hook. The dog was still going berserk, jumping against the fence and snapping his jaws open and shut. Damn. I was going to die. I knew it. I was completely powerless to defend myself. I was fully exposed, my body stretched across the fence like a silhouetted target in a shooting range. I only prayed that it would be quick and painless. In my mind, I knew I had failed. I had violated every rule known to police officers. I had set out on pursuit alone, without any idea of where I was. I failed to maintain radio contact. And I placed myself in a position where I couldn't control the outcome.

I turned my head back in the direction of the suspect and saw him kneeling with the gun in his left hand. He was banging it against his right hand. The gods had granted me the most opportune of all gun malfunctions, and I had seized a second chance. Calling on all of the strength I had left in my body, I pulled myself back to my waist and found the handle of my gun. Ripping it from my holster, I swung my arms down over my head, spun my torso around and pointed it at him.

"Drop the fucking gun!" I shouted at the top of my lungs. The trigger of my gun was at the point of release, and I had every intention to fire. But there was nothing there. Only a dark shadow was visible as he limped back across the yard and away from me. Goddamn. Not again. I tried desperately to focus my sights on him, which was next to impossible given the fact that I was pointed sideways, and he was moving too fast. I was just about to reach up and holster my gun when I heard the distinct sound of ripping fabric. I had only a second to cup my hands over the base of my head and twist my body as my pants tore free from the fence and I crashed against the frozen earth. Managing to twist just enough to prevent my head from hitting first, I landed flat on my back instead. Sharp jolts of pain shot up through my back and spread about my shoulders. Every ounce of air had been knocked from my lungs. My pants leg was torn from the crotch to the knee, and it was a miracle I hadn't gashed my leg open on the sharp barbs during my fall. My only thought aside from the extreme pain was the need to move, and fast. I rolled onto my side and gun in hand, I wobbled to my feet and staggered across the yard in the direction I last saw him run.

I soon found myself stumbling onto a sidewalk, and then out into the middle of a quiet, poorly lit residential street. The pain in my back was unbearable, and I was still having difficulty breathing. With my gun clenched in both hands, I searched down the length of the street, where I again located the suspect. He was far away, about two blocks and almost in the middle of an intersection. I could see him clearly. He was hunched over, almost in the same position as me. I could tell he too was in a lot of pain. His hands were empty. Slowly, he raised his face and stared right at me. He made no attempts to move.

"I got you, asshole. I got you," I said in a low voice as I tried to lift my arms. I couldn't do it. My entire upper body rocked with each labored breath I took. My head was spinning and my vision was blurry. I raised both of my hands and pointed my gun at him.

"Don't move or I'll shoot!" I screamed with the last words my lungs could summon. My arms were shaking violently as I tried to keep the gun up. Just another minute and I'll be able to move, just one more minute.

"No!" I mumbled as he slowly raised himself to his feet and turned in the opposite direction. "Don't move!" Within seconds, he made the corner and was gone.

"Please, please give me the strength to move," I said, trying to will the energy from anywhere in my body. I made it a few feet before the pain in my back became so intense that I felt like my body was on fire. It was over.

For the next couple of seconds, I struggled down the middle of this unknown street, barely able to move. I felt so helpless. I knew I had to accept failure as a part of the job. But knowing and accepting it were two very different things. I grasped my radio and rebroadcast a lookout for the suspect, hoping maybe another car might spot him. Several more seconds passed before I saw the flashing red and blue lights of a police car racing down the street towards me. Screeching to a halt, it came to rest at my side.

"What the hell happened," the officer yelled out his partially opened window.

"I'll explain it to you in the car. Can you give me a ride back to Saratoga and Montana?" I answered my breathing still deep and labored. "I left my car running there."

"Yeah, sure, get in," he said, hitting the power locks on the door. I climbed in and slumped down into the warm comfort of the seat. "I'm pretty sure another officer has taken care of securing your car. Are you sure you're all right?"

"Just...Can you just let the dispatcher know that cruiser four-sixty-five is on board and all right?" I said my eyes closed tightly shut. I didn't want him to notice the pain I was in. I was just happy knowing I would live to see another day.

CHAPTER SEVEN

The Buick Reatta caught both our eyes at the same time. Maybe it was the fresh damage on the front fender, or maybe it was the way the driver quickly slumped down in his seat as he passed us. Whatever the reason, Officer Noren and I simultaneously looked at each other and said the magic words: "Follow that car." Following closely behind, I checked the vehicles registration through the dispatcher. I joked with Noren, letting him know that if the Reatta was stolen and decided to run, there was no way we could catch him. Both of us were assigned to plain clothes vice unit, and had been more or less partners for the past year. We were in Noren's pea-green colored 1985 Crown Victoria, with a projected maximum speed of sixty miles per hour. And that was with the wind at our back. We called it the "war-wagon," and aside from its multiple cosmetic setbacks, which were many, it also possessed an interior roof lining that sagged so badly it came to rest squarely on the top of my head. But for about five hundred dollars, beggars couldn't be choosers, especially on a police department like ours, which couldn't even provide us with the basic necessities, such as typewriters and paper, let alone cars. So for us, the war-wagon was as good as gold.

"Tact unit twenty-two, on your tag, 4-5-7-8-3-S, there is no listing or record," answered the dispatcher.

"Tact twenty-two, I copy. Be advised, the vehicle is a blue colored Buick Reatta with damage to the right front fender. He's pulling into the east ally, thirteen hundred block of Thirteenth Street," I answered back. The Buick pulled slowly into the alley and continued towards the rear of a large apartment building. Noren hesitated before following.

"What do you think?" I asked.

"There's definitely something not right. I'm just not sure what," Noren answered in an unsure voice.

"Do you think it's stolen?"

"I'm not sure. But we should probably check it out anyway." We pulled in the alley just in time to see the Buick making a sharp left turn towards an underground parking lot. It wasn't uncommon for dispatchers to give returns on tags with no listing or record. This was the case with most temporary registrations. Regardless of their status, they never seemed to be entered into our computer system properly. That didn't mean the cars were not stolen. It just meant they weren't listed in the computer.

The Buick abruptly stopped in the middle of the alley. The driver sat motionless, staring straight ahead. We pulled behind him, slightly to his left. After a few seconds, he turned back to look at us and then pulled forward down a ramp leading into an underground parking garage. He stopped at a security box, which opened the gate to the garage. Again, he sat motionless, his car idling loudly.

"This shit isn't right. He's acting really nervous," I asked anxiously. "Why's he just sitting there at the security box?"

"Because he doesn't have an access card, that's why," Noren answered sharply. My attention was riveted on the Buick.

"I'll go check it out. Stay in the car in case he tries to run."

I slowly got out of the car and took a few steps towards the Buick. I kept my eyes on the driver, waiting for him to acknowledge me, but he didn't. He just kept staring straight ahead; his body still slumped down in his seat. I reached underneath my bulletproof vest and pulled out my badge, attaching it to a strap on my chest. We were working plain clothes, and despite my badge and arm patch, which displayed the Metropolitan Police logo, I was keenly aware that I was also wearing a black bandanna on my head and ripped jeans and could easily have been mistaken for anyone else but a cop. My right hand felt for my holster and gun as I circled around towards the rear of the car. I unsnapped the safety catch just in case.

"Look out!" Yelled Noren as the sound of screeching tires filled the air. The Buick slammed into reverse and sped back up the ramp directly towards me. I pulled my gun from my holster and brought up the sights towards my eye. I was too late. I barely had time to dive out of the way before the car whizzed past me. The last thing I remember was the awful smell of burning rubber as I dove head first into a patch of gravel on the concrete. Rolling onto my side, I saw the rear end as it sped past my legs, missing me by inches. I scrambled to my feet and raced towards our car. Noren had already spun it around and the passenger side door was open and waiting for me.

"Get in!" He yelled as I dove onto the passenger seat, my gun still clenched in my hand.

"God damn, that asshole tried to run me over," I shouted between gulps of air. "Did you see that fool? He tried to run me down!" I felt like I was going to pass out.

"Yea, I saw him. Are you all right?" Noren asked.

"I think so. My fucking ass is killing me. I think I dove into some broken glass." I dusted off my legs, picking the pieces of gravel from my arms and face.

"We'll, you'll have to check on that later. Right now, we're nailing his ass."

At a brisk forty miles per hour, Noren shot the war wagon out of the alley and into traffic on Thirteenth Street, fishtailing completely across the northbound lane. Cars skidded and swerved out of our way. I saw the Buick was just ahead, turning eastbound on M Street.

"Jesus, he's flying," I said, desperately fumbling for a seatbelt. It was stuck in the crease of the seat.

"He's got to be doing sixty or seventy miles an hour," Noren shouted back. His eyes were locked forward and I knew at this moment nothing would stop him from this pursuit. I had been in a few chases during my career, but nothing quite like this. First off, we were in an unmarked car, so no one around us had a clue as to what was going on. Second, I was with Noren, who took vehicle chases very, very seriously, and often likened his driving skills to being in the Indianapolis 500. He slammed the gas pedal to the floor, snapping my head back against the headrest. Still unable to locate my seatbelt, I locked one hand against the dashboard and grabbed my hand-held radio in the other.

"Tact twenty-two, we are in pursuit of a blue Buick Reatta. The car is traveling eastbound on M Street in the twelve hundred block," I yelled into the radio. I was screaming so loud, no one could acknowledge what I was saying.

"Tact twenty-two, repeat your transmission. You are coming in 10-1," answered the dispatcher. 10-1 meant I wasn't being heard.

"Calm down dude. Give them our location nice and easy, OK," Noren said as he stared intently ahead.

"That's easy for you to say. You don't have glass shreds stuck in your ass." I answered, feeling both terrified and silly at the same time. "Just keep driving, and don't get us killed, OK? I'll worry about the radio." We were racing down Thirteenth Street at an unbelievable speed. My heart was beating so fast I felt like I was hyperventilating. I knew that if we crashed we would probably die.

"Tact twenty-two, can you copy me now?" I said, taking in deep breaths of air.

"Tact twenty-two, loud and clear, is everything OK?" the dispatcher answered.

"We are in pursuit of a blue-colored Buick Reatta, traveling southbound on Thirteenth Street at a high rate of speed," I said, slowly beginning to calm myself down.

"All units, be advised Tact Twenty-Two is pursuing a blue Buick Reatta with Maryland registration 4-5-7-8-3-S. Last seen heading south on Thirteenth Street. What's the car wanted for?" The dispatcher asked.

"For assault on a police officer!" I shouted back. "Be advised he is now traveling east on M Street." We were now racing across M Street. The Buick was about three car lengths ahead of us and weaving in and out of traffic. He was easily doing seventy miles per hour, but we were gaining fast.

"Also, be advised he is now traveling on the wrong side of the road!" I screamed into the radio, telling myself to remain calm. Suddenly, he swerved all the way to his left and directly into oncoming traffic. Several cars swerved and skidded out of the way. One car, unable to swerve into a lane, shot onto the sidewalk before slamming to a stop. He then made a wide turn in the intersection of Eleventh and M Street, cutting back across our path of traffic and running the red light, then speeding south on Eleventh Street. Noren slammed the brakes, sending a sharp pain up my arm, then swerved across the two right hand lanes of traffic and made the turn in front of several parked cars.

"He's going south on Eleventh Street. He's still traveling at an extremely high rate of speed!" I yelled to the dispatcher. I could hear other cars telling the dispatcher they were responding to assist.

"Easy, Noren, don't get us killed." I pleaded, knowing he was only thinking of catching up to the Buick. Deep inside, I knew I would be doing the same thing. Both of us shared the same passion for catching criminals, at almost any cost, which was probably why we were partners. If I had to go, this would be the way to do it. And when I saw the Buick again swerve into oncoming traffic with us still following directly behind, I truly began to think this might be how my life would end. The sight of cars heading right at us gave everything a surreal effect as we swerved first left, then right, and then back to the left again.

"Relax. It's under control," Noren answered with a smile. I swear he had ice water for blood. Then he pulled us back into the right lane of traffic and floored it.

"Shit! Truck! Watch out!" I screamed as a large truck swerved out of our way, missing our front end by a foot. Ahead of us were cars swerving out of control trying to get out of our way. We were still weaving back and forth, passing cars on our right and dodging cars on our left. Just ahead was the Buick, still in the wrong lane and still speeding forward. I glanced out my window at the blurred faces of horrified people as they pointed and watched us fly by. I don't think they had a clue what was going on, only the look of sheer terror as our car raced past them at now close to eighty miles per hour. My head then slammed against the right side passenger window as I felt the incredible G-force of our car making a hard right-hand turn. I was sure we wouldn't make it. My eyes locked shut and I prayed we would not take out any other cars when we wrecked.

"He's going to crack up," Noren said as he yanked the steering wheel back around to his left and dramatically pulled us out of our turn. We fishtailed across the intersection to the left, leaving a long line of skid marks, then violently whipped back to the right, crossing sideways directly in front of several oncoming cars.

"He's going way too fast. He can't keep it up much longer," I said. We were now racing west on H Street. Traffic was extremely heavy. I looked at my watch, only now realizing that we were in the middle of rush hour.

"Hey Noren, its rush hour," I yelled. "This street is going to be packed and we're heading right into the middle of the downtown area."

"I know. We're not going much farther. He's not going to make it," Noren answered. "Take a look up ahead." I glanced ahead to see what he was talking about. We were rapidly approaching the intersection of Eighteenth, New York Avenue, and H Street. When defining the term "major intersection," this would be one that would immediately come to mind, especially at this time in the afternoon. On the far left were three lanes of eastbound traffic filled with cars either going straight or turning from Eighteenth Street. Directly ahead were three lanes packed with standing westbound traffic waiting at a red traffic signal. In the far right lane was a large Metro bus, which had stopped to discharge passengers at the corner. And to make matters even worse, on both sides of the street the sidewalks were filled with people leaving work for the day. The Buick had absolutely nowhere to go.

"He's not stopping. He's not stopping," I repeated several times, trying to will him to stop. At the speed he was traveling, no matter which route he chose, if he didn't stop, he was going to kill a lot of people.

"He's got to stop. There's no way he's going to try and bust that light. And there's nowhere else for him to go," Noren shouted. "He's boxed in. He's got to stop." For the first time, I could sense a little panic in his voice. The thought of witnessing this car crash into unsuspecting people made my stomach turn to knots.

"We have to stop, Noren. We can't continue. We've already pushed this too far!" I said, still staring ahead and praying.

As if on command, the driver of the Buick slammed on his brakes and came to a screeching stop inches short of the rear of the Metro bus. Clouds of smoke flowed from the rear tires as the car slid to a stop. He had spun to the far right, just behind the bus, and for a second, I thought for sure he was going to pull onto the sidewalk and ram through the crowd of people. He was desperately looking for a way out. Hesitating for a moment, our car still bearing down on him, he shifted to reverse and skidded backwards, heading towards us. The car directly behind him slammed his brakes and slid to the right and onto the curb. Noren caught this moment of opportunity, and before I had a chance to plead with him not to, I felt him hit the accelerator and pull into the center lane.

"Noren, whatever you do, which I know exactly what it is, don't you dare try to block him with my side of the car!" I screamed. I knew he wasn't listening. "Goddamn it Noren, don't block him with my side of the car. I have a girlfriend who would really like me to remain alive, OK? If you put me in front of his car, I'm going to kill you, do you understand?"

As these last words escaped my lips, he pulled directly to the left of the Buick, and then yanked the steering wheel hard to the right causing us to veer across the front of the Buick's path. Everything in front of me whizzed past at the speed of light. He was doing exactly what I had pleaded him not to, but I understood it was the only thing we could do. This maniac had to be stopped, and now was the time we had to make our move. It took only a few seconds for us to come to a stop directly in front of the Buick, with my side of the car now blocking his path. It took another few seconds for me to get a grip on what was happening. Shaking my head a few times, I turned and looked out the passenger window. The Buick was sitting only about twenty feet away, and for the first time, I could clearly see who was driving. He was staring right at me, his face completely expressionless. I was in such a state of shock that I failed to notice that his car was now slowly moving backwards.

For a second, nothing changed. His car, our car, and everything else had frozen in time. Then, without warning, everything changed, and the Buick was suddenly getting larger and larger, and I couldn't seem to understand why.

"Fuck!" I shouted as the Buick rammed full force into the passenger door of the war wagon. My body was thrown across the seat with an unbelievable amount of force. My radio flew out of my hand and landed on the driver's side floorboard. Everything went black as my face came to rest against the hard plastic of the dashboard. I heard the sounds of crashing metal, followed by skidding tires. I looked over for Noren, but he was gone. His door was hanging wide open. Still shaking from the impact and my head ringing, I pushed myself up and pulled out my gun. I glanced out the passenger window and into a crowd of citizens, who were screaming and running for cover. The impact had knocked our car 180 degrees around, and it was now facing forward. I had no idea if I was seriously hurt or not. I grabbed hold of the passenger door handle and pulled; Nothing. The impact had jammed it shut. I looked out the front windshield and saw Noren running down the street chasing the Buick, which was again moving in reverse, only now in the opposite direction. He had his gun out, screaming for him to stop. I scrambled across the driver's seat on my hands and knees, falling out into the street, broken glass stuck all over my body. My hands were bleeding. Lying on the hot concrete, I looked up just in time to see Noren diving head first across the road, landing on his shoulder and somersaulting forward. The Buick had spun around forwards and was again bearing down on me. Unable to get to my feet in time, I rolled my body sideways towards the safety of our car. My eyes were closed and I was sure I would soon feel the crushing blow of steel crashing against my body. At the last second, I launched myself into the car, landing on the soft velour seat. The Buick zoomed past, for the second time missing me by just a few feet. Moving quickly, I jumped out and raced towards the intersection where the Buick was now heading. He was just ahead, stuck in a line of traffic. For the first time today, I had a clear shot. I wanted so badly to pull the trigger I could taste it on my lips. This man had tried to kill me twice and I knew I could hit him. My sights were on the back of his head, and in a moment, as traffic began moving forward, my chances would be gone. Out of the left corner of my eye, I saw several men in suits running across the street, desperately looking for shelter. On my right, at the street corner, I saw men and woman running and screaming. Some were diving to the ground.

I continued forward, sliding across the hood of a stopped sedan blocking my path. My gun was still extended forward and I was screaming for people to get out of the way. Everything was happening so fast, and I quickly realized I was in tunnel vision, as everything around me, aside from the Buick, just disappeared.

I didn't take my shot. Instead, I stopped in the middle of the intersection in exhaustion and watched ahead as the Buick raced ahead of several cars and disappeared into the flow of traffic, knowing it would probably be gone forever.

Jumping up and down in anger and yelling every obscenity I could think of at the top of my lungs, I realized the insanity of this incident and how close I had come to getting seriously hurt. People all around stared at me like I was insane, standing in the middle of the street with bloody hands and a gun at my side. I probably was. The pain was finally starting to settle in.

An incredibly strong gust of wind knocked me back several feet as three Park police cruisers flew past me, sirens blaring. Our backup had arrived. With Noren and I officially out of the game, the Park Police chase continued across the Fourteenth Street Bridge, stopping only when the Buick managed to pull onto the far right access lane, barely escaping through a line of stopped cars. He continued his run into Virginia, where several Virginia State Troopers stood waiting. They pursued him towards the George Washington Memorial Parkway and then onto Interstate 66. From here, the chase continued until, while attempting to exit on a notoriously curvaceous exit ramp, only to realize his speed had finally caught up to him, the Buick flipped over several times, coming to rest on a steep grassy embankment. Somehow, the driver managed to escape from the wreckage and escape on foot. He jumped into a taxi, where he would once again lose the State Troopers in snarled rush hour traffic. However, his only mistake would prove to be a costly one. At the scene of the crashed Buick, lying on the roof of the upturned car was a District of Columbia driver's license. This license belonged to the man who had so masterfully executed his escape, and who was now casually making his way back into the city, confident he had eluded us forever. I found out later that night the Buick had been stolen from Reagan National Airport.

Early that Saturday morning, the day following the chase, while I was at home watching cartoons and eating a bowl of corn flakes, several members of the Metropolitan Police Department's Third District Prostitution and Tactical Unit, led by Officer Noren, responded to the address listed on the driver's license found in the stolen Buick Reatta. Knocking on the door with guns drawn, a frail man answered, wearing several bandages on his head and suffering from a badly fractured arm. His face showed a look of shock and disbelief, and he knew immediately he had been caught. He would go peacefully, muttering only the words, "You got me."

CHAPTER EIGHT

He was like a ghost. He was there, standing on the street, exposing himself to rush-hour traffic and any other poor soul unfortunate enough to pass by. Then, as quickly as someone could pick up the phone and call the police, he would disappear. After the first couple of calls, I was sure someone was playing a joke. I mean, not many people had the moxie to wander onto a busy street during evening rush hour, drop their pants and do their own personal interpretation of *A Chorus Line*. But then again, this was Washington, D.C., and after years of seeing just about anything and everything, nothing could possibly be beyond the realms of my imagination, absolutely nothing. Basically, in this city, if you could think of it, someone was probably doing it.

I was driving my little Honda Civic as fast as my 16-valve engine and heavy traffic would allow. For the first time in the past month, I was actually close enough to catch this guy. The dispatcher had just given the call for a man on the corner of Twelfth and N Street exposing himself. It had to be our guy. I was on Eleventh Street, just south of P, and within just a few precious city blocks. For a brief moment, I thought about taking a short cut and shooting west across O Street, and then south on Twelfth. But Twelfth was a one way, northbound street, and after already having several on-duty accidents, I was a little hesitant about again challenging oncoming traffic. I pressed down on the gas pedal and passed a Metro bus slowing down to pick up passengers. Several seconds later, I whipped onto N Street and headed towards Twelfth.

"Come on baby, just a few more seconds," I said out loud. We were so close I could taste it.

"Easy Arch," Baker answered excitedly from the passenger seat. "We're close this time. He'll still be there."

"He's gotta be," I said as I skidded to a halt on the northeast corner of Twelfth and N Streets. "I'm tired of losing this asshole."

"There he goes!" Baker yelled as he thrust open the passenger door and took off running.

"Damn!" I shouted as I pulled to the curb, grabbed my car keys and jumped out of the car. I took off behind. The man was running and had about a fifty-yard lead and was moving pretty fast. From a distance, I could barely make him out. He was pretty big, and his clothing looked old and worn. I called for backup on my portable radio and accelerated my speed.

"He's cutting behind that abandoned house!" Baker yelled as I whizzed past him. I saw the man veer off to my right towards a huge, old abandoned house.

"I see him!" I answered between breaths of air. The heavy summer humidity made running anything longer than half a block an almost impossible task. "That place is completely fenced in. He's got nowhere to go!"

I had checked this house out several times in the past. It wasn't at all uncommon for local drug addicts and homeless people to take refuge in any one of the hundreds of abandoned, boarded up houses scattered across the city. But this one was pretty secure. The owners had installed a chain-link fence around the perimeter, and boarded up all of the windows and doors. During my last check, which had been two or three months ago, I had determined it to be pretty impenetrable.

"Where the hell did he go?" Baker asked as we both cut the same corner where we had last seen the man running. It was as if he had vanished into thin air. "He was just here!"

"I have no idea," I answered. My hands were on my hips as I tried desperately to catch my breath. Several cars skidded to a halt behind us. Officers Ayala and Gonzalez exited and came running up.

"What's going on?" Ayala said as he walked beside me.

"You know that pervert, the dude who likes exposing himself to passing traffic?" I asked, knowing he would know.

"Yeah, what about him," Gonzalez chimed in. He was standing next to Baker.

"Well, he just took off running alongside of this house. We got the radio assignment and pulled up just as he was finishing," I answered.

"OK, he's got to be around here somewhere. Let's find him," Ayala said. That's what I loved about him. In his eyes, everything was so simple.

"Well, there's one slight problem," I said. "This house is completely fenced in."

"So maybe he cut around the rear and doubled back," Ayala countered.

"No way, I may not be a world class runner, but I'm certainly not about to get outrun by some homeless pervert," I said defensively. "He's hiding out, or he's some sort of ghost."

"He's in the house!" Gonzalez shouted from about twenty-five feet away. He and Baker had wandered over to the corner of where the side and rear of the house met. Baker was pointing towards the ground.

"How do you figure?" I shouted as Ayala and I jogged to them.

"This," Gonzalez said pointing to a huge hole in the fence.

"Damn. I guess our pervert is not as stupid as I thought," I said.

"So what do we do?" Baker asked.

"We go in after him," I answered. I had already gotten on my hands and knees and was making my way down through the hole. Ayala was directly behind me.

"Your nuts, you know that!" Gonzalez yelled as he pulled up the rear.

"So are you, or you'd have never joined this crazy department!" I yelled back as I reached the other side of the fence. I quickly jumped to my feet and brushed the broken glass and dirt off of my bare knees.

"I guess you're right," Gonzalez answered laughing. Basically, we were all crazy.

"This is not going to be good," Baker said as we surveyed a small hole on the side of the house which appeared to lead down into the basement. The entrance led down into a basement and was pitch black.

"Nope," I agreed.

"Hell no, I'm stopping right here," Ayala said, staring me in my eyes. "I know exactly what you're thinking, and you can forget it."

"Look, there's no way canine is going to get a dog down into there. The drop is too steep. And there's no way we're going to let this asshole get away," I said, feeling deep down inside like maybe he was right.

"I agree," Gonzalez said. "Let's just do it."

"I'm down," Baker added. His voice said yes, but the look on his face said something completely different.

"You all suck!" Ayala answered smiling. "Who's first?"

"I got it," I said quickly. I pulled my pistol from its holster and eased my feet into the hole. Hanging onto Baker's hand, I swung my feet around searching for the floor. Finally, I just dropped. Ten feet later, I hit the cold concrete with a thud, landing squarely on my ass.

"Are you all right?" Baker yelled from above.

"Yea, I'm fine. Just a little bruised," I shouted back. "It's about ten feet. I'll grab your legs as you lower yourself down."

"It's dark as hell," Ayala said as he dropped to the ground. He was the last one down. "Who's got the flashlight?"

"I've got one," Gonzalez said as he pulled his out.

"I've got a small one," I added, pulling out a mini flashlight from my pocket. Between the two, we barely had enough light to adequately make out our immediate surroundings, which was not very encouraging.

"Shall we continue?" I asked, knowing full well that I intended to scour the house until this man was caught.

"What the hell. You only live once," Ayala answered back. Pointing the light forward, I focused on a wooden stairway across the room. The others followed closely behind.

"This must lead to the first floor," I said over my shoulder. The old, decayed wooden steps creaked with each step I took. It was a miracle they didn't collapse under the weight of the four of us. There was a wooden door at the top.

"Open it slowly," Gonzalez said from behind me. I felt the pressure of Baker's body pressing against my back.

"Don't worry, I will," I answered as I slowly pushed the basement door open. "Give me some more light." I slowly moved the beam of my flashlight across the far walls of the room. It must have been a kitchen at one time. Now, save for a few piles of trash and junk, it was empty. Baker's light illuminated the room even more, and I could see scattered large holes in the walls leading into other even darker rooms.

"I think this house is a lot bigger than we expected," I said, thinking maybe it was time to reevaluate our plan.

"You're not kidding," Ayala chimed in. He had pushed past me and was standing in the entrance to the kitchen.

"Maybe we should wait for him to come out," Gonzalez said. He was still standing on the stairs behind me.

"I think if we move towards the front of the house, we'll get some light from outside." I said with false optimism, realizing that each window and door was boarded up and that very little light could get in from anywhere.

"So, what's it gonna be?" Baker asked. He was pointing his flashlight down a hall and towards the bottom of another stairway. Just then, the sounds of heavy but quick footsteps came from the ceiling above our heads.

"It's him," Gonzalez whispered softly. "He's on the move."

"Sure is. He's right above us. If we move now, we at least know which room he's in," Baker said, already moving towards the far stairs.

"Easy, dude, wait for us!" I exclaimed, following closely behind. "Everyone stick together."

"I'm right behind you," Ayala said. Gonzalez was bringing up the rear. Moving quickly but cautiously, Baker eased up the stairway towards the second floor. Everything now was deathly silent. I could hear Ayala and Gonzalez breathing behind me. The stairway led to another hallway, with 2 sets of doors on each side. I scanned my flashlight back and forth as I stepped onto the landing.

"Man, will you take a look at that!" I said as I focused the light beam on several huge, gaping holes in the floor.

"This sucks," Baker answered, gazing at the holes. "This place is like a death trap."

"Yeah, I know. I feel like we're in some kind of cheap Hollywood horror film," I replied quietly.

"Bite your tongue," Gonzalez said from the rear. "That means we'll probably all die." A soft rustling noise came from one of the rooms on our right.

"Over there!" Ayala said, pointing to an open door about twenty feet ahead. It was pitch black inside.

"I hear it!" Gonzalez said. He had pushed himself up to my back.

"Look out!" I screamed, jumping several feet backwards, as a flash of moving darkness crossed a few feet in front of us, running through the hallway from one room and into another. I almost knocked Gonzalez down the stairs.

"Let's move!" Baker and Ayala chimed simultaneously. Without hesitation, and with much stupidity, the four of us raced down the hall and into the room where the moving darkness had fled. Once inside, I frantically tossed my hand back and forth, trying to cover as many places in the room with my flashlight as quickly as possible. Baker and Gonzalez were plastered against a wall next to me, and Ayala was on one knee to my left. His gun was out and he was following the path of my light.

"I can't see a damn thing!" Ayala said loudly.

"Neither can I," Gonzalez shouted. Despite the paralyzing fear that was quickly taking over my body, I remained quiet, thinking only about finding the source of the moving darkness. My eyes caught a slight movement coming from the far corner of the room.

"I've got him!" I said, my words coming out in a low, garbled mess. My light came to rest on a man standing across the room. His back was against the wall and he was facing us. His clothes were old and tattered, and he had all of the appearances of someone who had been living on the street.

"Don't move!" I said in as authoritative a voice as I could muster under the circumstances. My gun hand was wobbling almost completely out of control. Suddenly, the most unexpected thing happened. The man smiled, and in his right hand, he dropped a set of shiny white fangs; two small fangs on the bottom, and two longer ones on top.

"You've got to be fucking kidding me!" Baker said, his voice raising at least two octaves. To my chagrin, I realized that the one thing the police department didn't issue us was a silver bullet.

"OK, this is some freaky shit," Gonzalez muttered from beside me.

"I think maybe this would be a good time to retreat," I agreed, meaning every word. I was already taking small steps backwards. Without warning, the man took off across the room towards a far doorway. All I could see was the outline of his dark body.

"Move!" Baker yelled, taking a few quick steps forward. I shined my light ahead as we ran across the old, frail floor. The boards underneath my feet squeaked with each step.

"Are you still with us?" I shouted, referring to Ayala and Gonzalez. I could hear them running behind me.

"We're right behind you!" Ayala answered in a tired voice. "Are we sure we want to continue this?"

"No," I yelled back. At this point, I had no idea what to do. So I just kept running.

"Over this way!" Baker yelled from ahead. I could hear the heavy sounds of running footsteps somewhere in front of us. We were close.

"I hear him," I answered. "He's just up ahead."

In my mind, I had no idea what we would do when we finally found him. I guess at this point, we were running on pure adrenaline. From a safety standpoint, we were violating every rule the Police Academy had taught us.

"I think I saw him cut in here," Baker said softly, pointing to another dark room.

"Are you sure?" I asked, coming to a halt a few feet behind him. I glanced over my shoulder and saw Ayala and Gonzalez standing behind me. Their eyes were as wide as flying saucers, just like mine. "Shhhhhh!" I finished and then turned back to Baker.

"Yeah, I'm sure. Besides, there's nowhere else for him to go. Look," Baker pointed his light ahead. The beam shone on a wall. It was a dead end.

"So what now?" I asked

"We've come this far, we might as well see it through," Baker answered.

"I've got to tell you, this is way fucked up," I replied. "I mean, I don't really believe in vampires, but what I saw just really hit me in a bad way. I don't think this guy is playing with a full deck."

"I don't either. We'll just be extremely careful," Baker answered. "Are you ready?"

"Yeah, on the count of three, we do it." I glanced back at Gonzalez and Ayala. They nodded in agreement. "One, two, three!"

Baker turned the corner and jumped to the left of the doorway. I followed immediately behind and jumped to the right. Ayala and Gonzalez stood in the middle. We had our guns drawn and pointed into the room.

"Don't move!" Baker yelled as he planted his light beam right on the man's face. He was crouched in a corner. His face was turned away from the light.

"Cover us, Ayala," I said as I began to move forward slowly.

"We got you," Ayala answered. Gonzalez was still standing next to him. As Baker and I moved closer, the man stood up and started to move away, until he ran out of room and cornered himself against the far wall. I was sure a brutal fight was inevitable, and I wondered how in the world I was going to explain two fang marks in my neck to my sergeant.

"We can do this the easy way, or the hard way. The choice is yours!" Baker said. "Either way, you're coming with us."

"Come on man. Make the right choice," I added, hoping he would comprehend the severity of the situation.

"OK," the man answered, his body still pressed against the wall. "Don't hurt me."

"Hurt you? Are you for real?" I said. Baker and I had both stopped about ten feet away from him.

"I'm not hurting anyone."

"Yeah, well you're really freaking the hell out of me," I shouted back. My brain was having a really hard time comprehending the matter of fact way he was speaking. It was as if he had suddenly become a normal person. Unfortunately, normal people didn't masturbate in the street, live in creepy abandoned houses, and sport plastic fangs in their mouths.

"Now turn around and put your hands over your head," he complied, and Baker quickly moved in and handcuffed him. Our little adventure was over. We took him back to the station and booked him. We left his fangs sitting there on the dirty floor, content to store this piece of information in my head as nothing more than a distant memory.

CHAPTER NINE

I knew the man had a gun. A hysterical prostitute running down the street towards our unmarked car, screaming and waving her arms frantically above her head, had quickly pointed to a bright red colored pickup truck parked half a block up the street.

"The man inside that truck, he's got a gun!" She screamed, tears flowing down her red, flushed cheeks. "He tried to kidnap and rape me!"

"OK, slow down, slow down," I said, keeping my eyes focused on the parked truck. I could see a man sitting on the driver's side. "Tell me exactly what happened."

"That asshole picked me up over on Twelfth Street," she began, her voice cracking nervously. "When I got in his truck, he stuck a gun in my face and pushed me down onto the floor. He told me if I screamed or tried to escape, he would shoot me."

"How did you get away?" I asked trying to speed up her story before the truck pulled off. I also needed to verify she was telling the truth, although at this point, I already suspected she was. I had learned over the years that prostitutes, although ruthless and conniving, rarely lied about things of this severity. It took an awful lot to shake them up this much.

"He pulled up to the curb, where he is now. He started telling me he was going to rape me. Then he saw your car pull by, and he started getting real nervous. That's when I pushed open the door and ran out. He's fucking weird, man, real weird."

"OK, stay here for a minute and we'll go check it out," I answered as I turned the ignition on. "Are you ready?"

"Let's go do it," Gonzalez answered, sitting next to me. He was smiling, and his gun was already out of its holster and in his hand. I slammed the gas pedal to the floor and pulled out into the dark street.

Within seconds, we were skidding in front of the truck, blocking him in. Seeing this, the man inside tried to lurch the truck forward, abruptly slamming on the brakes as he realized he had nowhere to go. I jumped out of the car and drew my gun from its holster, quickly fixing my sights on the center of his forehead. Gonzalez had already gotten out and positioned himself on the sidewalk behind a parked car. His gun was extended forward. We had him completely boxed in. Unless he decided to get out of the truck, he had nowhere to go. Now it was just a matter of patience.

"Put your hands up in the air where I can see them!" I shouted towards the open driver's window. He sat motionless, staring at me. His hands were below the dashboard and out of view. I had no idea what he was doing with them, or where his gun was.

"I said put your fucking hands up!" I screamed again. He was still staring at me with a blank, crazy look in his eyes.

I heard several voices coming from directly behind me. Quickly glancing over my shoulder, I saw a small crowd of people gathering a few feet down the sidewalk. Glancing across the street, I saw another crowd of onlookers standing behind a row of parked cars. This situation was quickly getting out of hand. If this man did have a gun, these people were going to be easy targets. I realized we had to try to end this as quickly as possible, even if it meant doing something really stupid, which is exactly what we did.

"Get out of the way!" I screamed at the on lookers. Then, leaving the safe cover of the front of my car, I quickly started making my way towards the driver's side of the truck. I kept my field of vision on the sights of my gun, which were now focused on the dashboard area. I prayed that if he pulled a gun, I would have enough time to see it coming. I tried to angle myself to the side, so that if he pulled his truck forward, I would have time to jump out of the way instead of having to shoot. I also didn't want any innocent bystanders getting shot. I could hear the steady grumbling of the truck's engine as I steadily eased forward. I prayed he was in park and wouldn't try to ram us.

From the corner of my eye, I saw Gonzalez moving forward with me. He never once took his eyes off the man. We were doing exactly what police officers weren't supposed to do. We had left cover and fully exposed ourselves to the threat. But I was convinced that this was our only course of action. We had to get this man in custody before anyone got hurt.

"Put your hands in the air where I can see them!" I shouted for what seemed like the one hundredth time. He would still not comply. Instead, he started slowly shifting his body in his seat.

"I said put your hands up where I can see them!" I shouted again. He still wouldn't comply. Then, ever so slowly, he leaned over to the passenger side, as if reaching for something, and disappeared completely out of my view. I was certain he was reaching for his gun and he was going to try to shoot me. My moment of decision had finally come. We had forced the issue by approaching the truck, and now I had reached an area of no man's land all police officers dread. I had to decide whether to shoot or not to shoot. Right or wrong, I would have to live with this decision for the rest of my life.

Without warning, the man popped back up in view. I desperately searched for his hands, but they were still nowhere to be found. The slack on my pistol's trigger was millimeters from firing.

I can't really explain what transpired next. I'm not even really sure how or why I made my final decision. For some eerie reason, I just didn't seem to care. Believe me, it was certainly not any heroic act of courage. I think it was more out of plain fear. I knew I could never live with myself if he didn't have a gun, and if I shot an unarmed man. So, I just decided to walk right up to the truck. He sat motionless, staring straight ahead as if in some kind of trance.

Sitting on the passenger side floorboard was a black colored semi-automatic pistol, only a few precious feet from his right hand.

"Gun!" Gonzalez screamed at the top of his lungs. He had followed me, but on the passenger side of the truck. I could hear people around us screaming and shouting. Gonzalez had reached the passenger door, flung it open and was yelling for the man not to move. I stuck my pistol to within inches of his face and reached down to open his door.

"Get the fuck out of the car!" I yelled, grasping his shoulder and pulling him out of the truck. He easily fell out into the street. Within seconds, I was straddling his body, my knee pressed into the small of his back. "I'm clear!" I said to Gonzalez as I holstered my gun and handcuffed the man.

"Hey Chris," I heard Gonzalez say from the other side of the truck.

"What is it?" I asked. I was still straddling the prisoner's body.

"She's loaded, with one in the chamber."

"I figured it would be," I replied, shaking my head. The seriousness of what had just happened hadn't fully sunk in yet. But it would later, as I sat in the station filling out the arrest paperwork, my knees wobbling so badly I had to hold them together with my hands.

CHAPTER TEN

"Check it out," I said quietly to Ayala. I pointed to a white pick-up truck, which had pulled to the curb across the street from us. It had Virginia license plates, and the markings of some car dealership were clearly printed across the driver's side door. "He's a long way from work for a lunch break."

"I see it," Ayala answered softly. I don't know why we were whispering. From inside of our unmarked car, no one could hear us anyway.

"So, what's wrong with this picture?" I asked Ayala, keeping my eyes fixed on the driver of the truck. The driver was desperately looking around, trying to find someone. He seemed incredibly nervous.

"You mean aside from the fact that he's got a Virginia truck and he's as white as white can be? Just about everything," he answered. "Look. There's a dude walking down from the corner of P Street. I think he's headed for our boy."

"Bingo. I see him," I said defiantly. "He's our dealer, black male, blue jeans, white shirt and black cap." I mumbled out loud as I jotted his description into my notebook. "And dude in the truck is our buyer."

"You think they'll spot us?" Ayala asked.

"I don't think so. Look at the driver. He's got his eyes fixed on the guy coming up to his truck," I replied. "It's the dealer we've got to worry about. And I think by now he would've made us."'

"It's going down!" Ayala blurted excitedly. I could see our dealer quickly climbing into the passenger side of the truck. My only concern now was if they were going to deal right here, or if they were going to take a drive around the block. I hoped it wouldn't be the latter. I hated trying to bust drug deals from moving vehicles. It was a royal pain in the ass.

"I think they're going to deal right inside the truck. Get ready!" I said, my hand grabbing hold of the passenger door handle. Now, it was just a matter of time. Inside the truck, the dealer was moving around, trying to get something from his pocket. I stared intently at his face. Quickly, he extended one of his hands forward and gave something to the driver. The driver examined the object, then handed the dealer something in return. The deal had gone down, just like clockwork.

"Let's go!" I yelled as I jumped out of Ayala's car. I clamped my badge onto the front of my jacket, pulled out my pistol and raced across the street. Reaching the front of the truck, I drew down on the two men inside.

"Police! Don't move!" I shouted, my finger taking the slack out of the trigger of my gun. The morning sun glared into my eyes, making it hard for me to see. I eased towards the center of the truck's front grill, carefully watching their hands.

"Get those hands up where I can see them!" I screamed. I heard tires screeching from up the street, which I knew was Ayala bringing the car around. He was positioning his car behind the truck. Everything was going just as planned. My only fear now was if they tried to swallow the dope, which meant I would have to get into the truck to try and choke it out of them. I hated that.

"Slowly, with your hands in the air, get out of the truck!" I commanded. I could see Ayala pulling in behind them. I glanced at the man in the passenger side. He stared straight ahead, a look of calmness covering his face. I figured he had been through this scenario before. That was good. Unfortunately, when I looked at the driver, it was a whole different story. His eyes were wild, and his head jerked back and forth. I could tell he was trying to figure a way out of this, which was not good. There was nothing more dangerous than a panicky criminal. At this point, I knew I was going to have to approach the truck. There was no way he was going to come out on his own. Quickly, I took several steps towards the driver's side, but I wasn't quick enough.

For the life of me, I could have sworn the truck's motor was off. I guess in all of the excitement, I never heard the gentle purr of the Ford engine as I stood stoically in front of it like a sitting duck. Like a charging bull, the full sized truck barreled ahead straight at me. My life became a blur as I took a giant step to my right and sighted my gun on the driver. Then, suddenly, I felt a sharp pain shoot through my left hip and my head jerked towards the sky. The truck's bumper had clipped me, sending my body into a vicious spiral. Spinning like a top, I felt the cold metal of the truck's body as it raced past me. I had no idea where I was or what was happening. Then, I felt myself become airborne, and I somehow landed in the bed of the truck with a sudden, bone crushing crash. I was now on my hands and knees. My gun slid across the plastic bed-liner and smashed against the rear of the passenger compartment. Completely dazed, my knees throbbing with intense pain, I crawled forward and pounced on it with both hands. I could feel the cool wind blowing through my hair and I was keenly aware that we were moving. Staggering to one knee, I pointed my gun at the back of the driver's head and banged on the sliding glass window. With a look of total shock, he turned to face me. His jaw dropped to the ground. The man in the passenger side stared back as well, his eyes the size of dinner plates.

The loud sound of burning rubber filled the air as the truck came to a skidding halt. My body slammed against the back window, my right shoulder bearing the brunt of the force. My gun again fell to the ground. The driver quickly opened his door and jumped out into the street. I jumped from the back of the truck and onto his back, both of us slamming onto the hard asphalt.

"Get out of the truck!" I heard Ayala yelling from behind me. He was screaming at the passenger. I saw him reaching into the truck and pulling him out. Then he flung him to the ground. "Are you OK?"

"No," I answered. I grabbed the driver by the back and yanked him to his feet. "What the fuck were you doing?"

"I'm sorry. I panicked!" He shouted his voice coming in short labored breaths. He was crying.

"Do you know what this is?" I said as I shoved my badge in front of his face. "Do you?"

"Yes, yes. I'm sorry," he answered. "I've never been in this part of the city before. I was scared. I thought you were trying to rob me."

"Yeah right, sure you did." I said as I handcuffed him and walked back towards Ayala.

"Boy. You are a nut," Ayala said from the other side of the truck. He had gotten the passenger handcuffed and was standing behind him.

"I suppose you haven't got anything to say, do you?" I said to the passenger.

"Man, I told him to stop. I told him you all were cops," he answered. "Man, you are crazy, you know that. You are plain crazy."

"Yeah, well, that's why they pay us the big bucks," I replied. I wasn't crazy. The city was crazy. I just happened to play a small part in the insanity. I leaned into the passenger side and scanned across the floorboard. "You're dealing days are over for a while my man."

"I don't deal in nothin'. I was just talking with my friend."

"No problem. You can tell it to the judge," I snapped back. I didn't have time to play games with him. I needed to find the dope.

"I didn't see either one swallow. And I don't think they tossed it out," Ayala said.

"Neither did I," I answered. "It's here somewhere." Then, as if guided by some unknown force, my eyes focused in on two small yellow dots sitting on the driver's side floorboard. I crawled in and grasped them in my hand. Sure enough, I could see the unmistakable markings of "4" and "K" on each side. They were Dilaudids, the rich man's heroin.

"I suppose you don't have a clue about these, either?" I said as I walked back to where the driver was sitting.

"Man, I ain't ever seen those before, I swear," he answered.

"How about you?" I shouted to the passenger.

"Those aren't mine. They must be his," he said, pointing to the other man. I turned back to the driver. My body was still shaking from the excitement.

"You fucking liar! That shit ain't mine!"

"Sir, you have the right to remain silent," I said. "Anything you say can be used against you in a court of law. You have the right to talk to a lawyer for advice before we question you and to have him present with you during questioning. If you cannot afford a lawyer and want one, a lawyer will be provided for you. If you want to answer questions now without a lawyer present, you will still have the right to stop answering at any time. You also have the right to stop answering at any time until you talk to a lawyer. Do you understand these rights?" I loved the sounds of these words.

"What am I being arrested for?" he asked. I couldn't believe he had the nerve to even ask.

"For being a fucking idiot, that's what for," I replied. I retrieved my portable radio from Ayala's car and called for a marked transport car.

After all was said and done, and our prisoners were on their way to the station, I collapsed on the sidewalk, my hip burning with intense pain. Ayala sat down next to me, smiling as always.

"Like I said, you are a crazy fool," Ayala said as he plopped himself next to me.

"Yea, I guess maybe I am. I guess maybe I am," I answered, thinking to myself. I stared ahead, just down M Street. A group of small kids were playing a game of three on three with a nerf football. One of the kids, maybe only ten years old, was running a perfect fly pattern. His teammate lofted a perfectly thrown long, crisp spiral that gently came to rest in his outstretched arms. He glided between two parked cars into the make-believe end zone for a touchdown.

"Hey Ayala, did you bring your Nerf football?" I asked Ayala, catching him off guard. He usually carried it in the trunk of his car for entertainment on some of our less busy days.

"Yea, why?"

"I thought maybe after we get the paperwork done, we could throw around a little bit."

"Yea, sure, you feel up to it?"

"I think I'll manage. Let's go." I limped back to Ayala's car. I wondered how in the world I was going to explain this in my paperwork. If I hadn't lived it myself, I don't think I ever would've believed it.

"Hey, Ayala?" I said as I sat in the car.

"What?"

"You think anyone will believe this?"

"No way."

"Not even down at the prosecuting attorney's office?"

"Absolutely not."

"Yeah, I don't think so either."

Slowly, we drove up Twelfth Street. I could see several prostitutes making their way towards their corners. It was going to be a long day.

CHAPTER ELEVEN

Ayala and I never heard the shot. We had been parked at the corner of 12th and O Streets, assigned to the unenviable task of moving any prostitutes we found out of the area. For whatever reason, tonight was slow, which was fine by me. Both Ayala and I had been in court all day and were struggling to keep our wits. I glanced at my watch and saw it was around 9:00 p.m. Only two more hours, and I too would be home sleeping soundly in my bed.

It wasn't to be that way: "Any unit available for the sounds of gunshots in the 13oo block of 13th Street!"

The radio dispatcher's voice boomed into the silence of the night. I whipped my car around and Ayala and I headed towards the scene, about three blocks from where we were. I could hear the distant sounds of sirens as other officers raced towards the area.

I was surprised at being called to a shooting in this neighborhood called Logan circle. I had worked this area for several years and though it certainly wasn't a quiet bedroom community, shootings were not an ordinary occurrence. Most of our problems occurred on the 13th Street corridor, between Massachusetts Avenue and Q Street. This area is best described as a study in stark contrasts. On one block, notably in the 1300 block of Vermont Avenue, stands a block of beautiful three story row-houses of various colors on each side of the street, immaculately maintained and cared for. On the south end is a large, moderately priced hotel and to the north, a beautiful bush circular park with several small, black wrought iron benches in the middle. Traveling east, a block towards 12th Street, surroundings become a bit dicier, consisting of poorly maintained row houses, subsidized apartments, liquor stores and vacant lots. This was Mecca for prostitution and a safe haven for many drunks, homeless, and vagrants. It was in front of the liquor store and adjoining alleyway that most problems would occur. This area had long been a favorite gathering place for small time persons plying the sex and drug trade. And on any given night, pimps would gather to share stories while their girls worked the neighboring streets. This was an area I would pass at least ten times during the course of my evening, stopping on occasion to move people along and clear out the prostitutes. I would also make a note to recognize any of the suspected pimps, knowing that despite our difficulty in catching them, I wanted to at least know who they were, and to let them know I was watching.

So as I wheeled my car into the block, I was fully expecting to find nothing out of the ordinary: Ayala and I figured some local hoodlum had probably set off a good string of firecrackers. What I did not expect to find was a man lying in a stairwell in a pool of his own blood.

When we arrived, Ayala yelled into the car radio that we needed an ambulance and some backup. I thought I could hear the dispatcher acknowledge our request, but I wasn't sure. We were both anxious, too intent on getting to the scene. Leaving the car idling in the street, I pushed my way through the crowd of about twenty people and made my way towards the stairwell around which everyone had gathered.

The injured man was slumped on the base of the stairs in a seated position. He was black and appeared to be in his thirties, but it was hard to tell. He was wearing jeans, soiled tennis shoes and no shirt. Seated to his right was a black woman, younger, perhaps in her twenties or early thirties. She seemed to be well dressed, and though I thought I might have recognized the man from the block, I was certain I had never seen the woman before. She was leaning up against him with both arms extended forward, holding a bloody clump of newspaper against his chest.

"He's been shot in the chest!" She said keeping her eyes fixed on the bleeding man. The newspaper had turned completely red.

"OK, we have an ambulance on the way," I answered.

"It's going to be OK. Just hold on," the woman was saying to the man in calm, soothing tone. The sound of her voice helped me feel more relaxed.

"He's bleeding to death," she whispered to me in a low voice, careful not to let the man hear.

"I know," I answered back softly. "He's going to make it. Just a few more seconds, and the ambulance will be here."

The woman directed her attention back to the wounded man. She was talking to him, telling him everything would be fine and that he would pull through. The man said nothing and sat motionless. I looked over my shoulder at Ayala, who was watching intently. I could tell by the look in his eyes that there was nothing else we could do but wait. The newspaper that had until this moment served as the only barrier keeping this man's blood inside was now completely soaked. Frantically, I looked around for something, anything to help stop his bleeding. My shirt, I thought. The shirt my girlfriend had bought me during a Bermuda vacation several years earlier, the one my friends accused me of wearing every day.

Without thinking, I pulled the shirt over my head and placed it up against the man's chest. I pressed as hard as I could to put pressure to help stop the bleeding. Soon, the shirt became soaked with blood. For a moment, I thought I was going to push right through him. His eyes were half closed, and his mouth was moving, as if he wanted to say something, but no words would come out. His breathing was very slow and irregular. On several occasions, I felt certain he had taken his last breath. I couldn't think of what else to do and started worrying to myself that the ambulance wouldn't come in time, or worse, had never been called. Sensing something else needed to be done, the woman beside me began to talk to the man, again telling him he was going to be fine. He again fixed his eyes on hers, his pupils darting back and forth. She placed her hands next to mine and we both held fast. I don't know what it was about this woman's voice, but somehow it made everything seem ok. For a few seconds, the man turned his head slightly and glanced at me then he turned back to the woman and began to focus on her. She was giving him something on which to concentrate. Everything else just disappeared, and my world became that of her voice. I wasn't sure who needed to hear her more, the victim or me. I guess it didn't really matter.

I don't know how long it was, maybe only a few minutes, but seemingly from nowhere, I felt several taps on my shoulder. Turning my head to the side, I could see the ambulance crew maneuvering into place.

"It's OK, we got it from here," one of the medical crew said staring down on me. I hesitated, not wanting to let go. Somehow I felt that if I did, everything might not be OK I looked over to the woman to see if she had let go but she was already gone. Just like that, she had disappeared into the night. I stood up and walked over towards Ayala, who had wandered back to the car.

There were many officers and other people running around. Somewhere back in the distance was a news camera crew, filming the events. I was embarrassed, standing in the street, my naked chest and arms covered in blood. I tried to walk away from the cameras, hoping they would not notice me. A police official walked up and asked me why I wasn't wearing a shirt.

"You're kidding, right?" I asked amazed at the question.

"Don't give me any crap, just get a goddamn shirt on right now," he said, staring me in the face.

"Do you have any idea what just happened?" I asked, still in shock over his order. I didn't have the heart to tell him I didn't even have another shirt. I'm sure I would have been disciplined for insubordination.

"I don't really care what happened. I just care how unprofessional you look parading around in front of the news cameras without a shirt on," he said sternly.

"OK, sir, whatever," I answered back. Then I just stared at him, having absolutely no idea what else to say. He walked away. I walked over to my car and retrieved a police windbreaker to put on.

"Are you all right?" Ayala asked as I stood next to my car.

"Yeah, I'm fine. Where did that woman go, the one with the newspaper?" I asked as I scanned through the crowded street, looking for her.

"She walked away. I'm not sure where she went," he answered. I could not find her. I was sure she was around, but I couldn't spot her in the crowd.

I never did get my shirt back. I was later informed by the Police Department that I would not be reimbursed because what I used it for was not deemed worthy of reimbursement. I learned later that night that the man who had been shot had a warrant out for his arrest. I also learned that he survived. I was glad. Not because of anything I did, but because of the restored faith this one woman had given me in the people of Washington, D.C. I was so accustomed to people not wanting to cooperate or get involved. I was at a point in my career when I desperately needed some reassurance, and this woman had stepped from nowhere to do just that.

CHAPTER TWELVE

On an ordinary December evening, with the thermometer barely above freezing and an icy cold wind from the north blowing swiftly across the city, James gently passed through my life. Without either of us knowing it, James and I shared a common link, an ironic bond with an intersection of streets in Northeast Washington, D.C. called Montello and Queen. An intersection well known for ruthless drug activity and more than its share of shootings and a place in the city neither of us would ever forget. A place each of us would arrive at for very different reasons yet would change both of our lives forever.

The deafening sounds of car horns filled the air. An occasional outburst of people shouting obscenities came from within several cars up ahead. I leaned out of the passenger window and glanced up Massachusetts Avenue towards 18th Street. All I could see was one hell of a long line of cars.

"What's going on? Rush hour shouldn't be this bad," Noren said as he gently let off the brake, our marked scout car inching a few feet forward. This was the first movement our car had made in over ten minutes.

"Patience, Noren. We have all night," I answered back, feeling just as frustrated. We had been stuck in traffic for nearly half an hour, during which time we had barely traveled one block. Dupont Circle, one of the city's busiest intersections, was about three blocks away, which explained some of the congestion, but I couldn't help but feel there had to be some other culprit to blame.

"Up ahead, on the right. Do you see that?" Noren stated, pointing to a long line of parked cars.

"What. I don't see anything," I answered ignorantly. I scanned the street up ahead, looking for what it was to which he was referring.

"There's a car double parked on the right, the one with the hazards on. That's what's causing this damn traffic jam."

I looked to the right and quickly spotted an old, raggedy brown-colored four-door vehicle blocking the far right lane. Because of this, there was only one lane of traffic open, and the cars stuck behind were forced to merge to the one open lane on the left. A man was sitting behind the wheel slumped down in the seat. Several cars swerved into traffic, stopping only long enough for drivers to yell obscenities through cracked windows. A long and loud procession of horns accompanied each passing vehicle. Noren pulled our scout car into the right lane and directly behind the disabled car. We waited several seconds, but the car ahead still didn't move. I reached over and hit the manual siren, which let out a piercing yelp. Again we waited several seconds. Still, the car did not move. The driver remained in his original slumped position.

"I don't understand why he just doesn't move, or acknowledge us," I said. "Something's wrong."

"Yeah, we should go check it out," Noren answered as he pushed open his door. I stepped into the bitter cold air and followed him towards the vehicle. I was amazed at the number of drivers who continued to blast their horns as they veered past, some coming within inches of striking us. Approaching the car, I could see the driver reaching down the side of his door. He was trying to reach something. I grasped the handle of my pistol and continued forward. I had no idea what he was reaching for. As we reached the side of his car, the driver sat up and glanced out the window. I could see tears rolling down his flushed red cheeks.

"Roll down the window, sir," I commanded firmly. He leaned towards me and again reached down beside the door. My sweaty palm clenched tighter on the handle of my gun. I sensed something was very wrong, and I was nervous. Why wasn't he opening his window?

"Open the window, sir. Open it now!" I shouted loudly. Something inside of me sensed that this man was on the edge, for whatever reason. He was still crying and fidgeting with the inside of the door. Finally, the glass began to descend and the window creaked open.

"What's going on?" I asked curiously, still quite nervous.

"Man, I just don't know. These people keep shouting and honking at me," he sobbed, his face showing every inch of the frustration his voice was projecting. "My car won't go anywhere, and I don't know what to do."

"It's OK. We just need you to move the car out of the street and we'll figure out what to do."

"You don't understand, man. My car won't move. It broke down a couple of blocks back. This guy, he was pushing me with his car and then he just left me here. Right here in the middle of all this traffic. He said he would help and he just left me."

"It's all right. We'll get your car moved," I answered back, trying to calm him.

"I can't push this car. I can't even walk because of my legs." He stopped short and began wiping the tears away from his eyes. I looked over at the passenger seat and saw a wooden crutch. I glanced back at him and then at his legs. They were folded at an awkward angle, almost as if they were separated from the rest of his body.

"OK, can you pop open the hood so we can check your engine?" I asked. Noren was already in front of the car trying to pull the catch open.

"No, it's busted from the inside. You need a screwdriver," he answered. He seemed much calmer now. I was thankful.

"Do you have a screwdriver we can use?"

"No. It's at home. I didn't think I would need it today."

"Well, then we at least need to get you out of the car until we can figure out what to do. Is there someone you can call to come and help you?" I asked, crossing all of my fingers in the process.

"Yeah, I can call my uncle. He lives over in Northwest. I think he's home now. This is his car. He'll know what to do," he answered.

"OK, let's get you out of the car," I said.

"I got a wheelchair in the trunk," he told us.

"Let me have the key. I'll get it out for you." He reached into the ignition and handed me the keys. I took them and went to the rear of the car. He reached over for his crutch and pushed open the door. I quickly gathered up his chair and Noren and I positioned it beside him. With ease I found to be amazing, the man scooted from the car to the chair, all in one swift motion. The sound of a honking car horn caused me to jump, and as I spun around I could see the dark-colored car racing past us, missing me by only a few feet.

"Thanks, asshole!" I shouted as he passed by. I could certainly now understand how someone could become so easily frustrated. "Some people are just too fucking impatient."

"It's way cold out here. We need to get you inside somewhere," Noren yelled as he wheeled the man onto the sidewalk. "We also need to get to a phone."

"There might be one we can use inside of that building," I said, pointing to an office building on the north side of the street. The lobby lights were still on.

"There should be. Let's go," Noren answered.

"Let me get the number." I asked James for the telephone number to his uncle's. "Stay by the scout car, we'll be right back."

"Don't worry, I'm not going anywhere," he answered.

His uncle seemed nice enough. I told him where we were located and briefed him on the situation. He said he was leaving right away, politely said good-bye, and hung up the phone. We headed back to the car.

"We need to get you someplace warm. You'll freeze out here in this cold," Noren said to James.

"It's OK I'll be fine. Is my uncle coming?"

"Yeah, he's on the way. We're going to wait with you until he gets here. We can wait inside of our car. There's no way we're leaving you out in this cold," I said sincerely. I remembered reading an article once about paralyzed people and their extreme susceptibility to the cold.

"OK, I'd appreciate that very much," he answered. Noren opened up the back door and just as swiftly as before, James slid from his chair into the car. I raced around to the passenger side, jumped in and immediately cranked the heat up to high. Now, all we had to do was wait. I jammed my hands in front of the heater and began rubbing them back and forth.

"What happened to your legs?" Noren asked innocently. I cringed as I heard him ask the question. Not because I wasn't curious myself. I'd be lying if I said I wasn't. But, I didn't have the guts to ask, I guess because I was expecting him to get angry. I was wrong.

"It happened back in '91, about four years ago," he answered casually. "I was shot five times. My right leg can still move, but my left leg, it's all messed up." He didn't seem the least bit angry or bitter.

"That's unbelievable. You're lucky to be alive," Noren said as he looked at me and shook his head.

"Yeah, you got that right. The bullets, they hit me all around my chest and back. One of the bullets, it cracked my spine. I'd show you the scars but..."

"That's OK," I interrupted. I didn't think I could really stand to look at the scars, at least not if I had the choice. "Where did this happen? Here in D.C.?"

"Yeah, over in Northeast, in the Trinidad area, " he answered. "At Montello and Queen Street."

My heart immediately skipped several beats. It had been a while since I had last seen these two streets, but I knew them well. Staring through the windshield, my mind drifted back to early January of 1992. I was assigned to a narcotics squad, and we patrolled just about every drug spot in the city. Back then, we often worked in the Trinidad area. One day, my partner Tim and I had stopped inside of a convenience store, right at the corner of Montello and Queen Street. Tim was at the counter paying for a can of soda. I didn't want anything, so I was content to stand near the back window, next to an old video machine. I gazed out the window at a group of men standing across the street. They were staring back at me.

"Check this out, Tim," I said as he stepped behind me. "These people across the street seem awfully interested in us being here."

"They probably have a drug stash around somewhere. They're waiting to see if we know where it is, or if we're going to look for it," Tim answered between gulps of Diet Pepsi. "As soon as we leave, I guarantee they'll walk back over this way."

"You know, this might sound kind of silly, but you remember Officer Washington? He used to be in Sector Three back at the Third District?" I asked.

"Yea, I remember him. What about him?"

"Well, when I was riding with him one day, he was lecturing me on the do's and don'ts of catching drug dealers. One of the things he said was to always check behind vending machines inside of these mom and pop stores. He said that was a favorite hiding place for drugs. That way, whoever they belonged to wouldn't get caught with or near them, but the dealer would have easy access to them whenever he wanted," I said, proud of my deductions.

"So what you're saying is that we should check behind this video machine right here, right?" Tim asked. He finished off his soda and attempted to toss it into a trash container several feet away. It clanged off the lip and bounced across the tiled floor. "Do you know how heavy these things are?"

"Nice shot, dude," I said, admiring his form. I ignored his last comment entirely.

"Screw you!" He answered smiling. Simultaneously, we both positioned ourselves on opposite sides of the video machine and pulled it away from the wall. As I was pulling my side, I glanced out the window again. The gang from across the street was gone.

"Bingo!" Tim said pointing at a crumpled up brown paper bag lying on the ground directly behind the machine.

"You think that's what I think it is?" I responded excitingly.

"Only one way to find out." Tim said as he reached down and picked up the bag. Gingerly, he began unraveling it. Slowly, the top of the bag opened up. Once open, Tim dumped its contents into the palm of his hand.

"Unbelievable!" I said as the penny-sized plastic bags cascaded down into the palm of Tim's hand. "That's the most crack cocaine I've seen!" Inside each small bag were small white and yellow rocks. They actually looked more like little slivers of chalk than cocaine. Finally, as Tim's hand began filling up, he turned the paper bag right side up.

"There's still more inside, he said. "This is some serious dope." He was trying to count how many bags he had poured into his hand. "There must be at least a hundred bags, maybe more."

"Somebody's gonna be awfully pissed we found this," I said, my voice trembling with excitement. Both of us knew someone would be held accountable for this missing crack, either the street dealer or the supplier. And whoever the street dealer was, he had probably gotten this stuff through consignment, which meant regardless of what happened to his dope, he still would be required to pay it off. So from an enforcement standpoint, even though we liked catching the dealers, sometimes making a recovery without the body was just as effective. The rest was left up to street justice, and sometimes that can be a beautiful thing.

"I can't believe someone would be stupid enough to leave this shit behind a video machine," Tim said laughing.

"You and I both know that if dealers were smart, we would probably never catch them," I interjected, laughing myself. "Hey, I've got an idea. Remember those guys from across the street? This has got to be their stash, right? Let's fuck with them a little and leave them a note. You know, just to let them know we've been thinking about them."

"You're a nut, Chris. You're just going to piss them off."

"So we piss them off a little. Maybe that's just what we need to do," I said defiantly. My mind was made up. I ripped a piece of paper from my notebook and began writing. When I was finished, I handed it to Tim for his approval.

"*Hey dumbass. Find a better place to stash your dope. Signed, Five-O.*" Tim started laughing. "You're crazy, you know that? How did someone from the suburbs end up so fucked up?"

"It's a long story Tim," I answered. "For now, let's put this note inside of another paper bag and crumple it up. We can put it behind the video machine in the same place we found the crack. Maybe when the owner comes back, he'll think his stash is still secure." At this point, I was laughing to myself hysterically. Once the bag was in place and we had pushed the video machine back to its original position, Tim and I returned to our scout car and drove back to the police station to put the drugs on the property book and into an evidence locker. From the station, the drugs would make their way to the Drug Enforcement Administration, where they would be tested and then destroyed.

The next day, as soon as Tim and I broke out of roll call, we jumped into our scout car and raced back to Montello and Queen. I couldn't wait to see the looks on the faces of the local gang as we pulled into the block. Judging by the smirk on Tim's face, I was sure he was enjoying the same thoughts.

It took only about twenty minutes, and as we pulled into the block, I was surprised to see the street was virtually empty. The gang from the day before was nowhere to be seen. A feeling of disappointment lumped in my stomach. Tim pulled in front of the corner convenience store and we both got out.

"This really sucks," I sighed with disappointment. "Talk about spoiling a good day's worth of anticipation." Deep inside, I guess I knew what we had done was kind of juvenile. But then, so was the whole drug dealer-police culture. Sometimes, I felt like we were all just a bunch of kids running around play-acting. It was hard to always remain entirely serious.

"Oh well. It was kind of funny," Tim answered. "At the least, I'm sure we really pissed off someone. That alone has got to be worth something." He was heading towards the store. I followed behind, still looking around for the street gang.

"What's up, fellas?" Tim said as we entered into the store. He was talking with two people standing in line. I didn't recognize either one.

"What's up, officer?" The taller one responded. He looked at me and began shaking his head. The other man, who was much shorter and stockier and standing next to him, started laughing.

"Why are you shaking your head?" I asked curiously. "And, why are you laughing?"

"Man, you two are the guys who left that note behind the video game, right." The tall man said, still laughing. "That was some move."

"Thank you. I must admit, it was one of our better days," I answered cautiously. I wondered where this conversation was going, and who these guys were.

"I was standing outside when this dude came to collect his shit," replied the short man. "I don't know him, mind you. Nor do I know anything about his stashes. I just seen him around the neighborhood, you know, him and his boys."

"So what happened?" I asked curiously. Tim was listening in as well.

"He went inside the store while his boys waited on the corner. He goes right to the back of the video machine. Then he comes running out with this brown paper bag in one hand and a note in the other. He runs up to this other dude and gives him the note. You understand? See, his ass can't even read! So, then he says, "What the fuck does this note say!" So, the other dude reads it, and says, "Hey dumbass, find a better place to stash your shit. Signed—Five-O." A slight smile spread across my face.

"So then what happened?" Tim chimed in. He was smiling more than I was.

"The dude who was reading the note started laughing, that's what. Then, the guy who gave him the note started jumping up and down and screaming, "They called me a dumbass! Did you say they called me a dumbass! I got their dumbass! I got their mother fucking dumbass all right!" So the other dude just tells him to calm down, tells him he was taken for a ride and to get over it."

"That's it?" I asked. "He didn't even have the audacity to threaten us?"

"That's it. That's the god awful truth," he answered. "He didn't threaten you, but I think you really pissed him off."

"Good. That was the plan," I said. "Mission accomplished." With that, I thanked them for the information and walked over to Tim and gave him a high five. Then I bought a coke so I could take a moment to relish in our little victory.

"Thanks again for the info. We appreciate it," I said as the two men walked out of the store. I wondered whether or not to believe their story. I guess it didn't really matter. It was fun just thinking about it.

"You ready to go?" Tim asked. He was holding a large bag of potato chips in his hand.

"Yea, sure, just give me one minute." I said, walking over to the video machine and glancing behind. There was nothing there. But hey, like I said, if they were smart, we would probably never catch them. Tim and I walked out the door and into the cold evening air. It was just starting to get dark.

"Take a look over there," Tim said. He was pointing to a group of about five or six men standing across the intersection. They looked like the same group I had seen yesterday. They were all huddled close together and every few moments, one of them glanced over in our direction. Finally, after a couple of minutes, they walked away and disappeared around the corner.

"They must still be dealing. Maybe they found another place to stash," I said. I headed towards a row house directly next to the convenience store. In between the store and the front yard of the house was an alley. Next to the alley was a brick wall, which was elevated about three feet and separated the first house from the alley. On the other side was a long row of houses, each with a small front lawn. The front lawn of the first house looked like someone had dumped a months' worth of garbage, with bags and bottles and assorted other items scattered all over the place. Mixed in with everything else was several crumpled up brown paper bags, not unlike the one behind the video machine.

"What are you doing?" Tim asked. He was standing next to the brick wall and the alley.

"I'm just going to check a few of these bags," I answered. "Why don't you give me a hand? They must be stashing their stuff around here somewhere."

"We'll never find anything. I'm sure they found a much better hiding place," Tim answered hesitantly. "But, what the heck, it's not like we have anything better to do." Tim hopped over the brick wall with a grace not befitting his large body and headed towards the opposite side of the yard. I stopped on the far end and started picking up bags.

The first round of shots sounded like firecrackers. At least, that is what my brain registered. Oh, they were loud all right, but not loud enough to get my full attention. However, on the second round, I froze in my tracks and stood up listening. The second round of shots sounded much more profound. I turned towards Tim, who was about twenty feet to my left. He was also standing upright, frozen in his tracks as well. For a moment, we just stared at each other, looking around for anything out of the ordinary. I'm sure neither of us could quite comprehend what exactly was happening, which was that someone was trying to put holes in our asses. Maybe we just didn't want to believe it. Maybe, we just didn't know what to do. Regardless, in a matter of seconds, all hell broke loose. Another string of loud bangs rang through the air like the Fourth of July, one steadily after the other. Despite the realization that we were being shot at, I still couldn't seem to move my legs. I was in denial. Staring right at Tim, I saw a patch of dirt explode from the ground only inches from his foot. It shot into the air and ricocheted into the side of the brick wall along side of the alley. That was all the convincing Tim needed. In a flash, he was sprinting for the other side, towards cover.

"Move your ass, Chris!" He yelled as he high jumped over the top of the wall and crashed to the hard concrete on the other side. I turned my body towards the wall and took a small step. I was too far away. Suddenly, another round of banging noises filled my ears. My feet were now acting with a mind of they're own. Instead of trying to make the sprint to the alley, which seemed miles away, I turned towards the street where our scout car was parked and took off in full sprint, diving headfirst into the side of the car. My head crashed against the metal door, almost knocking me unconscious. Scrambling quickly to my knees, I pulled out my gun and waited for the next round of shots. Abruptly, everything was now quiet.

"The roof across the street, I think they were coming from somewhere across the street!" Tim yelled from his hiding place. His small head popped up from behind the wall, his eyes darting back and forth. Then, as quickly as he had popped up, he quickly disappeared back behind the wall.

"I think you're right. Were they all shots? Some of them sounded a lot like firecrackers," I yelled back.

"I think they were a combination of both!" Tim shouted, again popping his head up just long enough to talk. "Someone is really trying to scare us!"

"I'm calling for assistance!" I answered, still scanning the roofline from across the street. "Stay where you are."

"I'm not going anywhere. You can believe that!"

"Four-sixty-five, we need assistance at Montello and Queen Streets, Northeast. We're being shot at!" I screamed into my hand held radio.

"Four-sixty-five, is everything OK at your location?" The dispatcher asked. "Any officers down?"

"Yeah, so far, no officers down. It's quiet right now. But we still need assistance," I answered, my voice cracking with fear.

Within seconds, every officer from our squad was on the scene. At least six cars pulled to the front of the block. Several other cars raced through the block and positioned themselves at the opposite end. For the next few minutes, everyone took cover and waited.

After a few minutes of silence, and feeling somewhat safe, I got up and quickly ran down to Montello Street where most of the scout cars had parked. I saw my supervisor pull in behind another scout car.

"What's going on?" He asked as he exited his car. I was out of breath and excited.

"Tim and I were up on the lawn looking for drug stashes when we heard shots coming from somewhere over there," I answered. I pointed towards the rooftops of a line of houses across the street.

"Are you sure they were gunshots?" He asked.

"Yeah, I am," I answered.

"OK We'll get a helicopter up and do a canvass. Are you sure you're all right?"

"Yea, I'm fine. Tim, he's OK too. But a shot just missed his foot by an inch. I saw the ground explode," I answered. My adrenaline was racing and my heart was still pounding.

Several minutes later, a police helicopter began making slow passes across the sky, shining a spotter light across the rooftops. It was getting dark and difficult to see clearly. We had pretty much sealed up the block from both sides and no one came in or went out.

For the next hour, we searched and waited, but to no avail. We weren't sure exactly where the shots had come from, or who had fired them. Eventually, we decided to give it up and returned to our scout cars to carry on with the rest of our nights work.

"I know that area well," I told James, slipping quietly back to the present day and out of my daydream. "I was assigned over there for a few months. Where exactly on Queen Street were you?"

"Right at the intersection with Montello, a few hundred feet from this convenience store," James answered. "Why?"

"No reason. I was just curious," I answered. What a strange coincidence. I didn't really feel like telling him my story. I don't think he would have been amused.

"It's OK, you know, my legs and all," James said, staring out the car window. "I was just the wrong man in the wrong place at the wrong time. They took me to D.C. General. I survived, so I guess I was lucky. Sometimes, I feel kind of sad. But then I think that there are a lot of people in this world who are worse off than me. I'm thankful. I got my own place, and in the spring, I'm enrolling at Prince George's Community College. I want to eventually study medicine. I'd like to understand more about spinal column injuries," He seemed like his mind was drifting elsewhere. Maybe he was having his own daydream, just like mine. Only his didn't have quite the same, happy ending. I wanted to ask him more, about the circumstances of the shooting. About what exactly he meant by being the wrong man in the wrong place at the wrong time. But I didn't. At a different time and place, maybe that would have mattered, but, not now. I didn't really want to know. Instead, I wanted to see this man for exactly who he was at this particular moment.

"His uncle is here," Noren said. I could see the car pulling in behind us. I reached down and touched my legs, wiggling my feet back and forth. I felt incredibly thankful. An inch here, or an inch there, that's all it really takes.

"I'm really glad we could help, James," I told him. "I really hope everything works out for you."

"Thank you, Officer. You know, you all aren't really that bad. I must admit, I used to really hate the police, always harassing people and shit. But you two are all right."

"Yeah, sometimes we are, aren't we? Here, let me give you a hand," I said as I pulled his wheelchair up to the door. He gently slid in and slowly wheeled away.

Sometimes, if we are very lucky, someone enters our lives and gives us a special gift of hope and appreciation, or perhaps just reminds us of what truly matters in life. Then, as quickly as they come, they are gone, leaving us with just a faded memory.

PART THREE

HOPE

"To expect or look forward to with desire and confidence." Webster's New American Dictionary

"The world is a beautiful place, and worth fighting for"

Ernest Hemingway

CHAPTER THIRTEEN

"We're screwed!" I said as I stared helplessly at the reinforced steel door in front of us. There were at least three deadbolt locks that I could see, and god knows how many I couldn't.

"I'm telling you, the last time we raided this place, all this guy had was a cheap, flimsy wooden door," replied Thomas, one of the prostitution detectives who was assisting us with this raid. We were getting ready to execute a search warrant for a house of prostitution, and we borrowed both of them from our downtown headquarters, using their experience since both had better then fifteen years on the job. I was certain they had not actually executed a search warrant for several years, but they knew this house, and they knew exactly what was needed to get our search warrants. And we had definitely relied on their planning, previous knowledge and advice in preparing for this raid.

"That sure doesn't do us a whole hell of a lot of good now," one of my co-workers shouted from behind us. I was in total agreement.

"Maybe he'll just answer the door," the other detective blurted sheepishly. "He's usually pretty harmless." I could tell they were both a little embarrassed at their poor planning.

"Oh, sure, maybe he'll just invite us in for tea as well!" Noren said standing in the rear.

"We've got one of our officers inside, and as much as we all know that these types of warrants seldom involve any real danger, I'm still not going to take any chances with his safety," I said, realizing I was, as team leader, ultimately responsible for the outcome of this raid. In order for us to make a case for an arrest, one of our undercover officers had earlier picked up a prostitute, who then took him inside this house. He paid the operator of the house, whom we were going to arrest, money for a room in which to have sex. Usually, it was ten dollars for an hour, and this was the basis for most of our prostitution warrants. We were pretty low budget, and in this city, which didn't take prostitution enforcement very seriously, we didn't have access to much in the way of surveillance cameras or recording devices. Now, our undercover officer was stuck inside this house, with a prostitute, trying to stall as long as he could, waiting for us to bust in.

So here we were, standing in front of 906 P Street in a grungy area of the city at roughly midnight on a busy Friday night trying to get inside an impenetrable prostitution house. Tonight had been the culmination of several nights' worth of investigation and surveillance. For the past two weeks, Ayala and I had sat half a block away, hidden safely within our car parked inconspicuously on a used car parking lot watching intently as wave after wave of prostitutes took their dates inside to rent a room. Each would stay about thirty minutes, then exit and leave, only to return later with new dates. Business was booming, and between the hours of eleven p.m. and three a.m. each night, it was all I could do to keep up and write down the descriptions of each couple. After the first night, it became clear to us that this was a pretty busy prostitution house, and that a search and arrest warrant would soon be inevitable.

"Hey Chris, we've got the two-man battering ram inside of our car," Baker said.

"You're kidding," I answered back. We had not discussed bringing a ram during our pre-raid conference, deciding to take the advice of the two detectives who swore we wouldn't need one.

"No really, it's in the backseat," Baker repeated again. "Sanchez and I thought it might be a good idea just in case."

"You are the man. I'll give you a hand," I yelled as we jogged to his car. We yanked the cumbersome iron ram out from the backseat and raced back to the front of the house.

"Stand back!" Baker shouted. Everyone moved to the side. We planted our feet, grabbed the handles on the side of the ram and started swinging it back and forth.

"On the count of three," I screamed, as our swaying motion began generating a good deal of force. "One, two, three!"

With a loud crash, the blunt face of the ram crashed into the steel door. Then, without causing so much as a dent, the ram came flying backwards. It was all I could do to keep hold.

"Damn, that door's not coming open easy," Baker cursed as the ram swung backwards. After going back as far as we could hold it, we swung the ram forward with as much force as we could muster, crashing it squarely into the door again. The ram bounced off and backwards, still without causing any damage.

"Harder!" I said, tightening my grip on the handles. Again we swung forward with all of our strength. Again the head of the ram crashed into the door, only this time causing the door to shake in its frame. A small buckle had formed at the handle. The door was starting to give.

"We've got it," Ayala said from over my shoulder. "Just a few more times."

I could hear movement coming from inside the house. By now, I was sure everyone inside was probably panicking and heading for every conceivable exit. Fortunately, we had officers positioned at the back of the house just in case. I knew we had to hurry, especially since one of our undercover officers was still inside and probably panicking just as well.

For the next ten or fifteen seconds, Baker and I swung the ram with all the force either of us could muster. The door had buckled so much, I could see light coming from inside the house from within a gap between the door and its frame. The door wanted to give, but the deadbolt locks wouldn't let it. My upper arms burned from the strain of swinging the fifty-pound lead ram. I could tell by the look on Baker's face that he was tiring as well. We couldn't last much longer.

"Mr. Walker, open the door now!" Detective Thomas shouted from behind me. I started laughing. I couldn't believe what was happening. Here I was, trying desperately to ram open a door and serve my first search warrant in a city noted for its violence and crime. And here was this veteran detective who was ordering a man who probably knew we were never going to get his door open to do just that, open the door. Had it not been for the undercover officer inside, I would have dropped the ram and fell to the ground in hysterics. Instead, Baker and I swung the ram back for one more series of blasts. We were going to blast this fucking door open if it meant dying in the process.

"One second. I'm getting it," replied a weak, old voice from the other side of the door. I heard the unmistakable sound of deadbolt locks turning as Baker and I started our last forward motion with the ram. There was no stopping now. Force and gravity were now in full effect. I only prayed that when the door opened, whoever answered from inside would be standing far enough away to not take the full brunt of our swing. Sure enough, about halfway through our forward thrust, just as the ram was achieving full power, the front door swung open. Standing in the threshold was a very small, frail old man with this weird little smile on his face. I was sure Baker and I were about to kill him. Using all the power I had left, I pulled back on the ram as hard as I could. The front of the ram swung upwards toward the sky, just missing the old man's chest by inches.

"Whatever you do, Baker, don't fucking let go!" I screamed as loud as I could, trying desperately to hold on. It was too late. Baker let go of his side of the ram and charged into the house, leaving me standing there as gravity slowly brought the ram back down to earth. I let go and tried to sidestep as quickly as my body would allow, but I didn't stand a chance. The rear part of the ram came crashing down on my left foot, smashing several of my toes in the process. I screamed in pain and fell to the ground, grasping my shoe. From my position wriggling on the ground, I watched as the rest of my unit raced into the house to begin the search. Tears filled my eyes as bolts of pain shot up through my leg.

From the moment I was able to regain my senses and get back onto my feet, everything around me became hazy and out of focus. Each beat of my heart brought an almost unbearable throb of pain to my broken toes. I limped into the house as quickly as I could and followed behind.

On my immediate right was a living room. With the exception of several basic pieces of furniture, like a couch and an armchair, it was empty. On the far end of the living room was a kitchen. It was also empty. Officer Jackson walked across the living room towards me.

"This area is all clear. Everyone else is upstairs." He said. "What the fuck happened to you?"

"Baker, dropped, ram, on foot," I said in short bursts. I glanced to my left and saw a staircase. I limped forward and headed upstairs. This part of the house consisted of basically just a long hallway with two doors on each side leading into several small bedrooms. It reminded me of a hotel. I painfully limped down the hallway and into the first room on my right. The room was really small, maybe ten-by-ten and the floor was covered with five soiled mattresses. Each was spaced about a foot away from the other, and sheets had been hung from the ceiling to act as dividers. Each mattress was covered with yellow and brown colored stains and dirt. I was sure they hadn't been cleaned in years. There weren't even any sheets or blankets. Roaches scurried across from one side of the room to the other. Next to each mattress, scattered across the floor were old, used condoms and condom wrappers. For a moment, this disgusting sight took my mind away from the pain in my foot. How in the world could anyone stand being in this shit hole? Standing against the far wall across the room were several prostitutes in various forms of undress. One girl was still naked. She reached over and began pulling on a pair of shorts. A guy was standing next to her buttoning up a dress shirt. His pants were still on the floor. He wouldn't look at me. Another man was completely naked and still had an erection. I assumed he was in shock, since he just stood there with his mouth hanging open, as if frozen in time. Several other men stood in the middle of the room with looks of utter disbelief enveloping their faces. In the far corner was a slender, tall blond with the biggest tits I had ever seen. I hesitated for just a moment, as this caught me off guard.

"Smile asshole, this is a raid," I said from the doorway. Despite the pain in my foot, I couldn't help but muster a laugh. This was a part of the job I truly loved. We had ruined everyone's night, especially one man, whom I had not noticed at first, but was standing in the far corner, with a steady stream of urine running down one of his legs.

"What the hell is going on?" a girl screamed in front of me. She was small maybe 5-2 or 5-3, and she had long, straight jet black hair and dark brown eyes. She also had the whitest skin I think I had ever seen. Her arms were folded across her bare chest. She was wearing nothing but a pair of black panties.

"Try a raid," I said, biting my lower lip in pain, trying to keep from staring at the blond with the breasts.

"You've got to be fucking kidding me," she answered. Her body was shaking in fear.

"No, I don't kid about such things. Get some clothes on, and tell your john to get his clothes on, as well," I motioned to the guy who had pissed all over himself. He didn't move an inch.

"Officer, Officer. I can explain," he said as he finally walked up behind the prostitute. "This is not the way it looks." Judging by the piss stain on his legs and pants, I hoped he was right.

"I don't give a shit how it looks and I could really care a less about you," I answered. "The only thing you should worry about is getting to a doctor and getting checked for diseases. Oh yeah, and also if we decide to call your wife," I chimed in after seeing the wedding band on his left hand. His mouth hung open and he stood motionless. "I'm sure she'd love to know what your activities were tonight."

"Please Officer, don't do that! Please don't do that!" He sobbed. Then he walked over to one of the mattresses and started getting dressed. The mattress was covered with urine stains and filth.

"Since when do the police raid prostitution houses? Don't you have better things to do?" The girl with the black panties asked. I recognized her from working the street. I had even picked her up several times, but she didn't recognize me. I was sure I would have no problems picking her up in the future. She was putting on a mini-skirt and was now fully clothed and starting to really get riled up.

"Not tonight, we don't," I answered casually. "And you should know just how much we like messing with ya'll." I turned around and started out the room. "Where else am I going to get paid standing around looking at naked woman?""

"Fucking asshole!" she muttered, not appreciating my humor in the least bit.

"Thanks a lot for the smashed toes, pimp," I said as I bumped into Baker in the hallway. He was walking out of another room down the hall. Officer Jackson, our crime scene technician was inside taking photographs of the mattresses and condoms for evidence. All of this would be important for court. There was no way I was going to seize this shit for evidence, especially used condoms, so photographs would serve just as well.

"Hey, I couldn't help it," Baker answered. "It slipped out of my hands." He had an annoying smile on his face, as if he failed to appreciate the seriousness of my situation.

"Yeah, and right on to my left foot." I shot back. I couldn't really get mad. It was just bad luck for me.

"I'm sorry. Are you all right?" He asked sincerely.

"Yeah, I guess. I'm sure I broke a couple of toes, but the pain is subsiding a bit now," I answered. "How's everything going so far?"

"Well, except for the front door fiasco, like clockwork."

"Is David OK?" I asked, referring to our undercover officer, whom had been trapped while we were assaulting the front door. He was the last person I wanted to see now and I knew I had a lot of explaining to do when I did.

"Yeah, he's fine," Baker answered. "He's a little pissed off about how long it took for us to get in, though."

"I don't blame him. I'll talk to him about that later." I slipped past Baker, stepped over a small pile of used condoms and headed towards the last room at the end of the hall.

"Take a look at this," Ayala said as I entered into the room. Unlike the other rooms, this one had just one regular king sized bed, and it was pretty clean. It must have been the owner's room. On the walls were hundreds of paintings and drawings of naked women. Some were no bigger than a post card and others were the size of large posters. Each drawing was of a local prostitute and I recognized quite a few of the girls from the streets. Some of them were so good; I thought I was actually looking at photographs.

"Pretty impressive," I said to Ayala. I leaned forward and pulled a few off the wall. "Hey, this blond chick is in one of the back rooms now."

"Yeah, I already saw her," he answered. "She's the one with the big tits, right?"

"Yeah that's her, what a waste, huh?"

"Yeah, I guess our defendant has hobbies other than selling rooms to prostitutes," Ayala had several pictures in his hand.

"Yeah, I guess so. Too bad, though, he must be at least sixty years old. I hate locking up old men. It's kind of embarrassing."

"Hey, it's a rough job, but somebody's gotta do it," Ayala answered. "I'm sure he's not acting like he's sixty when he's banging these girls." He was walking around the room looking at the pictures. I went back into the hall to assist Officer Jackson, who was herding all the girls and their dates outside, where a transport wagon eagerly awaited. Most of the prostitutes were busy gossiping amongst themselves, occasionally yelling out an obscenity to an officer standing nearby. They had been arrested many times before, so they were familiar with the game. As for the men, that's a much different story. They huddled together in mass; unsure of what would happen next, perhaps contemplating how they were going to explain our phone calls to wives and girlfriends.

When all was said and done, the owner, Mr. Walker, was charged with operating a Bawdy House, which is a misdemeanor offense punishable by only a three-hundred-dollar fine and one year in jail. He was sentenced to neither. He waltzed out of court with a suspended sentence, compliments of a sympathetic judge. I, on the other hand, would have trouble walking anywhere for the next month, having suffered two broken toes from the ram.

Little did I know this would be only the first of many houses our squad would raid over the next few years, each always the same, filthy mattresses, used condoms and a long line of respectable customers waiting to pay money to get in. Perhaps maybe even someone you know. Frightening, isn't it?

CHAPTER FOURTEEN

"Over there," Noren shouted. He was pointing to a woman standing on the corner of 12th and O Streets. "There's a warrant out for her arrest."

"Are you sure? What's she wanted for?" I asked. I was staring at her, trying to remember who she was.

"She didn't appear for sentencing in court last week. The Judge issued a warrant for failure to appear," Noren answered as he zipped our car through the intersection and brought it to rest a few feet from where the girl was standing.

"Are you sure?" I asked, knowing that he was. Spotting wanted persons was one of Noren's specialties and he was rarely ever wrong.

Now that we were close, I finally recognized her. She was wearing a red and black dress, over top of dark black leggings. Over her shoulders hung a dark blue flannel jacket with a hood, which she had pulled tightly around her small face. She was trying her best to hide.

"I just ran her name through the computer a few days ago. I'm pretty sure the warrant is still outstanding," Noren stated as he exited the car. The girl was now walking briskly away from us. I figured she had seen us.

"Hey Jade! Jade!" I shouted at the same time as Noren. We sounded like a stereo. Both of us were now walking after her, and had closed the gap to about ten feet. "Don't make us chase you," I pleaded. I hated chasing prostitutes. It was embarrassing having citizens watch us chase high heeled girls through the streets.

"What do you guys want?" Jade blurted out as she came to a halting stop in the middle of the block and spun around to confront us. Noren reached her first, and I followed immediately behind.

"We just need to talk with you for a minute." Noren had grabbed a hold of her jacket, as if reading my mind about chasing prostitutes. Just because she stopped didn't mean she wouldn't still be inclined to run. And she was wearing flat-soled shoes, which meant if she did, she was probably pretty fast.

"Where have you been?" I asked. "I haven't seen you around for a while. Not since the last time you were busted. "

"I was in the hospital. I just got out." She answered flatly. She wouldn't make eye contact. Instead, she stared down at the ground in front of her feet.

"Why were you in the hospital?" Noren asked, beating me to the punch.

"I don't work the streets anymore. I quit after you busted me. I'm just out here looking for a friend who said she'd meet me here," she answered quickly, obviously avoiding Noren's question. I had to admit, she looked much better than the last time I had seen her. She was wearing clean clothes and her weight seemed normal. I wanted to believe her when she said she was no longer working the streets.

"Come on, Jade. Why in the world would you meet your friend down here, especially on this corner? I know you don't live around here. And I'm pretty sure any friend of yours who is not engaged in any illegal activities probably doesn't live around here either. By the way, weren't you just arrested a few weeks ago for sexual solicitation?" Noren asked looking at me and smiling. I laughed. Noren was slick. He would never simply ask people if they were wanted or if they had missed a court appearance. That would give them a chance to lie. Instead, he would just keep asking questions, throwing them off guard until they admitted it. It was a good technique, one in which I often copied. It was always better to get people to admit that they were wanted, or at least to confirm a missed court date. This way, we had a pretty good idea what to expect when we checked with our dispatcher on the computer.

"Yeah, I think they put out a warrant for me for not paying some fine. They gave me a court date, something about a sentencing appearance, but I paid the fine the other day and my attorney said it was taken care of and I didn't need to go," Jade answered as she stared off into space. Noren had taken a few steps back. He looked disappointed.

"I'm going to run her name trough the dispatcher just to confirm," he said as he lifted his radio mike to his mouth. "I think she might be lying to us."

"So, why were you in the hospital?" I asked curiously, returning my attention to Jade.

"You know, I remember you now from last year. You used to have a ponytail, didn't you? And you drove around in a jeep. You looked much younger then." Jade answered, again ducking my question. She was good at trying to change the subject.

"Yeah, I did. I'm getting old, I guess, maybe a little too conservative as well. The police department will do that to you. I don't really look that old, do I?" I asked, feeling a little self-conscious, especially working with Noren. He was an avid body builder, with long blond hair, and standing next to him, I resembled a slightly taller version of Barney Fife from *The Andy Griffith Show*. Besides, nobody liked being called old, even if it was coming from a prostitute.

"No not really, I guess. But you used to look much better."

"A lot of girls used to have a crush on you. And your partner, he's gorgeous," she answered back. I was sure she was just humoring me.

"You still haven't answered my question yet, about being in the hospital," I reminded her, still not expecting an answer, let alone a truthful one. "So what was up?"

"Do you really want to know?" She asked back, a wry smile developing on her lips. "Can you handle it, copper boy?"

"Yes, I'm quite certain I can handle it, and yes, I do want to know."

"OK, you asked for it. Here, look." As she was finishing her sentence, she began slowly rolling up the sleeves of her jacket to just above her elbows. On each arm were at least ten or twenty small scars, each one covered with fresh tissue. They started on her wrists and lead up to her biceps. Each one was about an inch in length.

"Jesus. What the hell happened to you, Jade?" I asked, caught off guard by the sight of her wounds. My stomach started to turn.

"What do you think? I did them myself. Pretty nice work, huh? "Jade answered in a whiny, childlike voice. "Sometimes I get a little depressed and I like to do strange things. My doctor calls this self-mutilation. I'd rather like to think of it as stress therapy, and I think it's kind of fun. You know, you guys are too much. Why don't you go catch some murderers or something? Why are you always messing with us girls?" Noren was again standing next to me. He was shaking his head back and forth, which I took to mean Jade was no longer wanted on a warrant. She had cleared it just as she had said. I could see Noren was now staring at Jade's wounds as well.

"What the hell happened?" he asked.

"She cut herself," I answered. "It's stress therapy, ya know."

"Is there anything we can do for you?" Noren asked sincerely.

"Yeah, you can leave me alone. We're not hurting anyone," she answered angrily. "All you two do is go around messing with the prostitutes. Don't you have any greater aspirations than messing with us? Don't you have your own girlfriends?"

"Why don't you try going home, with your parents?" Noren responded sounding genuinely concerned. "You know that you'll eventually have to get off the street. If you don't, you'll end up like all the other girls, strung out and one step away from a grave," Both of us liked Jade. She seemed different from the other girls on the street. She was articulate and smart and funny. And she knew how to keep us on our toes.

"Can't do that, things are a mess at home, you know, even worse than on the street. It took me a long time to finally get out. I surely don't plan on going back."

"What's wrong with home?" I asked, hoping to learn a little more about her. But she just smiled and stepped a few feet back. I guess it would be her little secret.

"We'll check back at the station. If she's still got a warrant, we can come back for her," Noren said, turning to me.

"You know Jade, it's not as if we're out here just to harass you," I said, trying unsuccessfully to convince her that we really cared. "We're just trying to get you to stop, maybe think about doing something else. It's our job. You know that," I couldn't take my eyes off her arms. What could cause a person to do that to him or herself? I knew Jade didn't have a pimp, or any real enemies. And I had never known a customer to do this type of physical damage. They would rape, beat, and on very rare occasions kill the prostitutes, but never mutilate. So I was convinced that she was telling the truth.

"Maybe someday, I don't know," she answered in a low voice. "I guess I can't really do this forever."

"By the way, what's that mark on your neck? It's not a needle burn, is it?" I asked as I stared at a patch of red skin on the left side of her neck. I didn't figure her for a heroin junkie.

"No silly. That's just a hickey," she answered, her face turning bright red.

"Come on, jade, be honest," Noren said with a slight laugh. "Why would you have a hickey on your neck? Have you been dating high school kids now?" We both laughed.

"I'm serious. I got it last night," Jade answered, seemingly very much at ease with herself. "I was at this club in Georgetown having some drinks. I guess I got little too drunk and I started talking with this chick. Man, she was really hot. We talked for a while and we really hit it off. She asked me if I wanted to go home with her, so I did. And the rest is perverted history."

"So how much did you charge her?" I asked, enjoying her little story.

"You know I can't answer that officer," she answered sternly. "That would be self-instigation."

"That's self-incrimination Jade," I answered smiling. "I'm glad to see you've been reading up on constitutional law. So when did you start liking other women?"

"You know, we're not all a bunch of stupid bimbos. And I've always liked women. They are beautiful and caring people. I also find them to be intellectually superior."

"Girl, what's up with you?" Noren asked. "Intellectually superior? You've got to be kidding."

"It's like I said before. Sometimes I get depressed, so I do things, different things. I like to experiment," she answered, smiling and pulling down on the sleeves of her jacket. If I didn't know better, I'd swear I was now talking to a sixteen-year old girl. "Am I free to go?"

I wanted her to stay. I had many other questions I wanted to ask. But I couldn't. Even though she had opened up the lines of communication to areas I would have never wandered on my own, I really didn't think I was ready to go all the way. My sanity just wouldn't allow it.

"Yeah, go ahead. How about staying off of the street corner for a while, OK?" I answered, knowing full well that in a matter of hours, she would be standing right here on this same corner looking for business as usual. "OK?"

She didn't answer at first. She just casually turned her back smiling and started walking away towards 13th Street. Noren was already in the car, anxious to be on our way. It wasn't like we had anywhere to go anyway. It was only an hour before check off time, and soon we would be going home.

"You looked better last summer!" Jade suddenly shouted over her shoulder as I closed my car door. I laughed. I was struck by the ease and indifference with which Jade was able to talk about her lifestyle. I wondered if she really even cared. In her world, everything was fine, living life from day to day. Tomorrow was just a hazy, distant bur.

Traffic was pretty heavy for only three o'clock in the afternoon as we gently pulled our car into the street. Rush hour was still an hour away.

CHAPTER FIFTEEN

Sergeant Frank was our newly appointed supervisor. I knew who he was, having seen him around the station and I knew he carried with him an excellent reputation for being an "officer's" sergeant, which basically meant he was supportive of his officers and would do whatever was necessary to help them do their jobs. But since I had never worked for him directly, and had more than my share of asshole, incompetent supervisors in the past, I was not quick to give him the benefit of the doubt. So during the first week of his tenure with us, I was mindful to watch my step and do things by the book.

It was an ordinary Friday night, except that more than half our unit had taken off work, leaving only Sergeant Frank and three officers—myself, Ayala, and Gonzalez on duty. After a brief meeting, it was decided we would hit the street and case a few girls, indoctrinating Sergeant Frank to the basic bread and butter of our unit. Casing meant picking up a prostitute, getting an agreement of sex for money, and then making the arrest. It was easy, required little manpower and there were always plenty of hookers available. On any given night, we would case and arrest five to ten girls, depending on how busy the street was, and how much manpower we had. Because we only had four people tonight, we would probably only get two or three, which sucked because Friday was usually one of our busier nights. I elected to do the undercover work, and Ayala, Gonzalez and Sergeant Frank would provide my backup. I was going to drive my little Honda Civic CRX, which is every bit as small as it looks, and Sergeant Frank and Ayala would be in Ayala's beat up Ford Tempo. Gonzalez had a Chevrolet Cavalier. The plan called for Ayala and Sergeant Frank to hit the street and locate where the girls were working tonight. They would then give me a radio lookout describing a few of the girls and their locations to me. I would drive up, pick up a girl, and make a case. Once I made my case, I would give a pre-arranged signal, which usually meant activating my car's hazard lights and my backup unit would pull me over and make the arrest. Ahhhhh, the best laid plans of mice and men…

I pulled out of the police station confident that tonight would go smoothly. I was anxious to show Sgt. Frank how we worked.

"Archer, there's a girl standing at the corner of Eleventh and N Street. She's all alone," Ayala stated over the radio in his usual thick Spanish accent. "Go get her pretty boy."

"I copy that. What is she wearing?" I asked, turning my car around towards Eleventh Street. Ayala had a knack for picking out the nastiest, disease-ridden girls around for me to pick up. In a sea of perfect 10's, he'd hone in on the only girl with one leg a foot shorter than the other and one tooth in her mouth. I think he really got a kick out of fucking with me.

"She's a black female. She's got on a black mini-skirt, a white shirt and high heels."

"OK, I'm only a couple of blocks away. I should be there in a minute or two," I answered. "Where will you be so I know which road to take?"

"We'll be on N Street watching you."

"Copy." I eased my car into the block. Glancing out the window, I searched for anything out of the ordinary. The girl was just up ahead, standing exactly where Ayala had said. She was on the sidewalk, her face and body protected by the darkness of the night. As I pulled closer, I made eye contact and waved her to my car. She took the bait and eased from the shadows, walking slowly towards me. Hmmmmm, so far so good. No noticeable limps or missing appendages. Maybe Ayala was softening in his old age. I checked my rearview mirrors, making sure no one was sneaking up on me. That was a favorite trick of many prostitutes, and the cause of more than a few robberies. Everything was clear, and I thought to myself how easy this first case was going to be.

"Hey, what's up beautiful?" I asked, almost chuckling at how silly I sounded. No matter how many times I did this, which by now was at least a hundred, I still couldn't help but feel utterly ridiculous.

"I'm good. What you looking for?" The girl answered. She had walked up to the passenger side of my car and was leaning into the open window. I glanced at her face quickly, but it was too dark for me to get a good look. I reached up and clicked on the interior light of my car, but the damn thing didn't work.

"I'm trying to get some pussy. Can you help me out?" I asked, trying to sound as confident as possible.

"You ain't no cop, are you?"

"Nah. I'm a computer programmer out in Maryland," I answered. "I think the cops are just a bunch of assholes, always trying to ruin a man having some fun."

"You got someplace we can go to?" She asked. She was asking a lot of questions, which made me nervous.

"No not really, I was hoping you knew of someplace cheap."

"I do. Let's go," she answered as she opened the door and jumped into my car. As she sat next to me, I shot another quick glance at her face. I still couldn't fully make her out. It was too dark. I pulled away from the curb and headed down Eleventh Street.

"Make a U turn," She said abruptly.

"Right here?"

"Yes, right here." I checked the oncoming traffic and quickly spun my car around. I was afraid this would cause me to lose my backup, but as I checked my rear view mirror, I could see Ayala's vehicle right behind me. I was sure of this because I knew he had the only Ford Tempo in Washington D.C., pre 1985 and with only one functioning headlight.

"Where are we going?" I asked.

"It's just up ahead," she answered, pointing straight up Eleventh Street. I instinctively felt the right side of my body for my gun, forgetting that I usually didn't wear it for these types of operations. Sure enough, it wasn't there. I checked my rearview mirror again, and was comforted by the sight of my one headlight backup unit following directly behind.

"So, what kind of pussy do you want?" She asked, breaking a moment of calm silence. The question threw me off guard.

"It doesn't matter," I answered. "We can just have sex. You know, just straight, normal sex." All I needed was an agreement for the money, and I was good to go for an arrest and could signal for my backup.

"How about if I give you the fantasy blow job?" she replied with a slight growl in her voice.

All I had to do now was say yes and quote a price, and our first arrest would be complete. But no, I had to be a curious idiot, and a little voice inside of me kept asking over and over again, what in the world is a fantasy blowjob? Curiosity finally got the better of me.

"What the hell is a fantasy blowjob?" I asked.

"Baby, I'll suck everything from your waist down until you scream fucking bloody murder!" she yelled, only this time a much larger, guttural growl escaping from her lips. She then reached over and grabbed hold of my crotch with her left hand and proceeded to squeeze my balls into oblivion. Her grip was like a vice.

"Fuck that!" I screamed, slapping her hand away. "I'm not into this sado-masochist shit."

"You sure you ain't no cop?" She asked, her hand again grabbing my nuts and squeezing my crotch into another world.

"No…I'm not. Could you please let go of my crotch?" I whimpered between short gasps of air. The pain was immense. She finally let go.

"Pull into this alley here on the right," she said, never taking her gaze away from me.

"This one here," I asked, pointing to perhaps Washington, D.C.'s longest and darkest alley. My heart rate soared about a hundred beats.

"Yes, it's safe in here. We can do everything we want." There was no way I was pulling into this alley unless I had a case and an arrest was going to be made quickly. Having been sidetracked by the testicle grip from hell, I had forgotten to talk about money.

"OK, no problem. But I've only got fifty bucks. Is that enough for the fantasy blow job?" I said, realizing I needed to get this show on the road.

"Sure baby, that's more than enough." That was it. The price was all I needed for my case. I glanced into my rearview mirror, confirming that Ayala and Sergeant Frank were still behind me, and then made the turn into the alley. As I turned, I quickly activated my car's emergency lights and gently eased to a stop a few hundred feet deep. In another few seconds, we would make the arrest and I would be free from this alley. Life was good, except that I soon realized an important fact: apparently there was more than one red Ford Tempo in Washington D.C. with only one working headlight. And as the one behind me failed to make the turn into the alley and continued north on Eleventh Street, I felt the unmistakable horror of realizing I was now alone in this dark, secluded alley with some crazed chick who wanted nothing more in life than to give me a fantasy blow job. Panic began to set in.

"What's up, baby? You ready to get it on?" She said, her hands snaking towards my body. I smacked one of them away and pushed myself as far away from her as my Honda Civic would allow.

"What's the matter? Are you nervous?"

"You just don't even know the half of it!" I answered back, my mind desperately trying to think of a way out of this messed up situation. My backup would never find me here. Again, she reached for me, this time putting one hand against my chest, the other one heading for my pants.

"Just hold on a minute!" I screamed using my best Karate slaps to keep her hands at bay. "I'm not ready yet."

"Why are you so nervous? Don't you want to do it?"

"Of course I do, it's just I'm not quite ready yet," I stalled, sounding like an idiot. Something had to be done, and quick. As I was thinking, or should I say praying, she removed her shirt and stuffed it in her purse. If this wasn't a bad enough situation as it was I now realized this was not a girl, but a man. He had no breasts and more hair on his chest than I had on my entire body. I swore right then and there that if I survived this, I would kill Ayala in a most painful and horrible way.

"Listen, I need to get a condom, OK?" I said, trying to stall for time. I couldn't hide the ghastly look of disgust as I curled my face up at the sight of him.

"Sure, baby. One can never be too careful, that's my motto." God, I couldn't bear the thought of what this dude did to others after this mysterious and disgusting fantasy blowjob.

"Can you lean back a little? They're in my glove box," I said as I leaned forward and reached for the catch. I strained to keep from actually touching him, but thanks to my untimely small car, I couldn't help but brush ever so slightly against his legs.

"Oh my!" he said, almost making me vomit on the spot.

At this moment, I thought briefly about throwing my elbow into his face and making a break for it. But if it didn't work, I would be trapped in my car with no room to fight. Gently turning the glove box catch and pulling it open, I suddenly realized I had another, more pressing problem at hand. Sitting exactly where I thought I had put the box of condoms was my police armband, which was an orange-colored patch with the Metropolitan Police logo blazoned across in bright blue and yellow lettering. We used it to identify ourselves while working plain clothes.

"Ohhhh baby," the transvestite asked, leaning forward to get a better look. "What's that bright orange thing? Something for us to play with?" I shoved my forearm into his hairy chest and pushed him back while simultaneously slamming the glove box shut. If this dude figured out I was a cop, then all hell would break loose, and I was pretty sure my ass was going to get kicked. If not for the fact that this dude just looked scary as shit, then simply because I was so disgusted at the sight of him, I wondered if I could really muster the guts to actually hit him. I had learned during my years working prostitution, nothing was more dangerous or volatile as a transvestite who knows he is about to go to jail.

"Damn man, you don't have to get rough with me!" he blurted, still reaching for my crotch. "Come on, baby. What's in the glove box? I want to see."

"It's nothing. Really," I answered. "It's just something my girlfriend gave me a couple of weeks ago. It wouldn't interest you at all," I was desperately still trying to figure out how I was going to get out of this mess. I glanced into my rearview mirror, hoping maybe Ayala and Sergeant Frank were looking for me and might see my car parked in the alley. No such luck. Several cars drove by, but none stopped to look or slowed down to investigate. I had come to the conclusion that this was entirely on me, and I alone was going to have to figure this one out.

Then it came to me.

"My condoms are in the trunk. I have to get out to get them." I was shocked this might actually work. I guess intelligence was not a pre-requisite for being a prostitute.

"That's all right baby. I got some right here," he answered while pulling out a condom from somewhere in his nether region. "Look, they're ribbed!"

I was sure that my lips were now trembling and the expression on my face priceless.

"I need my own. I only use my own condoms," I blurted out, grabbing for the handle on my door.

"Fuck that shit," he said. "Something's not right here. Why you been acting so nervous?"

"I'm fine. I just need to get the condoms," I replied while quickly opening my door. As I stepped from the car, I reached under my seat for the portable police radio. I could just barely reach the antenna, but it was too far under the seat for me to pull it out. Shit. I jumped out of the car and walked towards the back. At least now I had some room to maneuver.

"Yea, I'm sure I left them in here," I said as I scanned my surroundings, trying to formulate an escape plan. My keys were still in the car and it was still running.

"I think you're lying. All this bullshit you been pulling since we got into this alley. I've seen this kind of shit before. You're a damn cop." He said as he slowly got out of the car. "But where's your backup?" Jesus, where did he get a brain from all of a sudden?

"Let's not jump to any conclusions," I answered back. "I think you're wrong. Now let's not get carried away here and do anything either of us might regret."

"Regret? Did you say regret motherfucker! I got your regret right here!" he screamed from beneath clenched teeth. "Do you think I would regret it if I kicked your ass for wasting my fucking time? Do you think I would regret it if I stole all your motherfucking money! Now where is the money you said I was getting? If you're not a cop, then give the shit up." He was slowly making his way around the car towards me.

"I don't have any money. And I'm not going to fight you, either," I answered, realizing this man was much bigger than I had first noticed. Damn, how in the world did I mistake him for a woman in the first place? I determined in my mind that fighting a transvestite in this alley was not worth the value of my car and that running seemed more the order for the day. I just needed to put as much distance between him and myself as possible. That way, he couldn't run me down. I still had a little speed left in my legs. I examined the best route of travel for my escape, deciding on the entrance where we had pulled in and prepared to push off from the back of my car.

"Screw you asshole, I'm outta here!" With these last few eloquent words, the transvestite took off running past the front of my car and through the alley away from me. He was quite a sight as he tossed his high heeled shoes into his hands in mid-stride, his mini-skirt flapping in the wind as he sped through the alley. He was heading towards Tenth Street. Damn, he was fast. I dropped to my knees and reached as far under the driver's seat as I could, grasping hold of my radio and pulling it free. I yanked the keys from the ignition, locked the doors and set off in pursuit. The only question now was how in the world I was going to explain this over the radio without sounding like a complete idiot. There was just no way. I was stuck. I had to do it.

"Tact twenty-two, I've got one running, black male dressed like a female in a black mini skirt and no shirt on, last seen running through the east alley in the 1800 block of Eleventh Street towards Tenth Street. I think he might have headed north on Tenth Street," I shouted, my body now running at full speed. He had long since exited the alley and headed up 10th Street.

"Tact twenty-two I copy that, any units to assist tact twenty-two with the pursuit?" The dispatcher answered. Several units acknowledged that they would assist.

"Tact twenty-two, what's the suspect wanted for?" The dispatcher inquired. I had been praying she wouldn't ask.

"Uh, uh, uh...the suspect is wanted for...prostitution violations," I answered, feeling humiliated. But wait, it would get even worse.

"Where did the suspect escape from?" the dispatcher asked. Jesus, what was up with her?

"From my car," I answered back, knowing that every officer monitoring the radio was now in a state of extreme hysteria. There it was. I had admitted to having let a transvestite escape from my car, and now, here I was, running around the city in plain clothes trying to catch him. I was ruined.

By the time I reached the end of the alley and onto Tenth Street, he was gone. And I was exhausted. Nothing quite managed to take one's breath away like talking into a radio and running at the same time. I looked down both sides of the street. There was no way he could have just vanished into thin air. I looked across the street just in time to see a marked scout car pull up.

"Hey Archer, you having a rough night?" I heard a deep voice say from the driver's side window. I couldn't immediately recognize who it was.

"Screw you, OK," I yelled back. And when I realized there was another officer in the car, I told him to screw his partner as well just for good measure.

"Uptight, aren't we? We all just have to know, what the hell you were doing with a transvestite in your car," the driver asked sarcastically. "And, are you off-duty?"

"Yes, I'm off duty, and to be real honest with you, I have this thing for men who dress up as women. I like to take them to dark, secluded alleys, then throw them out of my car and chase them down. It's a real turn on. You should try it sometime. Are you going to help me, or what?"

"Yeah sure, just relax. What was that lookout again?"

"He's a black male, dark complexion, wearing a black mini-skirt and no shirt. Oh, and high heels," I answered. I should have left out the high heels.

"Did you say high heels?" He asked. I knew better then to continue this conversation. I was just digging myself a deeper and deeper hole.

"Just do a canvass, OK. And when you find her—I mean him—let me know so I can do an ID." I finished my sentence and watched the scout car pull off. To add insult to injury, I finally recognized the other officer in the passenger seat as one of our new recruits. That was all I needed.

I flipped an imaginary coin in my head and decided to walk north on Tenth Street. After a few steps, a canine cruiser pulled into my path and an officer jumped out.

"Please tell me you're joking," he said abruptly.

"Look, I've already gotten enough shit from scout eighty-five. I'm tired, I'm humiliated, and I've got a suspect on the loose. Can you please just give me hand?" I asked.

"Yeah, relax dude. I'll get my dog and we can retrace his steps." He opened the back of his truck and out jumped the biggest, scariest Rottweiler I had ever seen. A long stream of gooey saliva hung from his mouth, stopping just a few inches short from the sidewalk.

"Hey man, what's up with your nasty ass dog?"

"What do you mean?"

"I mean, why the hell is he salivating all over the place? He looks like he's crazy," I said. "Has he been recently checked for rabies?"

"He's just excited. It's been a slow night and he's anxious to do some work," he answered back. His dog was eyeing me like I was a New York strip steak. I was certain if he got off his leash, I would be a dead man. The dog kept shaking his head back and forth, sending streams of saliva cascading through the air. If I didn't know any better, I'd swear he was trying to psyche himself up.

"Your dog's not playing with a full deck, is he?" I asked.

"He's all right. Just a little high strung," he answered. "Stop busting on my dog, OK."

"Well, just so you know, if that psychotic mutt comes anywhere near me, I'm going to shoot his ass, OK?" I was scared shitless of most police dogs. They were too high strung and unstable. Needless to say, I decided to take a wide loop around his dog and continued searching on Tenth Street. The canine officer walked back into the alley where my car was.

Now came the time I dreaded most. I was certain Sergeant Frank had heard the whole incident over the radio and was now heading my way. I was torn between being embarrassed, and being angry that Ayala had lost me. But it wasn't his fault. These things just happened sometimes. Unfortunately, they didn't usually happen the first week of breaking in a new supervisor.

As I was thinking of how I would explain everything to Sergeant Frank, I came across another alley entrance. At the opening of this alley was a huge pile of trash. I stopped for a moment to catch my breath and stared down the alley, hoping to see some movement. Nothing. Then, I walked up next to the trash pile, trying to figure out where to search next. Suddenly, a small corner of the pile moved. Not the whole pile, just one small corner. I turned my head quickly and froze in my tracks. Was it a rat? I couldn't be sure. Then it moved again. I focused on the area of the movement and saw a small patch of white clothing. It couldn't be. What an idiot! I had found my beloved transvestite, who had put his shirt back on.

I'd really like to say that I reverted back to some great police intuition, or that I used some form of innovative training, but in the end, it all boiled down to one simple, well placed kick. The hardest kick my right leg could muster, which was immediately followed by a loud yelp of pain. In a flash, the transvestite rolled out of the trash pile and sprang to his feet.

"I'm not chasing you anymore. It's over," I said as I stood a few feet away.

"Oh, so you're going to shoot me instead. Is that it?" He answered between gasps of air. What the fuck? I didn't even have my gun.

"No, I don't think I'll have to do that." I turned my head to the right just in time to see the huge Rottweiler brush past me. "Thanks. You're right on time," I said as the officer pulled his dog a few feet short of the transvestite.

"No problem. I really don't think he'll run now," he answered with a chuckle.

"OK, OK You got me. Just get that crazy, rabies infected dog away from me. I'm not going anywhere!" Screamed the transvestite, shaking from head to toe. I had a notion to just let the dog go and settle this right here on the street. But, rationality took over, and I slapped my handcuffs on him and walked him to the side of the street.

I never did have to explain this incident to Sergeant Frank. He simply pulled up to where I was standing with a huge smile on his face.

"I think I'm going to really like this job. What do we do next?" he asked, sounding like a little kid on Christmas. I heard Ayala in the driver's seat laughing.

CHAPTER SIXTEEN

There it was, sitting on the corner of my supervisor's desk. Just a plain, nondescript white envelope sitting along with several others, and had it not been for the word "Urgent" printed in bold letters across the top, I probably would have never noticed it. But I did, and with a burning curiosity, I picked it up and carefully examined it. It had already been opened; the letter inside having been carefully folded and placed neatly back inside. Gently, I pulled out the letter, unfolded it and began reading.

"THIS AD HAS THE POTENTIAL FOR VIOLENCE. I ARRANGED A MEETING. JUST AFTER ENTERING "TARA'S" APARTMENT, 1712 16TH STREET N.W., APT. #103, I WAS QUICKLY ESCORTED INTO A BEDROOM. (TARA) REMAINED BEHIND ME. THE DOOR WAS CLOSED AND UNDER POOR LIGHTING I SUSPECTED TARA WAS NOT FEMALE. I SAID THIS WAS A MISTAKE AND STARTED TO LEAVE—TARA STOOD IN FRONT OF THE DOOR & THREATENED VIOLENCE IF I DID NOT STAY. TARA SAID IF SHE COULDN'T, SHE HAD A FRIEND THAT WOULD MAKE ME STAY. AFTER A SHORT DISCUSSION, I WAS BEATEN VISCOUSLY. TARA IS EXTREMELY PHYSICAL & IS WILLING TO ENGAGE IN A VIOLENT ACT."

My heart raced as I folded the letter and slipped it back inside the envelope. There was no information about who the writer was. No name, no return addresses, just the letter itself, addressed to the D.C. Police Department, Third District. Enclosed with the letter was a copy of the personal advertisement from the *Washington City Paper* from which the writer had referred.

I quickly rummaged around the office in search of the latest issue. Usually, we kept one lying around somewhere. As luck would have it, I stumbled upon a month-old issue, which had been folded over and stuffed underneath some paperwork. Anxiously, I ripped through the pages, working my way to the personal advertisement section in the back. I quickly glanced through the captions; Men seeking women, Women seeking men, Men seeking men. Bingo, I found what I was looking for. It didn't take long for my eyes to focus in on the ad. In fact, it's almost as if it had found me instead. In dark typeset, about halfway down the page glared the heading "ENERGETIC TARA." I gently swallowed as I continued reading. German-American brunette, 5 ft. 9 in., long shapely legs. Come watch an X-rated video while I do my special hard work. Easy parking. Call ***-****.

At first glance, it seemed harmless enough. Maybe a little bizarre, but certainly somewhat subdued when compared to other City Paper personals. Yet, having read the anonymous letter, and now confirming the actual ad, I couldn't help but feel a tingling mix of fear and excitement. This was like the beginning of a movie, a strange tale just beginning to slowly take shape before my eyes. I knew immediately that I had to make the call.

Sometimes, when we had nothing else to do, Sanchez and I would play a game I called "What if's." Basically, we would sit down and imagine as many different ways to catch criminals as we could, only using slightly less than conventional techniques. What if we did this, or what if we could do that, we would ask each other. Sometimes we would read through the D.C. Criminal Code book and examine some of the more bizarre laws, their wordings and limitations and discuss to what level we could enforce them. I would challenge Sanchez with off the wall ideas, and mostly, he would shoot them down. But this was different. This letter, this *City Paper* ad, was right up our alley. Both of us had longed for something different than regular street level prostitution enforcement. Both of us wanted to explore more complex investigations, to flex our police muscles, so to say, and to establish our own level of prostitution expertise. And now, staring us right between the eyes was something new. In fact, we had never before discussed the idea of targeting a newspaper advertisement. Needless to say, I wasn't at all surprised when confronted with the idea of making the call; Sanchez simply smiled and said, "Let's do it."

On this chilly fall day, sitting at my desk with my feet kicked up, my palms so sweaty I could swim in them, I gently picked up the telephone, ready for our adventure to begin. Sanchez was seated next to me, a serious look enveloping his round, boyish face. I was nervous as hell. I knew it was just a telephone call, but I also knew that this was just the beginning, and that once the call was made, there would be no turning back. I took a deep breath and slowly dialed the number. The line on the other end began to ring. Once, twice, three times.

"Hello," answered the soft voice of a female.

"Hello, I'm calling about the *City Paper* personal ad, the one about Mistress Tara?" I blurted out, my voice cracking with tension.

"This is she. What do you want?" She asked calmly.

"I'd like to see what you offer," I answered.

"Do you like to watch X-rated movies?" She asked, catching me slightly off-guard. "I assume you read my ad?"

"Yes, I do," I answered quickly, not sure of what else to say. I was a little shocked at her frankness.

"Well, for a hundred dollars, you can watch videos while I give you a body massage," Tara explained in what seemed to be a very well-rehearsed speech. She obviously had gone through this before, perhaps many, many times.

"A hundred dollars? Can I get anything else for my money?" I asked, hoping she would commit over the phone. I wanted her to show her hand, and verify what Sanchez and I both suspected was a front for prostitution and sex.

"Well, we can discuss that in person, but first we should make an appointment," She answered quietly. "When would you like to come over?"

"How about this Friday night?" I asked, hoping a week would be enough time for Sanchez and me to arrange everything. There would be a lot of paperwork involved.

"Sure. That will be fine. Just give me a call around nine p.m. and I'll give you directions to my place."

"Why don't you just give me the address now, and that way I can just be there at nine?" I asked, a little confused by this turn of events. I had fully expected her to give me the address over the phone. Her reluctance added a bit of danger to the situation, and I was a little uncomfortable in having to basically wing it on Friday night. We wanted the chance to check out the surroundings and get an idea as to what to expect.

"Not till Friday. Good-bye." Click. The phone went dead. I sat briefly listening to the dial tone pounding in my ear. I glanced over at Sanchez and smiled. He looked confused. I felt just a little bit silly.

"How was that?" I asked sheepishly.

"That was good. We're definitely onto something. What did she say?" Sanchez asked.

"We're on for Friday night."

"What about her address?" he asked.

"She wouldn't give it to me. She said to call back Friday night at nine o'clock and she would give me directions."

"That sucks. Not good, either. We'll need to be on top of this and to make sure we have all of our bases covered. How did you want to handle this anyway?" Sanchez asked.

"Same as anything else, I guess. We'll call The Electronic Surveillance Unit and see about equipment, and keep our guys as a backup unit. I'll be in an hour early tomorrow if you want to meet and go over a game plan," I answered back, tired and ready to go home. My mind was racing a million miles per hour.

"Sure. I'll see you tomorrow," Sanchez yelled over his shoulder as he walked out of the office. I began to gather up my briefcase and jacket and headed into the parking lot towards my car.

I was in my office early the next morning, a chocolate covered donut in one hand and a piping hot cup of black coffee in the other.

"Hello, this is Officer Archer from the Third District Prostitution and Tactical Unit. How are you this morning?" I said into the phone, trying to swallow a mouthful of coffee at the same time. It was about eight, and I was trying desperately to wake myself up.

"I'm fine. What can I do for you?" The male voice on the phone answered back. Whoever he was he sounded much more awake than me.

"I was wondering what your schedule was like for this Friday night?" I asked. "We can sure use your help."

"Got a hot date?"

"I wish, unfortunately, its work related," I answered with a laugh.

"Not a problem, depending, of course, on what exactly you need."

"We're investigating a prostitution complaint. Well, actually, it's a prostitution and robbery case, something we dug up out of the *Washington City Paper*. We wanted to use myself as an undercover john, posing as a date. The target area is inside of an apartment building. What we need from you guys is some surveillance equipment and a couple of back up men. If everything goes as planned, once I'm inside of the place, the prostitute and an accomplice will try to rob me," I said, basically filling him in on what I knew, which wasn't very much.

"Where's this place located?" The E.S.U. guy asked.

"Well, that's a slight problem. I'm assuming it's an address here in the Third District since we received the original complaint. Unfortunately, when I called the number, the person who answered agreed to set up a date for Friday night, but she won't tell me where to go until I call her back right before," I answered, hoping this wouldn't be too much of a problem.

"OK, what time is this date set for?"

"Nine PM sharp."

"What we can do is give you a wire that you'll wear on your body. We can also give you a couple of guys who will monitor you from a van. I'm assuming you'll have people on your end to assist?" He replied.

"Oh yeah, definitely, at least four guys, probably more," I voiced back. "And they're all very good."

"OK, we're on. Call us on Friday when you get set up, and we'll meet you in your office," he answered. "Oh, and don't forget to get in your request paperwork by Friday. We need it in order to authorize the manpower and the equipment."

"Outstanding!" I yelled back quickly as he hung up. I placed the receiver down onto the phone and sat back in my chair. Things were moving along better than I had expected. I picked up the *City Paper* and slowly browsed through the adult personal ads while waiting for Sanchez to arrive. I couldn't believe what some of them were advertising. I wondered if Sanchez and I were opening up some sort of Pandora's Box by targeting the *City Paper*. There were so many advertisements, I wouldn't even know where to begin.

"Hey, what's up?" Sanchez shouted as he strolled into the office.

"Nada," I answered back, placing the *City Paper* down onto my desk. "I just got off the phone with E.S.U. We have a wire and a couple of their detectives reserved for Friday night. We just need to do the paperwork and make sure we get it in on time."

"Good. Did you have any problems?" Sanchez asked.

"Nah, not really. They're a little leery about not knowing the exact address, just like us, but there's nothing we can really do about that."

"So, what's the game plan?"

"Well, it should be pretty simple. We'll make the call on Friday night. I'll be wearing a wire when I make the entry. The E.S.U. people will be monitoring from inside a surveillance van on the street. You guys will be in cars or on foot monitoring on our regular radios. We'll use a code word so when I make the case and, hopefully, get robbed, everyone will know. They'll relay the information to you and the backup teams, and you'll advise when to come in and make the arrest. Simple, huh?" I must admit, it almost sounded too easy to be true.

"It sounds too easy to be true," Sanchez answered, reading my mind. "Something will get fucked up."

"Yeah, we both know it'll never go as planned. Nothing ever does. We'll just keep on our toes and deal with things as they come," I replied, knowing in my heart that Sanchez and the other officers I worked with had come through in the crunch time and time again. Deep down inside, I trusted them with anything, even my own life.

The weather report on Friday called for rain, but as I wheeled my car into the station's parking lot there wasn't a cloud in the pale blue sky. It would be dark soon and the late evening sun had long since disappeared behind the city's hazy skyline. My watch showed seven p.m. I was running late. E.S.U. would be waiting for my call. I slammed the car door and jogged to the back door of the station house, cursing under my breath as I struggled with the security lock. The damn thing seemed to never work unless you were running late. Once inside, I was met by Ayala, who was on his way upstairs.

"Relax dude. I already talked with E.S.U. They're on the way here. I just need to get some forms signed off on and we'll be ready to go," he said, obviously noticing the apprehension on my face.

"Thanks, Ayala," I answered. "I'm glad somebody's on top of things." I walked into the office. Terry and Gonzalez were sitting on a couch watching the news on TV. Baker was talking to his wife on the telephone. With the exception of Ayala, who had been with the department for nine years, the rest of us had less than five years on. We were, so to say, still very much rookies.

"Hey fellas, what's up?" I announced as I took off my gun and threw it into my drawer. I had already decided not to take it with me. I didn't want to run the risk of being patted down and having my cover blown. Even though I would like to have it in an emergency, I figured this was like most other prostitution assignments, a low risk operation, and I probably wouldn't need it.

"What's going on?" yelled my co-workers as they continued with their activities. I sat down and began rehearsing my lines. I was going to pose as a college student from Maryland who liked answering *City Paper* personal ads. I was also going to tell Tara that I regularly picked up street prostitutes. I didn't want her to think I was naive, and this would imply to her my intentions of wanting sex when answering her ad. I wanted it to be loud and clear that I was there for the sex, and nothing else. This would make getting the agreement for money and making our case much easier. I would use my real name, as I often did, which would cover me in case she asked for identification, which most prostitutes did. Once I was comfortable with my story, I sat back and waited for E.S.U. to arrive.

"OK, this is your wire device," stated the detective as he handed over a small recorder that looked exactly like a pager. Both E.S.U detectives were older guys whom I had never met. I didn't recognize either one of them, and I figured they had been with this unit for a long time, which comforted me deeply. I took the pager and turned it over in my hand. I couldn't believe this was a recording device.

"Are you sure this thing is going to work?" I asked, still turning the pager in my hands.

"All you have to do is place it on your belt like you would any regular pager. If you hit this button here, the pager will start to record and we'll be able to monitor it from our van. We'll be right outside in the street. Once you give us a pre-arranged code word, we'll come in. But we won't come in until you give us the word. Do you understand?" he said.

"Yeah sure, the code word I'll use is Batman. That's a word I'm sure I'll not forget. When I use the word Batman in a sentence, then that means I need help in a bad way," I answered. Batman was a nickname I had picked up the year before, compliments of my colleagues. I had made the mistake of sharing with my partners a story about a bat, which had somehow gotten into my house and terrorized me one night. Since then, the name and jokes had stuck. More importantly, I knew that in a stressful situation, this would be a word that I would remember.

"OK, that's fine," one of the E.S.U. detectives announced staring at his watch. "I think we're all on the same page. Gentleman, if you're ready, we should go ahead and make the call." It was one minute until nine. I popped the induction cord and tape recorder next to the phone receiver in order to record the conversation, and started dialing the number.

The phone seemed to ring forever. I was just about to hang up when the line was finally answered.

"Hello." The voice was female, the same one from the day before.

"Hello. This is Christopher. I had an appointment for tonight at nine o' clock," I said, my voice again shaking with excitement.

"Yes. Is it nine already?" Tara answered.

"Uh, by my watch it is. When can I come over?"

"Do you know where 17th and R St. N.W. is?" Tara asked.

"Yes, I do."

"There is a payphone there. Go to that phone and call me back." Then she hung up.

"Shit, she hung up," I cursed as I slammed the phone down.

"What's wrong? Didn't she keep the date?" Gonzalez asked from across the room.

"Yes, she did. The good news is she must live nearby because she told me to call her from a pay phone just a few blocks away, on 17th and R. The bad news is she still didn't give me her address. So we're still somewhat blind," I said. This was getting stranger by the minute.

"That's not a problem. We'll follow you in the van. If there is a problem, we'll be right there to assist," voiced in one of the E.S.U. detectives.

"The rest of us will be in unmarked cars. So following you definitely will not be a problem. She's probably going to have someone near that phone checking you out. We can keep an eye on you and they'll never know," said Gonzalez confidently. "We'll need a sledgehammer in case we have to break in a door, and everybody needs a radio on the surveillance channel!" With Gonzalez's last instructions in mind, we quickly left the office and I began the short four-block walk to the corner of 17th and R Street.

As I turned onto 17th and began walking south, I glimpsed over my shoulder to check for my backup. A nervous chill shot up my back as I realized that I could see no one. I prayed this was simply because they were far behind me, making sure they couldn't be spotted. Soon I was crossing over S Street.

Up ahead of me was a huge crowd of people. 17th Street was always pretty crowded, especially on this particular corridor, so I felt safe, yet I couldn't help but feel helpless in knowing that I was being watched and not knowing by whom. Every face I saw became a potential enemy, and every step I took was deliberate and cautious. I felt like I was stepping through a field of land mines. Finally, I reached the phone. There was someone on it.

"Excuse me sir. I really need to use that phone. It's very important," I proclaimed in as polite a tone as my nervous voice could muster.

"Kiss my ass fool! I was here first!" The man on the phone answered. He was taller than me, which considering my height is 6-4 is pretty damn tall. He weighed at least two hundred forty pounds and judging by his exposed biceps, most of it seemed to be muscle. He had on blue jeans, a white t-shirt and a black leather jacket. He was definitely not someone I wanted to mess around with. He turned towards me, probably expecting more of a confrontation. He was right.

"Sir, I'm not trying to be rude, but I really need to be on that phone," I said again. I glanced at my watch and saw it was now a quarter past nine. "It's an emergency."

"I guess you didn't hear me asshole. I said screw you!" He answered. I could hear him talking on the phone, telling his friend not to worry, that it was just some idiot trying to get on the phone. This infuriated me. Not willing to get into more of a shouting match, I casually reached over, grabbed the receiver out of his hand and hung up the phone. I had no time for this.

"You asshole, what the hell did you do that for?" he shouted. I pulled my badge out of my pants pocket and clipped it on my middle finger, extending it out for him to see.

"For the last time, I have an emergency and I must use that phone. What part of that sentence didn't you understand?" For a moment, I thought he was going to take a swing at me and I was going to have to fight. Instead, he turned and walked away, mumbling a few obscenities as he disappeared into a crowd of pedestrians. Maybe he was with Tara, I thought, trying to test me. I hoped not. If I had to confront him in a hostile situation, someone was going to get hurt, and that someone was most likely going to be me. Besides, now he knew I was a cop, and I realized my anxiousness might have just blown the whole operation.

"I'm on the phone now," I said as I picked up the phone and dropped a quarter into the slot. I didn't have a radio with me, so I had to assume my backup could hear me through the pager on my belt. "Some guy was using it, so I had to get rid of him. He's walking east on R Street wearing a black leather jacket and blue jeans. He's a bit taller than me and a lot heavier," I dialed Tara's number and waited.

"My, that was awfully quick," answered Tara.

"I was only a few blocks away when I called. I was at a friend's house. Lucky me, huh?" I answered, realizing I had made another possibly grave mistake. If Tara knew that the police station was only a few blocks away, then she would probably call the date off immediately, and we'd be shit out of luck. Fortunately, luck was something I had plenty of tonight.

"Well, Christopher, this is going to be your lucky night. I'm at 1712 16th Street, Apartment 103. As a matter of fact, I'm looking at you right now from my window. When you get to the front door, you'll notice a security lock. Dial 13 and I'll buzz you up. See you soon." Tara then hung up. I quickly slammed the phone down and looked towards the 16th Street skyline. I could see the rear of Tara's apartment complex. I gazed across line after line of windows, hoping to see something. But the windows were empty.

"I've got an address. 1712 16th Street, Apartment 103. We've got our first problem, though. There's a security lock on the front door," I said as I checked to see if the pager was on. It was. Just a little longer, I thought, and this would finally be over.

As I approached the front of 1712 16th Street, I noticed it had not one, but two separate security doors, both made of thick tempered glass. This would definitely be a problem. I looked around trying to think of a way to keep the doors open once Tara had buzzed me in. On a small patch of grass just to the left of the front walkway was a small tree branch. I picked it up and carried it with me to the front door. Once at the front door, I picked up the telephone receiver and dialed 13. After several rings, the door buzzed and I pushed it open. Tara didn't even bother to pick up the phone. As I approached the second door, I quickly broke off half of the branch and wedged it in the first doorway. It worked. The second glass doorway buzzed and I opened it, wedging the other half of the tree branch in its hinges to keep it slightly open. I walked up a small stairway and onto the first floor. Apartment 103 was the first door on my right. I swallowed and took a deep breath before knocking on the door.

"You must be Christopher," said the woman who answered the door. The contrast between the light in the hall and the darkness coming from within Tara's apartment made it difficult to see her clearly. She must have been aware of this, because she hid most of her body behind the front door. From what I could see, she seemed a few inches shorter than me, with long reddish brown hair. She was wearing nothing but a light blue bra, blue panties, a garter belt and black fishnet stockings. I stepped into the apartment, trying to get a closer look. Tara quickly shut the door behind me. All of the lights were out and the window curtains pulled tightly shut. I had trouble seeing anything in the vast darkness. The only light came from a small glimmer down a long hallway to my right. I looked back at Tara who was now just a shadowy figure in the darkness. I suddenly became very frightened. I wondered what it was that ever possessed me to do this in the first place. Had I finally embarked on something a little above my ability and sanity?

"It's OK Christopher. Just follow the light to the bedroom. I'll be right behind you," she said from behind me.

"Would that be the light at the end of the tunnel?" I asked softly. I made my way slowly, bumping into the walls as while trying to make out my surroundings. Tara's hand was on my ass, squeezing and pushing me along. I guess she was in a rush.

About halfway down the hall, I caught a quick glimpse of a dark object, which crossed directly in front of me and then passed into a large dark room to the left. It seemed to be the shadow of another person, but I couldn't be sure. I assumed this was the living room. For a second, I thought I heard the faint patter of footsteps. We were definitely not alone. Damn, if only I could see.

"Walk over to the bed and take off your clothes. I'll put in a video for you to watch while I change into something more comfortable," Tara said as we entered into her very poorly lit bedroom. Jesus, what could she possibly mean by more comfortable? She was practically naked as it was.

To my far right was a dresser with a small color television sitting on top. At the far left of the room was an old wooden bed covered with white sheets. Stacked neatly at the foot of the bed were several piles of videotapes.

"What do you like? Guys doing girls? Huh? Maybe you like the kinky shit, like girls doing girls. How about some female dominance videos. Yeah, I bet you like that. I've got just the video for you." Tara leaned over and picked up a videotape from the floor and placed it into the tape player. Suddenly, the room was filled with sounds of moaning woman, having sex. I kept my eyes on Tara, never flinching. I could barely make out her face in the darkness. Only every few seconds, as her profile crossed the path of light coming from the television could I see her clearly. She was large in stature, and very, very hairy. I was no longer just terrified. I was on the verge of a major heart attack.

"So what happens now?" I asked uncomfortably.

"Take off your clothes and we'll start with a massage," Tara answered. It was hard to hear her over the moaning sounds coming from the videotape.

"I'd just as soon skip the massage if you don't mind," I said as I began taking off my shirt.

"OK, what do you want to do then Christopher?" She asked, staring me directly in the eyes. I hated the way she said my name like we knew each other, as if we were old friends. She slowly began walking towards me.

"What do I get for my money?" I asked as I took a hundred dollars out of my pants pocket. She stopped a few feet away.

"For a hundred dollars? Do you like the oral stuff?"

"Oh yeah," I answered. "I love it." Tara moved quickly towards me and for a moment, I thought this would be it. She reached over and snatched the hundred dollars out of my hand and placed it into the top dresser drawer.

"Take off your pants," Tara said, obviously noticing that I was taking my time. "It's time to get it on." I placed my shirt on the edge of the bed.

"I need to use the bathroom, OK I need to piss before we start," I blurted out, trying to think of any way to stall for a few moments. I was beginning to undue the belt on my pants.

"The bathroom is just down the hall on the right. Follow me." Tara took my hand and led me down a dark hallway to the bathroom. The room had no door, just a sheet hanging from the ceiling.

"I'll only be a minute, OK?" I said as I entered and pulled the sheet shut behind me. I looked in the mirror and saw thousands of sweat beads running across my face. Damn, get a hold of yourself. You can do this, I repeated in my head over and over. Everything was going just as planned. I ran some water from the sink, gently splashing my face.

"Hey, Tara?" I called from behind the curtain. "Do you have any Batman videos we can watch?"

"What did you say?" Tara yelled back. She had gone back into the bedroom.

"I wanted to know if you had any Batman videos we can watch. They really turn me on," I yelled again. I glanced at my watch. Any minute now, my backup would come storming through the front door.

"You're kidding, right?" Tara called back.

"No, not at all. I have this thing for Batman. Ever since I was a little kid," I shouted. I turned on the sink, comforted by the flowing water, which was breaking the monotonous silence. One minute passed. Two minutes. Three minutes. No backup, no nothing. I glanced at my pager. It was still on. Suddenly, I heard heavy footsteps coming my way. I quickly unzipped my pants and pretended like I was urinating, flushing the toilet to add to the effect. Tara was getting closer.

"What the hell is taking you so long, pretty boy?" Tara yelled as she poked her head into the bathroom. For the first time, I saw Tara's face clearly. I was, to say the least, mortified. Her large cheekbones, sunken eyes and protruding forehead, now visible in the lighted bathroom, betrayed the makeup attempting to cover them. Mistress Tara was actually Mr. Someone.

"I'm sorry. I'm just really nervous. I haven't done this type of thing in a long time," I said, my whole body shaking as I noticed Tara's slight mustache and whiskers. "I could really use some Batman videos, or Batman comics to help loosen me up."

"What the hell is up with this Batman shit?" Tara yelled, her once soft feminine voice becoming deeper and deeper. "You're fucking weird."

"It's nothing, really. I'm just nervous," I answered, zipping up my pants.

"Just hurry up. I haven't got all fucking night."

Tara disappeared, leaving me alone in the bathroom. I looked desperately around for a weapon. Tara would be back soon, and I was sure this was going to get ugly. There was a plunger sitting next to the toilet. No, that wasn't good enough. I pulled open the medicine cabinet. Nothing. No weapons. I eased back towards the rear of the room, into the bathtub. I wanted to put as much space between the door and myself as possible. If I was lucky, maybe I could make a break for it and reach the front door. Then I remembered the shadow from the living room, and there was probably someone else in the apartment. Running blindly through the darkness was the worst thing I could do. My only hope was to stand my ground in the bathroom and stall for time.

Suddenly, I heard the heavy pounding of Tara's footsteps heading back towards the bathroom. My heart was beating rapidly and my palms sweating profusely. I braced myself against the shower wall and prepared to strike. The loud footsteps came to an abrupt stop directly in front of the curtain door. I waited silently, holding my breath. The deep sounds of my beating heart echoed off the tiled walls. Several seconds passed. My muscles tensed as I waited to fight. Thoughts of my family flashed through my head. I heard my mother's voice telling me to be careful. I always told her I had everything under control. Was I ever wrong. I was not in control. Not now. I had lost my advantage, my edge. And now I was stuck in this cold, cramped bathroom waiting to either live or die. I was not afraid to die. I just didn't want it to happen here, like this. I didn't want to see my name in the morning papers, below the headline reading "Police Officer Killed by Maniac Transvestite."

All was still deathly quiet. I could barely make out the sounds of Tara's labored breathing from behind the curtain. She was waiting and I assumed she was thinking of what to do next. Then I heard the first knock. It was coming from the front door.

"Police, open the door now!" shouted the loud, steady voice from one of my back up units. "Open the door now or we're coming in forcefully!" I took several deep breaths. Thank you, God. I wasn't out of the water yet, but things were certainly starting to look a lot better. I heard some shuffling around from within the apartment. Tara must be going to open the door. I could handle her for a few seconds, especially knowing that's all it would take for my backup to get in the front door. Quietly, I tiptoed to the curtain and reached forward to pull it open.

"Goddamn!" I yelled as the curtain moved and I found myself face to face with Mistress Tara. She had been waiting outside the bathroom curtain the whole time. I scrambled backwards, falling against the sink, knocking a can of shaving cream and several bottles to the floor. Tara was coming at me, her large hands reaching for my neck. The realization of death again blasted into my brain like a sledgehammer. My body was rubber as I pushed myself back and struggled with what to do. In the distance, I heard officers knocking on the front door and still shouting commands for someone to open it. Why didn't they just bust in?

"You're a damn cop! I knew it!" Tara yelled in the deepest, most masculine voice I had ever heard. "You fucking piece of shit! I'm going to kill you!" I knew all too well Tara's true sex now as I focused in on his bulging arms.

"I swear to God I'm not a cop. I'm just a student from Maryland!" I yelled, placing my hands in front of my face. "I have no idea what the hell's going on, but I swear to god, if you take one step closer, I'm going to break every fucking bone in your body. I don't know who, or what the fuck you are. But I'm not going out like this. Not here, not now. And if I do, I'm taking your ass with me!"

Tara hesitated for a moment, stopping just a few feet from where I was now hunched in position to fight. For what seemed like an eternity, Tara and I stood in the bathroom at a standoff—staring each other in the eyes, trying to decide who was going to make the first move. I think both of us were scared shitless. For the first time in my life, I think I was actually intimidating someone.

Suddenly, a loud crashing noise came from beyond the main hallway, and the apartment was filled with the sounds of screams and shouts. My backup had finally busted in the door. Tara turned quickly and bolted out into the hallway. I reached out to grab him, missing by just a few inches. I ran behind, slamming into several walls while fighting off the effects of my earlier panic. Following Tara down the hallway, I saw another flash of movement. I glanced over into the dark living room just in time to see a darkly clad body race over several pieces of furniture heading towards the kitchen.

"We got one running!" Someone shouted from near the front door.

"Where?" I heard and saw bodies racing through the foyer towards the kitchen. I stumbled into the living room, fumbling for my gun that wasn't there. Goddamn. Everything was happening so fast. I couldn't really focus on anything, just movements all around me. I focused in on the blurry vision of a man ahead of me, a very short man, as he raced into the kitchen and launched himself onto a windowsill. The kitchen light was on, and as I came into the entrance, another officer banged into my side and several more pressed into my back. In a split second, the man in the kitchen was gone, launching himself out the window and into the dark night sky.

"What the fuck?" I yelled, racing towards the window.

Gonzalez was the first to reach the open window. I heard a loud crashing noise as we I pushed ourselves forward.

"He's gone. That damn fool is gone," Gonzalez cursed, shaking his head in amazement. "I can't believe it!"

"What happened? Where did he go?" I responded, pushing him aside and looking out the window.

"Where do you think? He jumped the two stories and landed on the roof of that car." He answered, still shaking his head. He was pointing to a dark colored sedan parked on the street. "And then he was gone. Like some kind of ghost."

I looked down and saw the car he was talking about. We were two stories above the street and directly below were a small sidewalk, and a few feet beyond that was a long line of parked cars. I looked down the street to the left into the blackness of the night. I couldn't see anything. I looked to the right, towards 16th Street and a steady flow of traffic, and again saw nothing. He wasn't the first person to escape us, but it was by far one of the most dramatic. I backed away from the window certain any pursuit would be useless. There was no way I was going out that window.

"What's going on?" Baker asked as I brushed past him. He was standing with several other officers who had Tara pinned up against the living room wall.

"The other one got away. He did a swan dive from the kitchen window and vanished." I answered, staring at Tara. He looked at me for a second smiling, and then returned his gaze to the white wall in front of him.

"You're fucking kidding me, right?" Baker said.

"Do you really think I'd joke about that?" I replied, still shaking my head in disbelief. "I can't believe this shit."

"What happened in here?" Carpenter asked, a small grin escaping from the corners of his mouth. He was standing beside Tara.

"Exactly what we expected," I said. "A very well controlled state of fucking confusion. He's good to go for solicitation. The money's in the top drawer in a dresser in the bedroom." I was still trying to control the adrenaline that was pouring through my body. "This one was close, my friend. Too close. You get the next one."

"No, that's OK I'll stay with the females," Baker said, laughing. I laughed as well. I knew I would probably never hear the end of this, especially from the officers who were present. That was fine. I was still alive, which right now was all I really cared about. I was thankful. I walked into the bedroom and sat on the corner of the bed. I wondered how many "customers" had been on this very mattress, watching the same video I was now looking at. On the television screen, one woman was tied to a bed, and another woman was whipping her with a leather whip. What a job, I thought, trying to make sense out of the insane.

"Hey, Chris," shouted Ayala, who was with several other officers in the living room.

"What is it Ayala?" I yelled back, shouting above the screams coming from the video. The blond girl on the bed was currently in the throes of a major orgasm. I had to see this.

"Come out here in the living room and take a look at this."

"I'll be right there." After witnessing the orgasm, I reached down and turned off the VCR. Finally, the room was silent. I pulled out the tape and tossed it on the bed. For a moment, I thought maybe I might mash it into oblivion. I wiped the sweat from my forehead and made my way towards the living room.

"Over there, on the table," Ayala said, pointing to a wooden coffee table in the middle of the room, next to a plush brown colored sofa. Sitting on the table was a long butcher knife. Next to the knife was a small pile of marijuana. "I think I saw our window guy toss this when we first busted down the door."

Nothing really seemed to make any sense, and as much as I could speculate and theorize, the fact remained we had discovered nothing more than a sick transvestite and an unknown person who had a propensity for jumping out of windows. I wondered what really went on in this apartment during the night. From a personal standpoint, I don't think I really wanted to know. Our job was done.

I walked towards the front door, stepping aside as Carpenter and another officer escorted Tara through the door. Tara took one final look at me, mumbling something I couldn't understand under his breath.

"Yea, well fuck you too," I said, staring into his cold eyes.

CHAPTER SEVENTEEN

I guess I met Derrick through sheer coincidence. I know, at the time, I wasn't really looking for him, or anyone like him. If you were to meet him on the street, you'd have never thought he was anything more than just an average old man, probably someone's grandfather. But for me, he was much, much more.

It was a pretty routine and normal Saturday afternoon. Save for the blistering July heat, which in Washington has a tendency to scorch through each and every layer of your skin, things were pretty slow and tolerable. For the most part, Ayala and I had spent much of the afternoon sitting in our office being lazy and catching up on the past week's paperwork. Most of the rest of the unit was off, enjoying a good summer day. However, it only took a few hours for boredom to set in, and Ayala and I decided to take a quick ride around to check out what was going on in the neighborhood. We must have been on the street only ten minutes when I spotted a thin white girl wearing a red thigh-high mini-skirt and a white halter-top standing on the corner of Thirteenth and Q Streets, waving at the passing cars.

"I know that girl," Ayala said instantly. "That's this girl, Stacey. Sanchez cased her a few weeks ago."

"You know, you never cease to amaze me with that damned photographic memory of yours. You know everyone." I answered back. "I don't think I've ever seen her. Have I ever cased her before?" I could barely remember what I had for breakfast in the morning, let alone the hundreds of prostitutes I had picked up and arrested in my brief career. Ayala, however, could remember almost every girl who ever stepped onto the street. It was a pretty amazing gift.

"No, I don't think so. She's pretty new," Ayala answered smiling. He knew how poor my memory was.

"Good. Then I guess that means I can snatch her up now," I answered enthusiastically. I pulled my tiny white Honda CRX around the corner onto R Street safely out of her view.

"I don't know. She's pretty tough," Ayala answered, still smiling. "It took Sanchez damn near thirty minutes to case her last time, and all he got was an indecent sexual proposal."

"Hey, you seem to have forgotten who you are talking to. Am I or am I not the undisputed king of the sleazy, low down undercover prostitute super pimp pick up artists?" I said, trying to sound serious. My undercover curse, if you'd call it that, was looking too much like a suburban white kid, which ruined just about any narcotics work I aspired to do, but which worked wonders on the gullible prostitution crowd. Everyone loves a rich kid from the 'burbs, even if it's just for an hour.

"Yeah, right pretty boy," Ayala answered, this time laughing hysterically.

"OK, OK, so I can't seem to manage a single date in my off-duty time. But when I'm here, in the groove, nothing can stop me. Watch and take notes!" I said, reaching into the back seat of my car and retrieving the Amoco gas station shirt that was my trademark.

"Yeah, show me how it's done," Ayala said. "And make it quick. I don't really feel like staying late today." I caught the last part of his sentence as I stepped out of the car. The afternoon sun zapped my body as I pulled off my white t-shirt and tossed it on the driver's seat. I quickly pulled on the blue Amoco shirt, letting it hang down the front of my cut off blue jean shorts.

"Why don't you take all afternoon?" Ayala yelled from the passenger seat.

"Why don't you kiss my ass?" I shouted back. "Come on, get your lazy ass out of the car and follow me on foot."

"In this heat, are you crazy? I'll follow in the car."

"Come on, dude. I'll be quick. I'm sure she won't want to go too far, and besides, she'll never notice you if you just sort of hang out on the corner. She'll definitely notice you sitting in the car," I said as I started walking towards Thirteenth Street. Despite the wealth of experience we both had in doing this type of undercover work, I still felt a swarm of butterflies fluttering around in the pit of my stomach. "Give me about five minutes to find her and catch up."

"Got it," Ayala said, giving me double thumbs up. "And if you can't case her, you owe me dinner."

"You can put it on my tab," I said under my breath, chuckling lightly. I already owed him several years' worth of dinners. In order to pay off, I'd probably have to move in and be his personal chef.

I slowly rounded the corner of Thirteenth and Q and gazed down R Street. She was still there standing on the same corner as before. I was thankful it was still early and traffic was light. Had it been nighttime, she wouldn't have lasted two minutes before being picked up. I eased my way towards her, careful not to make eye contact too early. At first, as I approached her from behind, she didn't seem to notice me. Then, as I slipped past her, pausing for a second to catch her eyes, she turned towards me and smiled.

"Hey, pretty girl," I said, staring deep into her brown eyes.

"Hey," she answered in a low, barely audible voice. She was eyeing my body from head to toe. "Are you looking for something?"

"Yeah, I'm always looking for something." I answered casually. My forehead was dripping with sweat. "You know where I might find a date?"

"What kind of date?" She asked, this time her voice a little louder. She turned her head away from me and towards Q Street. She was looking for any sign of police presence. I tried to keep my voice steady.

"I want to do you," I said, my hands trembling in my pockets. No matter how many hundreds of times I had done this, I still couldn't help but feel both ridiculous and nervous at the same time. I was trying to be something I was not. Maybe it just wasn't my style.

"You mean you want to fuck me, right?" She answered giggling, reaching down with her right hand and pulling her mini-skirt up to her waist, revealing a neatly trimmed triangle of light pubic hair. "Do you like what you see?" My eyes were fixed on her crotch. I couldn't seem to keep from staring, which I'm sure looked quite silly. She quickly pulled back down her skirt.

"Yes, very much," I answered nervously. She had caught me off guard with her sudden boldness. "What is your name?"

"Stacey." Damn Ayala and his photographic memory. He was always right. "What's yours?"

"Mike," I said, glancing at the nametag on the front of my shirt.

"What's with the Amoco shirt, Mike?" Stacey asked, a wry smile escaping from the corner of her bright red lips. She slowly walked up to me, pressing the front of her torso against my groin. Her hands were at my waist, feeling for the gun I had left back at the station. "Are you 5-0?"

"Fuck no, I ain't no cop," I shouted. "I drive a tow crane over in Georgetown." I winced in pain as she grasped hold of my penis through the outside of my pants in a vice like grip. She squeezed it several times and then lightly brushed me back.

"I guess you're all right," she said as she started walking away. I shot a quick glance to the corner of Q Street and saw Ayala sitting on the stairway to a house. He had a huge smile covering his face. I guess he was enjoying the show. Give him a brown paper bag and he would have fit in perfectly with all the other drunks strung about the block. Slowly, I raised my right hand towards my head, in preparation of giving our pre-arranged signal to make an arrest. If I scratched my head, that signaled Ayala that a crime had been committed and we could move in to make the arrest. In this case, the violation was indecent exposure. Not quite the sexual solicitation charge we had set out for, but on this blistering hot summer afternoon, it would have to do.

"I got a place just down the street we can go to. It'll cost you fifty dollars for the fuck and another ten for the room," Stacey said over her shoulder as she started walking down R Street. "You're going to really like this!" She added as she reached around and squeezed her ass with her right hand.

I immediately dropped both my hands to my side. Now, the stakes had just gotten a little bit higher. One of our primary goals in prostitution enforcement was locating the many houses, or trick pads, that flourished in the city and served as low scale brothels. I hoped Ayala had not seen my attempted signal.

"I've got the money, no problem," I said, following behind. I reached into my pocket just to make sure. Things would get real bad if I didn't have the money. Five minutes later, we were approaching the front of the house.

"We're here," Stacey said with a giggle. She walked up to the front door and banged loudly. "Derrick! Derrick! Open the door. It's Stacey!"

"Are you sure this place is safe?" I asked. My eyes scanned across the front part of the house. The door seemed pretty solid, but it was wood, and I was fairly confident Ayala and the others would have little problem knocking it in if things turned bad. The house was three stories and the red bricks had long ago turned a dark orange brown and were old and rotted. On the third level, where I was certain we would eventually end up, were three large windows. I had been in quite a few of these, and always the bedrooms were upstairs. On the ground level where we stood were several large, full bushes, lining the front of the house rather neatly. I noted to myself that this could prove to be quite beneficial if I needed to make an emergency escape from one of the third floor windows and needed something to break my fall.

"Hi, Stacey," came the voice of an old black man who opened the front door. "Come on in."

"Hi Derrick, this is Mike," Stacey answered, quietly slipping into the darkness behind the door. "He's a friend of mine."

"Come on in, Mike," Derrick said as he motioned for me to enter. "Any friend of Stacey's is a friend of mine." I swallowed hard, took a couple of deep breaths and walked into the dark hallway. From behind, I heard the loud thud of the front door slamming shut and then being locked. From this point, I had exactly ten minutes to get what I needed. A second too long and my backup would come storming through the front door. Fortunately, that had only happened once before, but that's another story.

"Mike, this is Derrick. He lives here," Stacey said as we reached the top of a flight of stairs and entered into a living room area.

"What's up, Derrick?" I said, extending my hand forward. He took it into his hand and shook lightly. His hand felt weak, cold and clammy, as if it would break if even the slightest amount of pressure were applied. Now that we were in the light, I noticed just how old he really was. His wrinkled face and feeble body told me he was well past sixty. He moved slowly and with a slight limp. His eyes squinted, giving me the impression that his eyesight was very poor. He had on a pair of old, tattered blue work pants and an oversized white t-shirt. His feet were bare and creaked as he made his way across the old wooden floor.

"Do you have the ten dollars?" Stacey asked, reaching her hand out.

"Yes, here." I reached into my pocket and pulled out my money.

"I'll take the fifty now, too," she said, her eyes staring at my hands greedily.

"OK," I answered. I counted out sixty dollars and handed it to her. Stacey took the money, pulled out a ten and handed it to Derrick. Derrick took the money, continued across the living room towards an old easy chair which he just sort of fell into.

"This heat is not good for an old man," he said in a coarse, scratchy voice.

"This heat basically sucks for everyone," I said from across the room. "I'm sweating my ass off."

Stacey had since walked past me and down the hall. At the end of the hall was an open door leading to what I suspected was a bedroom, and I saw an old, dirty, stained mattress sitting near the door. She pulled her white halter-top off, exposing very large, perky breasts. Not bad for a hooker, I thought.

"I told you you're going to like this!" she shouted down the hall. She turned towards me and began slowly rubbing her nipples with her hands, moving her crotch in a circular, grinding motion. She seemed to really like her line of work. "Why don't you go ahead and take off your clothes and we can get started." I glanced at my watch. Three minutes had already passed. I had to move quickly.

"OK, but I have to use the bathroom first," I yelled back. "OK?" I had to stall for a moment to figure out my way to escape. Once Derrick had taken the ten dollars, I had gotten enough evidence to retrieve a search and arrest warrant for operating a Bawdy House, a misdemeanor similar to a House of Prostitution. Now, all I had to do was figure a way out that would not arouse any suspicion. This was often a task that was easier said than done. These were criminals, and to them, blowing your nose

aroused suspicion.

"The bathroom is the first door on the right down the hallway," Stacey said, turning away from me. She was slowly pulling her mini-skirt down from her waist in a mocking strip tease. "I hope you don't have no problems getting it up!"

I definitely had to move fast. I headed into the bathroom and pulled the door shut behind me. The bathroom was pretty nondescript, albeit just as filthy and drab as the living room. Moving quickly, I yanked a handful of toilet paper from a roll next to the sink and pulled a pencil out of my back pocket. Using the sink counter as a surface, I quickly and meticulously drew a rough sketch of the inside of the house, from the front door all the way to the far bedroom where Stacey now was. I wanted to do this while my memory was still fresh. This information would be important when we returned to execute the search warrant. When I was finished, I stuffed my pencil back into my back pocket and shoved the sketch in my front pocket. I was just getting ready to flush the toilet when I heard Stacey walking past the door and into the living room. She started talking with Derrick in a low voice. I cracked the door open ever so slightly and strained to hear what was being said.

"I need my shit today, Derrick," Stacey said sounding irritated. "You promised."

"I'll have it for you later tonight, by eight o'clock," he answered. "My regular man won't be around till then."

"OK Hold it here for me." Stacey said, sounding irritated. "I'm tricking this other dude who'll pay top dollar for that good shit. I'll be back for it later after I turn a few more tricks."

"OK Like I said, it'll be here for you after eight." Derrick answered casually. "I'm sorry I couldn't get it for you earlier."

"You my man, Jess. Just keep hooking me up baby."

I checked my watch. Almost seven minutes had passed by and I was quickly running out of time. If I didn't make my move soon, Ayala would be storming through the front door. I reached over and flushed the toilet. Then I pushed open the bathroom door and headed back into the hallway.

"Stacey, you're not going to believe this," I said as I bumped into her in the hallway. She was now completely naked, and was reaching for the front of my belt.

"What's that baby? You shoot your load already?" She answered, placing her hands on her hips. My eyes kept wandering down to her breasts. I felt like a high school kid watching his first R-rated sex movie. Stacey, who was obviously noticing my gawking, just smiled.

"I just got paged for a job, so I gotta go," I said, bracing myself for an argument. "You can keep the money."

"You're damn right I can keep the money," she answered sternly. "There ain't no money back guarantee on this little piece of pussy."

"Sucks for me, I was really looking forward to seeing what you can do," I said, trying to sound disappointed. I knew I would try to pick her up again some other time.

"Well, Mr. Amoco man. You are kind of cute," she answered.

"Maybe I can arrange a little discount for the next time."

"Hey, check this out. Maybe next time, you can do something else for me," I suggested, hoping I could move the conversation into the area of drugs without sounding too obvious.

"What's that?" Stacey asked.

"I got this strung out chick I mess around with from time to time," I said, formulating my story in my mind on the fly. "She's really into Heroin big time. Man, the things she will do after a few hits of Heroin."

"Damn, I can understand that," Stacey answered. "Check me out another time, and I'll see what I can do." She headed down the hall and into the bedroom, slamming shut the door behind her.

"What's a guy like you doing messing around with Heroin?" Derrick interrupted from his seat across the room. I had almost completely forgotten he was in the room. "I don't see no track marks on you, and you don't seem like no junkie."

"Are you kidding? I don't touch that shit," I answered as I entered into the living room. "But, I know this girl in Maryland, man, is she hot. She's really into it, you know. I try to hook her up since I'm in the city all the time. She's a fucking sex goddess, I can tell you that much."

"Well I know Stacey ain't gonna be able to get you jack shit, especially since she gets all of her stuff from me."

"So then I should talk to you?" I asked hesitantly. I checked my watch. Ten minutes had since passed. I was on the verge of making my first potential big time drug connection, and if Ayala came bursting in the front door now, all would be wasted. I had to let him know I needed more time.

"Did you just hear a crash?" I asked Derrick abruptly as I quickly made my way towards the front windows.

"I didn't hear shit," Derrick answered, still sitting back in his easy chair. His feet were kicked up on a small wooden end table, which he had placed under his feet. "But that don't mean nothing. My hearing ain't been worth a damn for years anyway."

"It's probably nothing," I said. "Just sounded like a little fender bender. I'll check it out." I gently pulled open a stained yellow curtain and glanced across the street. Today, I was a very lucky man. Ayala was positioned directly across from the house, standing on the street corner, his portable radio poised at his mouth ready to call for backup. I was just in time. I waved my hand up to my head to get his attention and quickly held up five fingers, signaling for five more minutes. He nodded his head in acknowledgment and brought the radio away from his mouth. I dropped the curtain and eased over towards the downstairs stairway and prepared to leave.

"See anything good?" Derrick mumbled from his chair. "I don't hear no sirens yet."

"Nah. Probably a hit and run or something," I answered. "There's nothing out there right now."

"Hmmmm."

"Oh, by the way, you're probably not interested in this kind of shit, but I have a lot of friends in the suburbs with a lot of cash. If you can get me some good shit, I can certainly make it worth your while."

"Think so?" Derrick asked sounding vaguely interested. "I can always use the money."

"Definitely," I answered. "But hey, right now I gotta book. How can I get in touch with you?"

"Just come by the house. Knock three times so I know it's you."

"Great. I'll be by next Saturday, if that's OK with you."

"No problem," Derrick answered. I sensed his voice was beginning to trail off, each syllable getting lower and lower. If I didn't know better, which I didn't, I'd swear he was falling asleep. "Oh, and by the way. Stay away from Stacey. She's bad news." I caught the last part of his sentence as I started down the stairs. What had started out as just another routine day had suddenly become something much more intriguing.

The following Saturday couldn't have come fast enough for me. I had made plenty of drug arrests during my career, but never as a buyer, and I had done hundreds of undercover operations for prostitution, but I had always longed to do real undercover drug work. And now I had my first really good opportunity. I had planted my hook, and I was sure Derrick trusted me. I parked my car about three blocks north of R Street at the intersection of Thirteenth and T Street. This was far enough where even if he was outside, Derrick couldn't see me. But, it was another blistering, god awful hot day, so I was sure he was inside, sucking up air conditioning. Sanchez pulled his small, red Pontiac Fiero several cars behind. I gave him a thumbs up signal, un-tucked my Amoco shirt and shoved my portable radio under the driver's seat. I quickly slammed the door shut and headed towards Derrick's house. My eyes scanned the street corners for any sign of Stacey. I was certain if I ran into her, my chances of getting Derrick to sell me some Heroin would be shot. First off, she would want a date, which I had no time for now, and second she would want to act as a middle man for the transaction, which under better circumstances, might have proven beneficial, especially if she or Derrick were that well connected in the local Heroin trade. But prostitutes, especially basic streetwalkers were rarely so highly connected, and usually could be counted on for little more than a bag of two. And I had yet to make out just how much Derrick played the role in the local Heroin scene. Regardless, it was in my best interest to avoid Stacey if at all possible and simplify the matters at hand. I caught a glimpse of Sanchez as he zipped past me in his Fiero, searching for a better vantage point. He continued down a block, then quickly made a U-turn and pulled to the side of the road. From this spot, he could see just about everything. Gonzalez was parked in the alley directly behind Derrick's house, just in case something didn't go as planned. I felt pretty relaxed and was sure everything would go as expected.

"Hey Derrick!" I shouted towards the upper windows as I rapped on the front door three times.

"Who is it?" Derrick shouted from directly behind the wooden door. I jumped back a few steps, startled at his quick response. For a second, I almost felt as if he might have been waiting for me.

"Yo, it's me, Mike," I answered. Derrick pulled open the door and waved me in. "How's it going?"

"OK, I suppose," Derrick answered in a scratchy, hoarse voice. He was wearing the same ragged clothes as last week.

"You sound sick," I asked. "Maybe I should come back later."

"No, No. I'm fine," he answered as he painfully dragged his old body up the stairs. I followed closely behind, checking my surroundings for anything that might look out of the ordinary. Everything was fine. The house was quiet and still, and I was pretty sure we were alone. Derrick eased across the living room and plopped down into his favorite easy chair. I stood on the top stair, gazing down the hallway towards Stacey's bedroom. The door was shut.

"Don't worry, Mike. No one else is here," Derrick said from his chair, obviously noticing my darting eyes. "She's working the street."

"That's fine," I answered, trying not to sound scared. I had very little experience with these types of encounters, no real formal training and was basically winging it. "Do you live alone? I mean, aside from Stacey?

"Usually." He said, staring towards the front windows. "Actually, Stacey doesn't really live here. Sometimes, she or some of the other girls stay a night or two, but never for very long." I stared intently at Derrick's face, etching its harsh, pained image into my memory. He looked much older than when I had first met him. Just my luck, my first chance at nailing a drug dealer and he had to be a senior citizen, and a sickly one at that.

"You must get kind of lonely, being here by yourself and all" I said, wondering how to ease into the conversation of buying Heroin. "Although I guess it must get kind of busy on the weekends with all the hookers and shit."

"Yeah, it does sometimes, but I got some friends to keep me company. Right over there," Derrick said, his long, frail fingers pointing to a large wooden bookcase sitting near the entrance to the kitchen. It was filled with dozens of hardcover books.

"That's quite a collection," I said as I walked towards the bookcase. "You like to read?"

"Sometimes I think that's all that keeps me alive," he answered. I knew the minute I heard these words escape his lips that he was deathly serious. A man after my own heart, I thought to myself. If I had a dollar for every book I had read, I'd be a very rich man.

"Me, too," I answered, gently moving my fingers along the spines of each book. "It seems like the only thing left in this world where we can really, really escape the bullshit of everyday life, and yet still use a little imagination," I said. I scanned the titles across the top shelf. "Movies just don't do that anymore."

"I always liked reading, even when I was a little kid," Derrick sighed. I could tell he was daydreaming a bit.

"Me too," I replied. I was amazed at the selection of books Derrick owned. There were the usual bestsellers, but also classics, including *Crime and Punishment* by Fyodor Dostoevsky. "Dostoevsky? That's some pretty heavy shit Derrick."

"Never read it. But, I've heard it's really good."

"It is."

"Maybe you can read to me sometime?" I froze when I heard his last sentence. Read to him? He had to be joking.

"Are you serious?" I said, my voice stuttering noticeably. "You want me to read to you?"

"Of course," he answered in most serious tone. For the first time since we met, his expression belied that of an old, sickly mind and took on this sudden look of lost youthful exuberance.

"Why would you want me to read to you, Derrick?" I answered, giving him my full attention.

"Because my eyesight ain't so good anymore and I can't really read to myself that much."

This was an unsettling turn of events, and I wasn't sure what to say next. I knew it would be hard for me to refuse, that this might hinge on whether he'd sell me Heroin or not. But at the same time, I knew I couldn't really allocate enough time to be sitting in this house reading books to a Heroin dealer. This seemed to me, at least in my primary assessment to be beyond the scope of my authority. Yet at the same time, I needed to buy as much time and trust with Derrick as I possibly could, especially if he had access to any serious amounts of drugs. I took a moment to ponder my dilemma and decided it was best to take a few days to think it over.

"OK, I'll tell you what. I gotta get going. I got this date with a girl who won't even mention my name on her beautiful breath unless I show up with some Heroin. Hook me up this time, and when I come back next week, I promise I'll come a little early and read to you a bit. But, I can't promise I'll be able to stay for long," I said, realizing I was starting to get myself into something maybe I wanted to stay away from.

"Sure," Derrick answered as he wobbled out of his chair. "For a moment, I'd thought you'd forgotten."

"We'll start with this," I blurted, while turning to the bookcase to grab a book. I pulled out a copy of *The Talisman* by Peter Straub. I had read *Ghost Story*, which he had written several years earlier. I figured as long as I was going to read to him, I might as well pick something I might enjoy as well.

"Just the book I had in mind, something scary," Derrick said, now standing right in front of me. "How much you want?" I reached into my pocket and pulled out four crumpled up twenty-dollar bills.

"Two good bags," I answered as I held out the money. "How much?"

"I can get them for forty. I'll keep the rest."

"I figured you would. Let's go," I said, taking a few steps towards the stairway.

"No, no, no. You gotta stay here," Derrick yelled. He stepped in front of me and placed his wrinkled hands on my chest. "My people only deal with me. They won't give me nothin' if they see you hanging around."

"I thought you had the stuff here?" I asked, feeling very stupid. I had absolutely no idea how this was supposed to work.

"Of course not. I'm not a dealer. I'm just a middle man who knows where to get the shit from." Derrick said. "Just wait here. Thirty minutes, tops."

"No problem," I sighed. Derrick turned away and headed down the stairway. A few seconds later, I heard the front door slam behind him. I was alone. I crashed on an old beaten up green couch across from Derrick's easy chair. For the first time since being inside this house, I took the time to get a good look at the inside of Derrick's house. I was surprised at just how filthy and disgusting it really was. I know Derrick was old, but I still pegged him for being at least a little clean. I felt sorry for him. I wondered what it must be like, to be old and alone and living in a house littered with trash and dirt. Packs of roaches scurried across the floor in groups of five and six, disappearing behind a plastic bag in the kitchen. Large spider webs covered the corners of every wall. Plates covered with old, moldy food lay scattered across the kitchen countertops and the kitchen floor. I jumped up and grabbed *The Talisman* from the bookcase and dusted off the cover. I guess if I had to live like this, I would be reading every second of every day, too. I would create my own little fantasy world, somewhere far away from the reality of this everyday life. I slowly opened to the first page and began reading to myself.

The sound of the front door opening snapped me back to reality. I heard Derrick's labored body making its way up the creaky, old stairway. I placed the book on a table in front of me and stood up. Checking my watch, I realized he had been gone for over thirty minutes.

"What's up, Derrick?" I said as he rounded the corner and came into the living room. His face was covered in sweat and he was breathing very hard. "Is everything OK?"

"Yes, everything is fine," he answered. He reached into his front pocket and pulled out two small zip-lock bags, each filled with white powder. "Here's your stuff." He handed it to me.

"Thanks," I answered as I grabbed the packets and examined them. I wasn't any sort of narcotics expert, but I had seen enough Heroin and cocaine in my career to know this was more than likely the real stuff. I stuffed the packets into my front pocket. "I gotta book Derrick. That girl's waiting for me."

"Sure, Mike. I'll see you next week," Derrick said as he limped past me and made his way towards his easy chair. His body fell into it with a loud thud. I couldn't believe the chair didn't collapse. "Don't forget about your promise, OK?"

"About the reading?" I asked as I eased towards the stairs.

"Yes," Derrick said, his eyes closed and his breathing starting to slow down.

"Sure, I won't forget." I started walking down the stairs and soon I was out the front door and back into the blistering hot sun. I jogged to Thirteenth Street and headed towards my car. Sanchez whizzed by, smiling as his Fiero turned on T Street and out then out of sight. Several seconds later, I too was in my car and speeding towards the police station.

"How did it go?" Gonzalez asked as I walked into our office. Sanchez and Ayala were sitting at their desks.

"Two bags of Heroin," I answered as I plopped down at my desk. I grabbed a wad of paper towels and wiped the sweat that was dripping down my forehead. I reached into the top drawer and grabbed a Heroin test kit. I needed to make sure this was the real stuff.

"Great!" was the unified response of everyone in the office. I opened the top of the test kit, which was a small plastic vial with a liquid substance inside that produced a chemical reaction upon contact with dicytilated morphine, the active ingredient in Heroin. If the drug were real, the chemical reaction would produce a certain color, which in this case was a deep purplish brown. I steadily opened one of the small bags of Heroin, which were about the size of a penny and poured a few granules of the powder into the test vial. Closing the top of the vial, I cracked open the chemical fluid and shook it up. Immediately, the mixed fluids inside turned from a vanilla white color to the purple/brown I was looking for. I let out a deep sigh of relief. The stuff was real.

"Did you see where he went to get this shit?" I asked, staring at Sanchez. I was holding up the test kit towards the light.

"He went to the Giant parking lot on 9th and O Street," Sanchez said. "It was hard to keep an eye on him with only two cars without him noticing us. Anyway, he met up with about four or five other guys, younger guys, and I think they must have sold it to him."

"OK," I answered. I couldn't really expect them to be sure. We hadn't really been prepared for Derrick to leave the house and go to another location to get the Heroin, so we really didn't have enough people on the street to follow him. The important issue was he had access to the drug, and he had sold it to me. We had now made an iron tight case against him for distribution of a controlled substance, and we still had him for the Bawdy House, which had started the whole investigation in the first place. I was content. Things were going pretty well, despite my reservations over Derrick's age and apparent health condition. The bottom line was he was a drug dealer, and I hated them all just the same. So when the time was right, he was going down, and I would feel none the worse for being the one pulling the strings. I went home that night and slept well, dreaming of the next Saturday and how much Heroin Derrick could get.

After several days of blistering, dry heat the following week finally brought some much needed rain. Saturday was by far the worst, and the water hit the streets with a vengeance. I was at the corner of Thirteenth and T Streets in Ayala's car, waiting for the torrential downpour to subside a bit. It was about two o'clock in the afternoon. Finally, I just gave up. I jumped out of Ayala's car and sprinted to Derrick's house. I desperately prayed he was awake. I didn't want to be stuck in the rain outside his door waiting for him to answer. As luck would have it, I only needed to knock three times before Derrick swung the door open and invited me in. I didn't hesitate and quickly followed him upstairs to the living room.

"You look wet as hell!" Derrick laughed as we entered into the living room. "You gonna get sick boy."

"Yeah, I know. Thanks," I snapped back. "I couldn't find a decent parking space."

"Here," Derrick said. He tossed me a towel he had retrieved from the kitchen. I quickly started drying my face, and then worked my way down my rain soaked body.

"Thanks, I needed that." Derrick wasted no time in slumping down into his easy chair. Sitting on a small table next to him was the book. He picked it up, and with a huge smile tossed it across the room to me.

"Whoa, be careful!" I screamed as I just barely caught the book in my arms.

"Just testing your reflexes, Mike. Are you ready?"

"Sure, sure, give me another second to finish drying off," I answered. I finished with the towel and tossed it on the couch. As I eased onto the couch, I thought I heard several, almost inaudible moaning voices coming from the bedroom down the hall. They gradually became louder and louder.

"What the hell is that?" I asked. I looked down the hall and saw Stacey's bedroom door was closed.

"Don't mind them. That's Stacey and one of her tricks," Derrick answered casually. "They've been in there well over thirty minutes. They should be done soon."

"Great," I said sarcastically. The moans were interrupted only by the unmistakable sound of the headboard banging against a wall and the loose bed springs squeaking up and down. I noticed Derrick had placed a folding chair a few feet from him, to which I quickly relocated. I could tell he was really looking forward to this. "This will be kind of distracting with those two going at it, don't you think?"

"Don't pay them no mind," Derrick said as he closed his eyes and slumped back even lower into his easy chair. Any lower, and his ass would be on the floor. "Read loud, OK Mike. My hearing's not so good anymore either. Besides, you need to be louder than those two lovebirds down the hall."

"No problem," I answered laughing, as I turned to the first page and began to read. "Just don't fall asleep." For the next thirty minutes, Derrick and I escaped into the wonderful world of *The Talisman* and for all intents and purposes, I never really once thought about what had brought me to this house in the first place some three weeks ago. As much as I tried to keep my mind on what I was trying to accomplish, I couldn't help but feel a sense of enjoyment in reading to this old man. In his lonely world, I was a friend. Even though he knew so little about me, he seemed to trust me unconditionally, which I didn't understand. Little did he know that eventually, I would arrest him, but for now, I refused to think about that and kept my mind on the matters at hand.

"OK, Derrick. I have to get going in a few minutes," I said as I folded over the last page I had read and closed the book. I placed it on the table next to me. "Can you get me some stuff?"

"Thanks Mike. You read great," Derrick said as he slowly opened his eyes. "I'll get it for you now. Same as last time, right?"

"Sure. Same as last time," I answered. I handed him the eighty dollars. "If I needed a larger amount, you know, for some of my friends, can you get it for me?"

"I can get you whatever you need Mike," he answered.

"That's great," I answered, hoping I wasn't pushing my luck.

"I got to tell you something though, Mike. I'm not the person you probably think I am," he answered. I didn't understand what he was trying to say, nor could I think of what to say back. I checked my watch and saw I was running out of time. It had taken quite a bit of explaining to get my supervisor to authorize thirty minutes for me to read to a drug dealer. Not to mention the kidding I got from my co-workers. So I left this conversation open for another time.

"I was just curious," I said. "I'm sorry if I offended you."

"I'll be right back," Derrick said as he headed for the stairs. "And, you didn't offend me."

"OK," I answered. I sat down on the couch and waited. Five minutes later, the bedroom door opened and out came a naked Stacey and an older white man wearing a nice, clean gray business suit. He had a fat, ugly red paisley tie that barely made it halfway down his protruding belly.

"Hey," I said, staring up at Stacey. I wondered if she would recognize me. "Couldn't wait for me, could you?"

"Mike. What's up?" she answered, appearing a little shocked to see me. "You here for some pussy? I got a little energy left, if you know what I mean." She did her now infamous grinding routine again for me.

"No, not today. I'm waiting on Derrick," I answered smiling. "He's picking up something for me. Man, when you say you charge for the hour, you really mean it, don't you?"

"Who the hell is that?" The man in the gray suit asked. "You told me we were alone."

"Bite me asshole!" I cut in before Stacey had the chance to answer. I hated johns more than I hated prostitutes, and I didn't have time to be arguing or explaining myself. I bit my lip a bit, realizing I couldn't act like a cop and needed to subdue myself. But, it was just way too much fun fucking around with suburban business idiots who were fucking around with hookers and I couldn't resist just a little intimidation.

"Hey, Mike, don't be a jerk," Stacey shouted back. "He's just nervous. This was his first time with a girl like me."

"I'll bet," I stated, again sarcastically, turning my gaze to the fat guy. "I'm sure you've never fucked a prostitute before, right?" I could see the unmistakable glistening of a wedding band coming from his left hand. "Does your wife know what you do?"

"Hey man, I didn't mean to offend you," he said, his body shaking nervously. He looked to the side of me as he was speaking. "I just thought we were alone."

"Yeah, no problem, just take a hike before I throw your sorry ass out," I said. I got up from the couch and took a few steps towards him. I thought for a second that if I couldn't arrest this asshole, I'd just clock his ass for good measure. I wanted him and Stacey out. It was bad enough listening to them screwing around for the past hour. I didn't feel comfortable with them around, and when Derrick got back, they would just complicate things.

"Easy Mike, we're going," Stacey said as they made their way towards the stairs. "Tell Derrick I left his money on the nightstand, OK?"

"Sure, whatever," I answered indifferently. When I heard the front door shut, I returned to the couch, cooled off a bit and waited for Derrick. Thirty minutes later, he returned.

"Here," Derrick said, handing me two plastic zip-lock bags of Heroin. He had another one in his hand.

"What's that for?" I asked curiously.

"That's mine," He answered quickly.

"I didn't know you messed around with this shit," I said as I slipped the two bags into my pocket.

"Off and on, my brother, off and on," Derrick answered. "I've been trying to kick the habit for almost as long as I can remember. I've been going to the hospital and getting some of that liquid methadone shit, but I'm out right now." Liquid methadone was a drug people took to get down from Heroin.

"Damn, that sucks. I'm sorry to hear that," I said.

"What do you care?" Derrick snapped back, sounding a bit irritated. "Your friends are doing the same shit as me, only they're young enough to stop."

"I'm sorry. I didn't mean to offend you," I said. "How did you get hooked anyway, if you don't mind my asking?"

"After the war," Derrick answered. He had since made it to his easy chair and was sitting back, his feet kicked out in front of him.

"The Vietnam War?" I asked stupidly.

"World War II," he answered, laughing hysterically. "Man, how young do you think I am, anyway?"

"I was thinking maybe fifty," I answered, lying through my teeth. I knew he was much older.

"Man, you crazy. I'm a helluva lot older than that."

"How old, then?" I asked.

"Don't worry about it young boy, it's not important," he answered. "Anyway, during the war, I was shot several times in the stomach and back. Ever since then, I've been either stuck on Heroin, morphine, Dilaudids, and Methadone. You name it. If they couldn't give it to me, than I was buying the shit on the streets." I was taken back by his story. I suddenly felt like the biggest jerk in the world. Not only was my soon-to-be defendant for distribution of Heroin a sickly old man, but he was also a war veteran who had been shot. This wasn't supposed to work out this way. I was supposed to be nailing young, violent gun-packing assholes that were dealing dope to school kids, not timid old men who probably didn't have but a few more years left to live. But I couldn't stop now. The wheel was already rolling, and I was standing behind it pushing faster and faster.

"Look, I really gotta get going," I said, breaking a few seconds of silence. I didn't know what else to say and I wanted to leave.

"You want to do a few hits for the road on me," Derrick said, holding out his packet of white powder.

"Come on man, I told you I don't mess with that shit. Besides, my girl is going to split if I don't get back," I said, trying to sound convincing. "Maybe next time."

"OK, Mike. I guess I'll see you next week," Derrick said as he got up from his chair and headed to the kitchen. I guess he was going to get high. "Don't forget we're on chapter two next week."

"I won't forget!" I shouted over my shoulder from the bottom of the stairs. I pushed open the front door and sprinted as fast as I could for my car. This was an ugly, depressing turn of events.

I took a lot of ribbing from my co-workers during the next week. I must admit, I couldn't really blame them. The situation I was in was precarious, at best. I decided to see if Derrick could get some larger amounts of Heroin, and if he couldn't, then just wrap up the case and move on. I didn't want to nail him too bad if he couldn't lead us to something better and my conscience was tearing me up. Every time I thought of Derrick, instead of seeing a hardened menace to society, all I saw was a frail old man who seemed to be more of a victim than a criminal and even though I knew he was getting his Heroin from other sources, our office was in no position to tackle the lengthy process of tracking the source line beyond a few more contacts. I had to face the reality—our unit was formed to enforce prostitution, and that was what the department expected of us. Anything else was simply a sidelight and a much lower priority.

The following Saturday welcomed a return to the blistering heat that had become a trademark of the summer. It was decided during a squad meeting that we would press Derrick for a large amount of Heroin. If he couldn't deliver, then we would take him down on the charges we already had. Fortunately, we would hit him after getting arrest and search warrants, instead of locking him up immediately. I didn't want to be present when this happened. Deep down inside, I knew he couldn't get much more than a few bags of dope. He was a neighborhood junkie, and he probably had any number of local contacts that supplied him with what little he needed, but I was sure that was where the line was drawn. Anything more, and people would become suspicious, and Derrick's lifeline would be cut in a heartbeat. It just didn't make fiscal sense. Derrick was in no position to challenge any of the area's big-time dealers. So I knew that today would be the last time I would see him as "Mike", his friend. After today, he would know me only as Officer Archer, the man who walked into his life, befriended him and then ripped his meager existence to hell. I wanted this to be over as soon as possible.

"Hey, Derrick," I said as I walked past the open door and headed up the stairs. Derrick was behind me, his body moving a little bit slower than usual.

"Hi Mike. How's it going?" His breathing was labored.

"I'm fine. Are you OK?" I asked, pausing at the top of the stairs to give him time to catch up. "You don't sound well."

"I'm pretty sick. But I'll be OK," he answered. "Are you ready to do some reading?"

"I'm always ready to do some reading," I said. I walked across the living room and took a seat in the same folding chair I had sat in last week. Derrick labored behind me and plopped into his easy chair. I picked up the book and began reading chapter two.

"Hey, Derrick," I said after about twenty minutes of reading.

"Yeah, Mike?" he answered. I thought he had fallen asleep.

"I'm curious about something, but I don't want you to get mad at me when I ask you," I said, trying to think of a tactful way to ask what I wanted to ask. I had to know why he sold Heroin. I needed to have my assumptions verified. I had to know he was a piece of shit dealer who deserved to be locked up.

"Go ahead, I won't get mad," he said. His eyes were still closed. I wondered if he even knew what I was really saying.

"Why do you sell me Heroin? I mean, other than the few dollars you make, what do you get out of it?" I asked, just letting the words flow out of my mouth. "I know you told me the other day that you wanted to be my friend. What did you mean by that?"

"Why do you ask?" he said. His body didn't move, but his eyes were wide open and he had an attentive look about his face.

"Because you don't seem to fit the stereotype of what I imagined drug dealers to be," I replied.

"What is that stereotype?"

"I guess I'm not so sure. I just know that you don't fit it," I answered. "Maybe the young, gun-packing gangsters I read about in the papers."

"Well, I'm not a dealer. I told you that. I'm just a man of opportunity," he answered. "If something presents itself, and I can make a few bucks, then I gotta go with it."

"And do your customers always read to you?" I asked.

"Are you kidding? Of course not. Just you."

"And why me?" I asked.

"I don't know. I just trust you. There's sincerity about you that I really like," Derrick answered. He had turned his head towards me and was staring at me. "Does it bother you?"

"Not at all. I guess I'm just trying to understand you a little better," I answered.

"What's to understand? I'm just a tired old man who's gotten a poor hand out of life. This is the hand I was dealt, and I'm just trying to make it as best as I can."

"Yeah, I guess that sums it up for all of us," I said, reflecting on the many tragedies that had happened during my short life. Suddenly, I felt very close to Derrick. I could relate to what he was feeling.

"Don't think too much about it, Mike. Life is funny sometimes. I know I'm not going to be here for much longer, but I've done the best I can. I've never hurt anyone, and I never will," Derrick said, his eyes now staring out the living room windows. "I'm not the person you probably think I am. I'm just a person getting by."

"I understand, Derrick," I replied quietly. I realized now exactly what this man was. He wasn't the drug dealer I had envisioned and wanted him so badly to be. He wasn't the violent murderer I had seen and read about before joining the police department and wanted so badly to take down. He was just an everyday man, struggling with the life that had in many ways been dictated to him by forces beyond his control. And in my mind, the thought of arresting him and putting him in jail made me sick to my stomach. But that was my job. Not to judge or to sympathize, but to gather facts and make arrests. I cursed what the city of Washington, D.C. had done to me. It had bestowed on me the burning desire to dedicate my life to preserving justice and catching criminals. Then it up and threw people like Derrick at me, shattering my images of what was really right and wrong. Just what was justice, anyway? What did justice mean to Derrick?

"Is everything all right?" Derrick said, snapping me from my thoughts.

"Yeah, I'm fine. I was just thinking about some things," I answered solemnly. I wanted to tell him what I was thinking, but I knew I couldn't. "Listen, I gotta run. Can you get me a couple more bags?"

"Sure," he answered. I handed him the money. Derrick took it and headed out the door. I walked over to the window and pulled aside one of the soiled curtains. Derrick had turned east on R Street and was slowly limping out of sight. Soon, he was gone, and I walked back over to the bookcase to put away the book. I knew I wouldn't need it anymore. For the first time, I noticed a series of small-framed pictures sitting on the top of the bookcase, each covered with a thin layer of dust. I picked one up and dusted it off with my shirtsleeve. It was an old black and white picture of several men wearing military fatigues. I looked closer and then I recognized one of the men, standing off to the side. It was Derrick. He had a stern look on his face, a look of confident but lighthearted seriousness. Most of all, he looked very proud. He seemed so very far away from where he was now. I set the picture back down on the shelf and feeling very depressed, I eased towards the couch and sat down. It was definitely time for this to end.

"That didn't take long," I said as Derrick reached the top of the stairs and entered into the living room.

"Yeah, look, I'm sorry, but I couldn't get nothing," he answered. "There wasn't no one out there."

"Hey, don't worry about it," I answered. I breathed a sigh of relief. I was certain this man would never have been able to get me any amounts of Heroin worth continuing the investigation. "I'll catch you next week, O.K? Oh, and keep the money. You need it more than I do."

"Thanks, Mike," Derrick answered as he limped to his chair and fell back into it. "Chapter three, right?"

"Yeah, chapter three," I said. "I'll see ya." I took the steps two at a time, and in a flash, I was out into the afternoon sun jogging to my car. I was certain this would be the only point in my career that I was actually happy not to have bought any drugs.

Later that afternoon, we decided I would get the warrants on Monday and we would arrest Derrick later in the week. That was fine by me. He wasn't going anywhere.

I waited in my car several blocks away as officers approached Derrick's house with an arrest and search warrant in hand, charging him with two counts of distribution of a controlled substance and for operating a Bawdy House. After several minutes, two officers escorted Derrick out the front door, his hands handcuffed behind his back. His limp was more profound now, and out in the late afternoon sun, his body looked frailer than ever. He looked as if he could have just melted away into the street or blown away in the wind. I had taken his last piece of dignity away from him and shoved it in his face. They walked him to an awaiting scout car and pushed him into the back seat. Then he was gone. I wheeled my car up Thirteenth Street and headed back to the station to finish the paperwork.

I was sitting at my desk when they finally brought him in. My Amoco shirt hung on a coat hanger next to me. His eyes hit mine the instant he entered through the doorway, and the look that covered his face is one that I know I will never forget. It was a look I can't quite describe, no matter how hard I try. It was a look that pierced deep, and left me with a feeling of complete emptiness. I got up from behind my desk and walked towards the doorway, paperwork in hand.

"How could you do this to me, Mike?" Derrick said as I slipped past him, never once taking my eyes from the doorway ahead. Those were the last words I would ever hear him say.

CHAPTER EIGHTEEN

Just by looking at her, you would never have figured Lorelei for a prostitute. She could have been mistaken for a tourist maybe, clad as she was in plain white tennis shoes—or just another resident of the neighborhood. She preferred jeans and a sweater to the more flamboyant attire of most hookers, and she shunned the faux-fur look. If the weather got cold, she slipped on a nylon jacket.

The strange thing was she always seemed to be moving, as if being set in motion by some unseen and concealed force. Most prostitutes stake out a particular street corner, but not Lorelei. She preferred to wander about, sometimes back and forth between her small apartment on M Street and the 11th Street corridor. She was not beautiful, yet with shoulder-length blonde hair, a slight frame and piercing blue eyes, she commanded the attention many of the other prostitutes could not. And in a part of the city where most prostitutes got involved in drugs—either as users or sellers, often selling themselves as a means to support their habit, Lorelei seemed to be clean.

Business came easily to her, and she gradually became a constant presence on the street. Day and night, seven days a week, Lorelei would walk the streets, sometimes stopping at the corner of 12th and O Streets, NW, waving to the cars as they drove by, blowing kisses and flirting with anyone who would stop long enough to look.

It took me some time to learn Lorelei's real name. As a police officer, I had been working in a prostitution unit for about three years, and I was used to getting the run-around from streetwalkers. Part of my daily routine consisted of identifying prostitutes and developing ways to get them to stop. Sometimes that meant making arrests, but it didn't take long to discover that most of the women I would pick up simply reappeared on the street, sometimes within a few hours. Perhaps it was the money, or more likely it was the desperate feeling of hopelessness that kept these women from seeking out a better way of life.

With Lorelei, I thought, perhaps I should try a different approach: a more therapeutic technique wherein I convince her of the error of her ways. A bit naive, I knew, but well worth a shot. In the ever-increasing revolving door of street prostitution, there had to be a better way than making arrests. Yet despite my eagerness, I had little idea of what I was getting myself into.

Each time I approached Lorelei, she would give me a different alias. Then she would giggle out loud and walk away, mumbling "Five-O" under her breath, a way of signaling that she knew, despite my street clothes and unmarked car, that I was a cop. It was like a game to her, but gradually she began to engage me, maybe just as a way of passing time. Once in a while, she would offer surprising bits of information about her past. Never enough to draw any conclusions, but enough clipped remarks to suggest she had had a rough childhood and difficulties with her parents. But certainly nothing out of the ordinary. With insight and power she would talk occasionally about the horrors of prostitution—the violence and danger that always lurk when you're climbing into a car with a man you know nothing about.

She seemed more self-aware than other prostitutes and sounded confident when explaining how she alone had chosen her own path. Being a prostitute was about making money, she would tell me, nothing more. Although I believed there had to be more to it, Lorelei would only allow small glimpses of her past, leaving my thoughts and conclusions about what drove her through personal speculation. I sometimes thought maybe she was afraid of her past, and couldn't comprehend the future. Only today mattered, and how she was going to survive.

Over the course of a year, I began to notice slight changes in Lorelei's activities. She was gradually coming out onto the street earlier and earlier in the day, a time slot usually occupied by drug addicted prostitutes. She seemed to pay less attention to her appearance. Her once flowing blonde hair looked several shades darker and was often matted against her head. Her eyes, once curious and sharp, now seemed distant and cold. Where before she had stood alone, working her corners like a symphony conductor, now Lorelei hunched timidly, sharing her space with several other girls. She was using drugs now, I concluded.

Sometimes, I would see her walking with people I suspected to be drug dealers. As I wheeled my car toward them one afternoon, the dealers took off running, escaping into the mouth of an alley. I took little notice. It was Lorelei, standing innocently on the sidewalk gazing at her feet, in which I was interested. I slipped from behind the wheel of my car and gradually approached her. I wanted to tell her she was too pretty, too smart to be working the streets, but I knew it would mean nothing to her. She had probably heard it many times before from people much closer to her than I. And I knew in the back of my mind there were many complicated practical questions to be answered even if she took my advice. Where would she go? What kind of job could she get? Jobs were for people with self-esteem and assuredness. Lorelei had neither. I was learning about the sometimes-fragile thin line separating those of us who succeed from those who slip between the cracks.

So on this hot summer day, I settled for idle chitchat, trying to find out a little more about what made Lorelei tick. As we talked, I noticed small purplish red marks on Lorelei's arms. I guessed she was shooting heroin as well as smoking crack cocaine, something I had caught her doing before. Today, I would let her go with another lecture. But from this moment on, I couldn't help but think that Lorelei's days were numbered. Like an emptying hourglass, her time seemed to be slipping away right before my eyes. I wondered how much longer she could survive on the streets.

Once or twice a week, I would catch her standing on the corner of 12th and O Streets, plying her trade. She looked weak and frail, her clothes dirty and always the same. My lectures had long since lost their slim appeal, and I guess I became just another insignificant facet of her lost life. She would direct her attention to the flow of traffic, searching for the supplier of her next fix. Her eyes showed desperation, and I figured at this point she would probably do just about anything for a few dollars. This must have been the thought of the man driving the new Acura Legend who pulled up beside her and opened his passenger door for Lorelei to get into his car. For twenty dollars, he would get any sexual experience he desired, and Lorelei would get her next hit of dope. For a fleeting moment, a slight sparkle filled her eyes. She was accepted once more. For some reason, I wondered if this might be the last time I would see Lorelei, or if perhaps she might just disappear like the falling autumn leaves. I remained in my car, wondering why police officers had to see these things happening and what we could do to stop them. My mind drew nothing but blanks.

Two weeks later, I received a call from the manager of Lorelei's apartment building. Lorelei, the landlord complained, was using her apartment for prostitution. Maybe I had one more shot to help her. It didn't take long for me to build enough evidence to confirm this, and soon I found myself standing outside her front door gently knocking, arrest warrant in hand. She opened it without hesitation and I think she knew immediately that she was going to be arrested. She grabbed a jacket and walked past me. "I would like to talk with you when we get to the station," she said matter-of-factly, leaving me feeling confused but hopeful. Perhaps she finally wanted off of the streets, I thought, and was going to turn to me for help.

That night, Lorelei and I spoke for several hours. She explained to me that it was time for her to move on, to start looking for a regular job. She knew it would be hard, especially without any money, but she said she was tired of working the streets, and felt like life had something more to offer her. Maybe I was just looking too hard, but I felt she had a certain sparkle back in her eyes, and in her voice I could sense an urgency that convinced me she was serious. I asked her what had changed her mind, but she wouldn't explain. She just said it was time. I felt incredibly close to her that night. Not quite like friends, but more out of respect. She had shared a portion of her life with me, and sought me out to talk to about changing her life around. Not because she had to, or because I was a police officer, but because she simply wanted to, maybe because she trusted me. I was content. I had reached someone not because of the badge I carried and the authority it gave me. Instead, I had reached someone with my heart, something much more powerful than a badge or the power behind it.

I went home that night pleased about how things were turning out, convinced that a small but significant battle had been won. I was used to seeing the constant flow of new girls entering the world of prostitution. Seeing one get out for a better life was something I had yet to witness. Maybe, just maybe, there was something in police work beyond putting my handcuffs on people and placing them under arrest.

For several weeks after that night, I searched the streets for Lorelei. I wanted to see how she was doing. I wanted to hear about her successful escape from the streets. I knew she had been evicted from her apartment building, but she had assured me she would have no problem finding another place to stay. I believed her. In a way, I was happy not to see her. This meant she was off the street, and even though I wanted to talk with her, it was good she was nowhere to be found. I told myself she figured it was better to stay out of the city, for her own safety.

One night a few weeks later, I came to work just as I always did, arriving in my office to plan my schedule for the evening. I was feeling empowered lately, boosted by the thought that the more personal approach to law enforcement was working, that I might have the power within me to pull at least some of the prostitutes off of the streets. Where once my confidence had wavered, now it held steady and strong. I was eager to hit my beat for the first time in over a year, ready to make a difference.

Only it wouldn't quite turn out that way. Later that night, under a broad and dark sky punctuated by thousands of bright stars, Lorelei's lifeless body was found, having plunged several stories from the roof of a nearby building. It hit me with deadening force how naive I was to think Lorelei could change her life so easily. Or that I could be the one to make the difference. I suppose I should have known something was wrong, but I didn't. In my foolish, perfect world, I wanted so hard to believe.

I never did find out what it was in Lorelei's past, or life, that would bring her to sell her body on the streets. Whatever it was, it obviously convinced her that being a prostitute was her only route to survival. Finally, she had escaped the life that so betrayed her.

CHAPTER NINETEEN

I was sitting in my car at the corner of 13th and L Streets, a commercial area of the city, desperately fighting off the slow onset of sleep. On most nights, usually after midnight, this was my little corner of the world. Not much to speak of, but for a few hours anyway, it was all mine. I usually parked on the northwest corner, where there was a large empty parking lot which afforded me the best view of L Street. L Street was a major part of what we called "The Strip," which covered the areas of the 1200, 1300 and 1400 blocks of L Street and the 1200, 1300, and 1400 blocks of Massachusetts Avenue. This was where most of the hookers worked. From here, I could see the girls working on both sides of the street. Tonight, thankfully, was very slow. Most of the girls had already been arrested and would spend the next few hours in a jail cell. For those who escaped, they had probably sought out a new location far, far away from me. Well, at least three or four blocks, and as far as I was concerned, that was far enough. A few pimps crossed in front of my car, paying me little notice. They were probably wondering where their girls were. I laughed. Soon, their cellular phones would ring, with messages from girls pleading with them to come to the police station and post bond. Then, in a matter of hours, they would be back on the streets again, hustling to make up for several hours of lost time. That's how it worked, just one big, huge vicious cycle. Sure as day turned into night, and then back into day again, prostitutes worked this little section of the city. It really didn't matter if we were here, or a tornado swept down from the sky. This was their turf, and they weren't giving it up easily. I found this out the hard way, after four years of dedicating my life towards eradicating them. It was a battle everyone was losing.

Killer Joe, who was a pimp straight out of Eddie Murphy's *Saturday Night Live* skit called Velvet Jones and his book on how to be a pimp, crossed casually in front of my car. He was wearing his trademark red suit with patent white leather shoes. A white hat concealed his greasy, long black hair. I laughed. There was this strange, fashion time warp thing going on here, and the stereotypes about pimps and tacky seventies clothing really did ring true. I was surprised to see him walk so brazenly across my territory. He had to know we had most of his girls locked up, especially since they had been the first to go. I guess he'd be shelling out the bucks tonight.

"Hey, Archer, are you on the air?" Gonzalez's voice came across the radio.

"Yeah, go ahead," I answered, picking up my portable radio from off the floor.

1300 M Street?" He asked. His voice was drowned out by the sounds of passing cars. I assumed he was standing on the street.

"Yeah, what's up?"

"I think we got a new girl out here. Can you come take a look at her?"

"I'm on my way. Give me a minute, OK," I answered curiously. It had been awhile since we had spotted any new girls. Pimps were usually pretty good about keeping them out of our sight. I started my car and pulled quietly onto 13th Street. But before I pulled off, I had some unfinished business to take care of.

"Hey Killer Joe!" I shouted out of my cracked open window.

"What the fuck you want, man?" he answered back. "I ain't doing nothing but going for a walk." He always looked like he wanted to fight.

"Well, you might as well start walking your sorry, pimp ass up to the Third District. We have all your girls locked up, and they need bond money to get out," I yelled, a huge smile enveloping my face. This would cost him in the neighborhood of a thousand dollars, which was just a drop in the bucket for an average pimp, but I guess it was just the fact of having to pay to the police that seemed to piss them off so much.

"You know I ain't got no girls. I stopped doing that shit years ago," he shouted back, and I heard him mutter the words *fuck you* under his breath.

"Sure you don't," I said, still smiling because I knew that pissed him off big time. "Well, I thought I'd just let you know anyway, you know, in case maybe you're a little bit curious as to why the street is so empty. So, if that's really the case, and you don't have any girls, then how about taking you're sorry, I'm-not-a-pimp ass up the street and off of my street. Got it? Or you'll get your ass locked the fucked up."

"Fuck you!" He muttered again as he crossed the street and walked away. "Locked up for what?" He was quickly moving away from me and I knew his words were just for show. If I stepped out of my car, he would be gone in a flash.

Most pimps thought we were stupid. I could see why. Washington, D.C. has never really concerned itself with prosecuting pimps, or with prostitution for that matter. These crimes were always an afterthought, which made sense having been the murder capital of the states for three years running. Basically, it was a free for all, with our small, ten-man unit serving as one of the only barriers between sexual law and lawlessness. So, most knew they could get away with just about anything. And quite often, they would flaunt this fact right in front of our collective faces. But I didn't mind. Our squad would cause more than our share of anarchy over the years within the prostitution establishment, which was all that I could really ask for.

"Is that her?" I asked Gonzalez, as I exited my car and pointed to a short, blonde-haired girl standing on the corner of 13th and M Street about twenty yards away. She was standing next to another girl with long jet-black hair.

"Yeah, that's her," Gonzalez answered.

"Please don't tell me that's Jasmine standing with her."

"Yeah, it is." I'm sure Gonzalez anticipated what I was going to say next. "She's breaking her in." Breaking her in meant showing her the ropes. Most pimps would put new girls out with older, seasoned veterans. They showed the girl what to do and what not to do. Most of all, they taught the new girls how to be totally obedient to the pimp. Pretty soon, they depended on the pimp for everything, money, clothing, food, shelter, and worst of all, self-worth. That's how most girls were hooked, through a slow process of control, need and dominance.

"Has she been warned already about being in the street?" I asked.

"Yeah, about twenty minutes ago," Gonzalez answered.

"If we have to, we can take her in for failure to obey." This was our catch-all charge, which allowed us to basically sweep the streets regularly and arrest prostitutes for a night. "She can't be more than sixteen or seventeen years old. Maybe if we talk to her, off of the street and away from Jasmine, we can try and help her," I answered, wondering if I was really prepared for what I was getting myself into.

"No problem. I talked with her a little bit already," Gonzalez agreed. "I think we might be able to get to her if we move quickly. She's very confused. I think there's a chance she might want out. The problem is getting her away from Jasmine."

"OK, let's give it a shot." With that, I jumped into my car and Gonzalez followed me to the corner of 13th and M. Both girls were still there, waving to passing cars.

"What's up, Jasmine? Long time, no see," I said getting out of my car. Both girls started walking away up 13th Street. "Oh, no you don't. Don't go anywhere. I want to talk with you."

"Damn. Can't you leave us alone for just one night?" Jasmine answered in a whiny voice, kicking one of her high-heeled shoes into the ground in disgust.

"I'll leave you alone as soon as you promise me you'll quit working the street, OK?" I shot back. Both girls had slowly made their way back towards Gonzalez and me. I looked closely at the other girl, but didn't recognize her. She had to be new, and she looked really young. I couldn't place her exact age, but from where I was standing, she couldn't have been older than eighteen.

"You know that's never going to happen," Jasmine responded. "We're not hurting anyone. Why don't you go and catch some real criminals?"

"Like drug dealers and murderers, right?" I answered, cutting her off in mid-sentence. I had been down this path before. It was a no-win situation, so I figured on ending it now. "You know that our job is enforcing prostitution. We already have people who enforce narcotics and lock people up for homicides. Besides, then I would miss out on all this perverted great fun!"

"You suck, you know that. Nobody gives a shit about us," Jasmine answered in a slightly irritated voice. I was getting to her, at least from an antagonizing standpoint.

"That's where you're wrong. We care. That's why we do what we do. Wouldn't you like to just walk off the street right here and now... forever?" I asked.

"Yeah sure, sometimes. But that's just dreaming. I'll never quit."

"Then how about you're new friend there?" I asked, pointing to the blond haired girl. I detected a sense of fear covering Jasmine's once confident face.

"She's not hooking. She's just hanging out with me until I'm done," Jasmine said quickly, not giving the girl a chance to speak.

"I suppose you really expect me to believe that, right? Can't she speak for herself?" I answered, staring the blond girl in her deep blue eyes.

"Sure she can. Just not to you assholes," Jasmine blurted back, laughing slightly. The blond girl looked very afraid. She shielded herself behind Jasmine, her hands clamped tightly together, trying to keep us from noticing them shake.

"It's OK You don't have to listen to her," I said, moving myself to an angle where I could see her. "I know you're new out here. And I also know that it's not too late. You can come with us now and we'll get you out. I promise," I said. The word "Promise" echoed resoundingly through my head, over and over again. I had never made this promise before, partly because few prostitutes ever trusted us for help, but mostly because I really wondered if I had the ability to deliver on it. But there was something about this girl, with her innocent face and ice blue eyes that seemed different. She wanted out. She knew that she did not belong here.

"She's not going anywhere!" Jasmine quickly cut in. "She's not hooking, I told you. I'm just watching out for her for the night." She was doing her best to protect what she thought was her property. But she was going to fail. I knew that our only real chance was to get them separated.

"Watching out for whom? For your pimp, so he can break her in slowly? Or are you just showing her how the system works all by yourself?" I yelled back. I glanced back at Jasmine's friend. "The choice is yours. You can walk away with us, right here, right now. Or you can stay with Jasmine, and end up just like her. Stuck with no life, and death staring at you around every corner, and in every car you hop in."

"I told you asshole, she's staying with me. Isn't that right?" Jasmine turned to the girl, waiting for a confirmation. The girl walked a few feet away and in a voice that was barely audible whispered, "I've got nowhere to go." I looked at Jasmine and knew by the expression on her face that she had not heard what the girl had just said.

"Gonzalez, can you get Jasmine away for a few minutes so I can talk with her?"

"Sure," Gonzalez answered as he made his way towards Jasmine. "Come on girl. You and me, we're going to have a little talk."

I was now standing alone with the new girl. The more I looked at her, the younger she became. She was somebody's daughter, standing out here in the street, about to become just another fucked up statistic. I felt myself getting angrier and angrier. If Jasmine's pimp had shown up right now, I would have beaten him to a within an inch of his worthless life.

"We can help you get a place to stay. A safe place," I said cautiously. "Maybe, we can help you get back home."

"I don't know. I'm so confused," she replied, her eyes staring at the ground. "I can't go back home."

"OK, you don't have to. You just need to get off the street, right here, right now, one step at a time. This is the first step." I could tell she was really being honest and was really confused. She didn't have that air of distant arrogance most prostitutes had, one which served to mask the fear and depression deep within. Perhaps she believed the story Jasmine and her pimp had sold her, about all the money and friends she would have, about her new "family" and how much they loved her and how she couldn't trust anyone from the real world. I had seen it happen with so many other girls. It was an attractive lure, if you were stupid enough to believe it.

"These people, they're not your friends. It's just a business to them. And for them, you're nothing more than a way to make money. They will take it all, and you'll be left with nothing. Do you understand?" I asked, trying my hardest to drive my point home.

"I guess so. Can you really help me?"

"Yes, we can. We'll do everything in our power to get you a place to start over. OK?"

"OK But you can't let Jasmine know what's going on. Promise me you won't let her know that I told you I wanted help?" A few small tears slipped from her blue eyes. Her voice betrayed the age she was desperately trying to convey. She now sounded every bit like the child she was.

"OK, but you have to come with us now," I said, knowing time was of the essence. If her pimp even knew she was talking with the police on this level, and had contemplated leaving, he would beat her so badly she'd never come back.

"I can't."

"You must," I replied, feeling like I was so close, but that she was slipping away. I knew that Jasmine already had an idea of what was going on.

"I'll get back with you, OK? I just need some time to think," she said, wiping the tears off of her flushing red cheeks. I didn't know what to do. I was losing her, at least for now. Then I remembered Gonzalez telling me earlier that both girls had been previously warned about standing in the street and waving at cars. This was an arrestable traffic violation, and since we had seen both girls doing the same thing a second time, they could be arrested. I hated myself for using this law as a means to buy more time, but I had little other choice.

"I'm arresting her for failure to obey a lawful police order," I yelled at Gonzalez, who was still standing with Jasmine. "Can you call a transport?"

"Sure, no problem," I could tell by the smile on his face that he agreed with what was going on.

"That's fucked up. You can't just arrest her for nothing," Jasmine started yelling.

"Watch me!" I yelled back. The blond girl looked more confused than ever. She started shaking again, only now worse than ever. I wished I could explain to her why we were doing this.

"You want to be a prostitute. No problem. Now you'll be treated just like one. See how a few hours in jail suit you," I said, my voice sounding as serious as it could. I hated doing this, but I had little choice.

"Why are you arresting me? I didn't do anything wrong," she sobbed. I locked my handcuffs on her skinny wrists.

"We'll talk at the station," I said as I walked her to the back of the transport car. "Take her to the Third District cell block," I said to the uniformed officer in the car. Gonzalez cut me off as I made my way back to my car.

"What's going on?"

"She wants out. She told me. She's just scared. She has no place to go, and she's afraid of Jasmine and her pimp. You know that if we let her go tonight, we may never see her again. But, if we have a chance of convincing her tonight, then we can maybe get her out," I said, trying to convince him, which I knew was silly. Gonzalez had one of the biggest hearts on the department, and would do anything to help anyone.

"I agree. She's just a kid. At least this way, we get her away from Jasmine for a night. Maybe, once we get to the station and away from the street, we can talk some sense into her," Gonzalez answered.

"I'll meet you back at the District," I said as I jumped into my car and headed towards the station. Gonzalez quickly made his way to his car and followed closely behind.

She was sitting in a small holding cell where we did most of our interviews, legs crossed and hands folded neatly on her slender waist, when Gonzalez and I arrived.

"Are you all right?" I asked as I walked into the doorway. I knew she wasn't. I'm sure she had no idea about what life as a prostitute meant, nor did she have any idea what to do next.

"I guess. So what happens now?" She questioned calmly. "Where's Jasmine?"

"Don't worry about Jasmine now. How about telling us your name," Gonzalez said as he gently nudged past me, a notebook and ink pen in his hand.

"It's Julie."

"Where do you live, Julie?" I asked.

"I don't have a home. I told you that already."

"Where did you live?" I asked. "Before you ran away and wound up on the street. You had to come from somewhere."

"My folks live in Rockville…Maryland," she answered. This caught me way off guard. This was my hometown, where I had grown up.

"Where in Rockville?" I asked, trying to keep the questions flowing. Gonzalez was busy writing everything down.

"Just in Rockville, OK. Why are you asking so many damn questions?"

"Because we want to help you, that's why," I answered. "We need to know these things to help us figure out exactly what to do. I know you're scared. I'd be scared too. You have to understand that Jasmine doesn't care about you. Her pimp doesn't care about you. The guys who try to pick you up, even they don't care about you. Hooking is not a glamorous job, and it's not going to take any of your problems away."

"Is that why you brought me in here?"

"Partly. I know it sounds silly, but Gonzalez, and any other officer from our squad you may meet tonight, care about you. We're not here to just lock you up. We're here to try and get you some help. Do you want us to help?"

"I guess if you can. I just don't know what you can do," she said. "Things are pretty fucking hopeless."

"They're never as hopeless as they may seem, Julie. Trust me, I know," I replied, thinking briefly of my own life. "How old are you?"

"I'm eighteen. Why?" she answered.

"We need to know, so we can call somebody," Gonzalez said from behind me. "There are different places, but some are for adults, and some are for juveniles. Maybe we can call your parents?"

"No way, that's the worst thing you can do," she shouted.

"Why can't we call them?" I asked. "I'm sure they're very worried about you and wondering where you are and if you're all right."

"Because, they threw me out of the house and told me not to ever come back, that's why. That's what got me here in the first place." Julie started crying, her hands again covering her soft, flushed face.

"Maybe we can talk with them. What if we could get them to take you back home?" I asked desperately. I couldn't believe they had actually thrown this girl out onto the street. "Would you do that?"

"There's no way. I've run away so many times before. This was my last chance."

"They're your parents, Julie. I'm sure they love you very much. Maybe if we could just talk with them for a while, we can explain the situation to them," I asked, hoping this was the best route to take at the moment. These situations were extremely shaky, given that her home-life may have been the very reason she was here with us now. We could never be certain what we might get ourselves into when talking about a person's home, such as sexual molestation by relatives, or alcoholic and abusive parents. Nothing was beyond the realm of imagination. But, we'd never know if we didn't at least try.

"They won't take me back. I'm telling you. I've fucked up too many times."

"I can talk to them. Trust me. I've done this plenty of times." I said, lying through my teeth. I had never even attempted this before. It was one thing when calling wives to tell them their husbands had been arrested for soliciting undercover police officers or fucking hookers. However, talking to parents was a completely different animal. I sensed the way Gonzalez was staring at me out of the corner of his eye that he was thinking to himself, "Don't you dare get us in over our heads with promises we can't keep." I really had no clue, but I prayed that I wasn't.

"It isn't worth it, officer. Just finish the paperwork so I can get out of here," Julie said abruptly. "Leave my parents out of this. I fucking hate them anyway."

"Look, we can't let you back onto the street. Not like this. We're going to have to call them anyway," I answered defiantly. "Let's just give it a try. Nothing to lose, right?" For a few moments, the three of us stood silent in the bleak, cold confines of the holding cell. The line had been drawn. Gonzalez and I had made our best pitch, and now it was just a matter of whether or not Julie would break. I don't think any of us expected what happened next.

"Maybe you can just call my mom and tell her that I love her and that I'm OK?" Julie asked in a soft voice. I could barely hear a word she had said.

"That's a good place to start. We can do that for you," I answered, excited at the sudden turn of events. "Wouldn't you like us to say something else to her, as long as she's on the phone?"

"Do you really think you can convince her that I love her and want to come home?" Julie asked, tears still rolling down her cheeks. Despite her tears, I saw a tinge of excitement and hope cross over her face.

"Yes. I think we can." For a moment, Julie's eyes lit up and she smiled. Then it quickly disappeared. "I know we'll do everything we can."

"Here's the number." She handed me a piece of scrap paper which Gonzalez had given her earlier to jot down her personal information for arrest paperwork. I took it in my hand and Gonzalez and I left for our office.

"Are you nuts?" Gonzalez said as we entered our office. "What if she's right and her parents really don't give a shit about her? Huh? What if you made her a promise neither of us can keep? Have you thought about that? Huh? The damage we do here can be devastating."

"You think I don't already know that? I haven't a clue what to do if this doesn't work. But I know we'll think of something. We always do," I said. "How many times have we prayed that maybe just one girl might walk off of the street to look for a better life, instead of just rotting out there before our eyes. I know you've felt that."

"All the time man, all the time." Gonzalez answered shaking his head. "I'm pissed off just like you. And I'm not saying we shouldn't try. I just think we should be careful about the promises we make."

"I know, I know, you're right," I said. I reached for the phone and dialed the number.

"Hello?" A woman answered in a soft, sleepy voice. I was surprised she picked up on only the second ring.

"Hello. My name is Officer Archer. I'm a police officer in Washington, D.C," I said. "I'd like to talk with you for a moment about your daughter Julie. But before I go any further, I want to assure you that everything is fine and she's all right."

"Yeah, what about her?" The woman said. I was shocked by the seemingly lack of concern in her voice. "You do realize that it's almost two o'clock in the morning."

"Yes ma'am, I know exactly what time it is. Listen, I'm sorry to bother you at such a late time, but I'm concerned about your daughter." I hesitated for a moment, unsure of what to say next. I didn't want to come right out and let her know that we found her daughter out on the street hooking.

"Welcome to the club. What's she done this time?" the woman asked. "Did she hurt anyone? Did she hurt herself?"

"No, no, it's not what she's done," I replied, still amazed at her nonchalant attitude. I guess Julie had been right about her parents' lack of concern. I was confused and knew I needed to choose my words carefully. This was no longer about trying to empathize with her, as I had originally hoped. Now, it was going to be a battle of wills, and I had dramatically assumed the role of family counselor. This was a hat I never really wore too well and I figured the best thing to do was to just get it out and hope for the best. "We found her on the street with a prostitute. She was, she was…"

"That doesn't surprise me!" the woman said, cutting me off in mid-sentence. I guess she had noticed me struggling with how exactly to phrase it. I sensed she didn't want Julie coming home, but I felt maybe this was just an initial reaction of frustration, or just plain old shock. This had to be one hell of a blow to any family, and I couldn't begin to imagine how I'd feel if the roles were reversed.

"Ma'am, your daughter wants to come home. She's really upset. I think the best thing is to come and pick her up," I said, believing she had to have some feelings towards her daughter. "This is a difficult time, and this is what's best for her. She needs this."

"We can't do that," she answered.

I was dumbfounded. I never expected this, even though it was an obvious potential outcome, one in which Julie had already forewarned us about. But, common sense said otherwise, and my idealistic sense of right had compelled me to truly believe this was not a viable alternative and would not happen. I just couldn't believe that anyone, under any conditions could leave a child in this situation, no matter how bad it was. Now, I was pinned against a wall of my own making, and with little idea of how to move forward.

"Listen, ma'am. I know this must be rough on you," I said, trying to bring some semblance of sanity back into the situation. "But I just got done spending the last hour talking with her. She's upstairs in one of our holding cells crying her heart out. She says she loves you and wants to come home." The woman on the other end began to sob. Now was the time to increase the pressure. "I have to believe this is genuine and there is a reason why she wants to come home. No matter how bad things are right now, they can get better. Trust me. Please."

"I can't talk with you anymore, sir. I appreciate what you have done, but our therapist has advised us to not take Julie back anymore," she said between gasps for air. Then the phone went silent and I was sure she had hung up on me. I knew now this was not going to end on a good note. I knew this situation was well beyond anything I could understand and I did not have the ability to negotiate Julie back home. Just take a magic marker and write the words failure across my forehead. What in the world had I been thinking?

"Hello, sir?" a man said from the other end of the line.

"Who are you?" I asked politely.

"I'm Julie's father. You can't call us here anymore. Do you understand? You've upset my wife. She can't handle this," he said bluntly. I guess he didn't care either.

"That's fucking bullshit!" I screamed into the phone, completely losing my composure. I tightened my fist as hard as I could, trying desperately to maintain a sense of professionalism.

"This is not our problem anymore," the father said coldly. I despised the calmness in his voice, and I wondered just how many shots of liquor it took for him to wrench his heart out from within his body and then flush it down the toilet. Fuck composure. Fuck professionalism. There is no composure when you have a teenage hooker sitting in a jail cell crying her eyes out, and her parents are on the phone trying to explain to me why it's not their responsibility and that I should just go fuck myself because I'm sitting here on the phone trying to explain to them just how insane this whole fucking situation is.

"You chose to bring a girl into this world, sir. And right now, she's confused and scared and she needs her family," I argued. "Like it or not, she is your responsibility. You are her father. Does that mean anything to you?"

"Listen, I know you think you are doing the right thing. And I appreciate that. But we've been through this before, many times, with our therapist. We have to take a hard line approach now," he answered back. "That's our only hope."

"OK let me try and get this whole thing straight. I have your daughter sitting upstairs in a jail cell. She's cold, hungry, and scared. She's crying her eyes out and wants to go home. If you don't come and get her, she's going right back onto the street where God only knows what will happen to her. And you and your wife don't have the common decency to come and get her. Is that what you're telling me?" I asked, my voice shaking with anger. "That this is your only selfish hope?"

I knew this was bad. I was sure I was fighting to get Julie home because this was what she wanted, and this was the best thing for her. But deep inside, I also wondered if I was just frustrated and only arguing because I had made an asinine promise and wanted so desperately to see it through. I had no idea about anything that predicated how and why Julie felt the need to run away from home, to put herself out into the street or why her parents felt the need to keep her away at this time of need. Maybe it was somehow justified. Maybe I was pressing for an issue that would ultimately be a huge mistake for everyone involved.

"Officer, you just don't understand. We've tried so many times before. We can't take this anymore," the father stated, drawing a defiant line. His mind was made up, and I was sure there was no changing it.

"Don't give me that shit! So you just keep on trying for as many times as it takes. That's the deal. There's always hope. There's always a chance. How can you just give up on your own daughter?" I yelled again. Gonzalez was standing next to me shaking his head, surely feeling my frustrations. I knew, having listened to every aspect of the conversation that he was as angry as I was. I wanted to explain to Julie's father about all the times I had called my parents, sometimes in the middle of the night, asking them for help. About the time I came home after quitting college after only one week with no job, no money, no direction and no idea of the real world. And how, just as my life seemed to be going nowhere, it all suddenly began to come together. How, with the help and support of my parents, I was able to find my place and finally grow up. Had they not been there for me, maybe I too might have ended up on the street doing god knows what.

"Sir, I'm going to hang up the phone now. Please don't call us back," her father said.

"I can't believe this. Don't you dare hang up the fucking phone," I screamed. I couldn't believe I had resorted to cursing. "I can't believe you're going to let this happen to your daughter." I could hear his wife in the background sobbing. I felt so helpless.

"I can't talk anymore. I'm sorry. Thank you for what you're trying to do." He hung up the phone and the sound of the dial tone reverberated through my head. For the next several minutes, I stood with the receiver next to my ear staring off into space. I guess I was expecting him to pick back up the phone and tell me this was some sort of bad joke.

"Motherfucker! Goddamn motherfucker!" I exclaimed as I slammed the receiver against the wall.

"What the hell are you doing, man? Get a grip on yourself and calm down!" Gonzalez yelled as he yanked the phone from my hand. "What are we going to tell Julie?"

"I don't know. I'm still can't believe that...they just hung up the phone," I said. "I can't believe they hung up on me." I sat down. I had never felt so much frustration, so much confusion in my career. I thought of my own parents, and how they would have come for me no matter what the circumstances. "I was certain they would come for her."

"Me too. Julie's not going to take this very well," Gonzalez said, a look of deep thought covering his face. "It just doesn't make any sense."

"I know. I can't tell her. Can you imagine what it must be like to know your own parents won't come to help you when you call out for help?"

"No, I can't," Gonzalez answered, staring into space. "But I think I might have an alternative answer."

"What is it?" I asked.

"Maybe we can take her to a shelter for the night, maybe that place called Sasha Bruce, and let everyone cool down a bit. At least we can buy some more time. Maybe we can try and call Jennifer at the HIPS program and see what they can do. You remember how she said she could help us if we needed it, right?" HIPS is the acronym for Helping Individual Prostitutes Survive, a somewhat new and controversial program established by an ex-prostitute who worked helping encourage and support street prostitutes getting off the street. Over the past year, this program had been very successful. But, they had also been a deep thorn in our side as the constant line between law-enforcement and rehabilitation kept being drawn and then redrawn. Our relationship with them had been quite tumultuous, to the point where philosophically, we were at opposite ends of the spectrum. As police officers, no matter how much we believed in rehabilitation, at whatever cost, we were ultimately bound to enforce the law. As a non-governmental, privately funded public assistance organization, HIPS had the good fortune of not being bound by these same constraints of law and had adopted the attitude that as police officers, we were more a part of the prostitution problem as opposed to being a part of the solution. This caused a riff as we had no other real tool then making arrests, while HIPS tended to lean more towards alternative resources, which quite often meant avoiding arrests altogether. Despite the sight of their van streaking around the city informing prostitutes about our undercover officers and interfering with many of our operations, I respected them greatly. They were, without a doubt, the only real agency that gave a rat's ass about prostitutes, and despite our best police intentions, their only real hope of a life beyond the street.

"Might work," I answered. "But Sasha Bruce House is only for juveniles. Didn't Julie say she was eighteen?" I was sure she had. "And also, remember there's no guarantee anyone from HIPS will even want to work, let alone trust us on this one."

"Yes, I know. She did say she was eighteen," Gonzalez answered. "But we should still give them a call. We've got absolutely nothing to lose on this, and everything to gain. What's that girl's name again, Jennifer? Maybe she can help. Do you still have her number?"

"It's in my wallet," I said reaching into my back pocket, my mind tossing the idea around inside of my head. Gonzalez was right. This was a good plan. "And don't forget, Julie is going to have to volunteer to go. They won't take her unless she is willing."

"Yea, I know. That's going to be the hard part. We're gonna have to convince her that someone can still help her, even though her parents won't."

"See if you can keep her preoccupied while I give Jennifer a call," I said, picking up the phone. "I'll be up in a minute."

"I'll let her know what's going on," Gonzalez said softly. "Good luck." I knew Gonzalez would explain the plan to Julie better than I could. He had this knack for making bad situations often seem much better than they actually were, and he had an unbelievable gift for making people laugh. He also had one of the most positive attitude's I had ever seen.

"Hello?" Jennifer answered. I had woken her up.

"Jennifer? This is Officer Archer, from over at the Third District," I said.

"Hey Archer, how are you doing?"

"I'm good; well, actually, I'm not doing that well. I'm sorry for calling so late, but I have a problem maybe you might be able to help us with."

"OK, I'll do the best I can," she answered. "Does this mean the big bad D.C. police department is finally willing to admit that you need our help?"

"Come on now," I replied. "You know I basically believe in what you're doing. It's a struggle for us as well, but you know we all want the same thing. I wish sometimes we had a little bit more leeway like you."

"I know, I know. One day, we'll figure it all out. Tell me what you have."

"Listen, we just picked up a new girl working the street. I'm pretty sure it's her first night out, and she's really, really scared. Jasmine was breaking her in."

"What's her name?" Jennifer asked curiously.

"Julie," I answered. "Do you recognize the name?"

"No, not off of the top of my head. What does she look like?"

"She's about five three, with a medium build. She's got blond hair and really, really blue eyes," I answered, hoping Susan might know her. That would make things a lot easier.

"I don't think I know her off the top of my head," Jennifer said after a few moments of silence. "So, tell me, what's the problem?"

"We've talked with her for about an hour now. We convinced her to let us call her parents to come and pick her up. Only, there was one slight problem."

"The parents didn't want her?" Jennifer asked, anticipating what I was going to say. "As if those assholes ever do!"

"Exactly, and worse, I promised her I would get her home," I said, feeling more helpless than ever. "I think that was probably not a very good thing to do."

"How old did you say she is?" Jennifer asked.

"She's eighteen. Why?" I responded.

"That's not going to work. We could have taken her to the Sasha Bruce House, but she has to be a juvenile. They won't take anyone over eighteen," Jennifer said, sounding a little depressed. "That would have been the best alternative. At least there, no one can visit without permission. That would alleviate any hopes of her pimp coming tonight to snatch her out."

"Yeah, we already thought of that. We're running out of answers over here. To make matters worse, I've got her here on a bullshit failure to obey charge. As soon as her pimp finds out, he's paying her out, and god knows what might happen then."

"Who's her pimp?"

"I'm not sure. I think Jasmine has a few, so there's no telling who's breaking this one in."

"Well, one thing we do know. You can't let her back on the street. Jasmine will definitely scoop her back up in a heartbeat," Jennifer said. She was right. "And we'll pretty much lose her after that."

"I know. I'm trying, I just don't know what else to do," I answered. "Lock up is not a good option right now."

"How about another shelter?" Jennifer offered.

"We thought of that as well. But any other shelter and she can just leave. Or worse, Jasmine and her pimp can find her. Juvenile is the only place we can safely store her until tomorrow morning," I said, still racking my brain for ideas.

"Listen. Let me give you my pager number. Get her to a shelter and call me back. I'll make sure I'm at that shelter first thing in the morning and we'll get Julie out of here. We'll just have to go with what we got, and pray for the best," Jennifer said. "Maybe she'll stay." I was thankful that I had called her. There was no one in this city that cared more about prostitutes than HIPS.

"OK I'll call you soon," I said quietly. "And, thank you."

"Don't thank me until we get her out, OK?" Jennifer said as she hung up the phone. I set the receiver down and made my way upstairs to the cellblock.

Judging by the sounds of laughter coming from the holding cell, I knew Gonzalez was weaving his magic with Julie.

"What's up, Gonzalez?" I said as I entered into the room.

"Nada. Nada," Gonzalez answered. "I was telling girlfriend over here what the deal is. She understands. And I was telling her some stories about the job."

"I'm really sorry Julie. We tried, but I guess it just wasn't enough. And don't believe a word this man tells you. He loves to exaggerate," I said smiling at Gonzalez.

"I exaggerate? That's, how do you say it, the kettle calling the coffee black? Am I right? Am I right?" Gonzalez stated. We all laughed.

"It's OK. You tried your best," Julie answered in a sad voice. "That's more than anyone else has done for me in a while. I appreciate your efforts." She was trying to laugh, thanks to Gonzalez and his jokes, but I could tell she was still frightened.

"I made you a promise I couldn't keep," I said solemnly.

"But you still tried. I knew they wouldn't come for me."

"There still might be another way. It's a long shot, and requires some luck, but I think it just might work. Are you up for it?" I asked her, assuming she was pretty tired and untrusting of any other options we might present to her. I really kind of expected her to just give up. If I were she, I probably would have given up long ago.

"Yes. What are we going to do?" She answered, a small smile appearing on her face. She seemed to have found a new sense of excitement.

"The first thing we do is process your paperwork and get you out of here. We'll let you out on a personal recognizance. I'll talk with an attorney downtown and get your case disposed of so you won't have to come back to court. That's the easy part," I said.

"I hate to think of what the hard part is," Gonzalez chimed in.

"So do I," Julie said.

"It's not that bad. It will, however, require you to lose a few years in age, Julie," I said. Gonzalez looked at me in confusion. "And you'll have to be a good liar."

"I get it," Gonzalez said shaking his head back and forth.

"I don't," Julie said, shaking her head as well.

"We're going to take you to a shelter. The problem is this particular shelter only accepts juveniles. And you're, unfortunately, not a juvenile. But it's the safest one, so we want to take you there. You'll just have to tell them you're only seventeen years old," I explained.

"OK, I can do that. But once I'm at the shelter, what happens next?" Julie asked.

"A woman named Jennifer will meet you first thing in the morning. She's going to help you."

"Who is Jennifer, and why should I trust her?" She asked defiantly.

"Because she understands exactly what you are going through," I explained. "And she's the best chance you have. You have to trust us."

"Do you really think she can help me?" Julie asked.

"If you trust her, and do exactly what she says, then yes, she can help give you your life back," I said confidently. "But remember, you have to do exactly what she tells you, even if it doesn't make any sense. She knows what she is doing. And most of all, she's your friend."

"OK I'll do it," Julie said immediately. "But I'm scared."

"It will be fine. Jennifer will take good care of you," I said, glancing over at Gonzalez.

"Good choice!" Gonzalez echoed smiling. "Welcome to the rest of your life girl."

It took about thirty minutes to complete the arrest process. I wanted to call Julie's parents and tell them to kiss my ass, that she was going to succeed without their help, but I didn't. I did, however, enjoy the thought for a few brief minutes. Once our paperwork was completed, we called Jennifer and gave her the information. Then we ran our idea through our supervisor Sergeant Frank, who approved the plan. Perhaps other supervisors might have said no, opting for the more conventional approach of saying it's not our responsibility or duty to escort prostitutes to shelters. But not Sergeant Frank, he was one of us. He cared. So I was not at all surprised when he gave his approval and finished it off with a simple "Nice work fellas!" as Gonzalez and I walked Julie to our car.

The drive to the shelter lasted less than ten minutes. Ten minutes to embark on a brand new life. At four o'clock in the morning, there was little of the busy congestion most of these roads saw during the daylight. Surprisingly, the drive was mostly quiet. Julie remained in the back seat, her head tilted against the seat headrest. I'm sure she was sleeping. She certainly deserved the rest. Maybe she was dreaming of what lied ahead. I couldn't even begin to comprehend the emotions she must have been feeling. Gonzalez sat next to me in the front seat, staring out the passenger window. I could tell he was exhausted as well. So was I. I was relieved when I finally pulled our car to the front of the shelter.

"We're here," I said loudly, even though I knew everyone was aware we had arrived.

"Keep your fingers crossed," Gonzalez said to Julie as we exited from the car and walked towards the front door. "Just act natural."

"They have been for the past three hours," she answered giggling. I laughed as well. A small light in the lobby came on as I tapped lightly on the front door. Seconds later, an older black woman answered it.

"Can I help you?" she said as she rubbed the sleep from her eyes.

"Yes, I think you can," I explained as I pulled out my badge and showed it to her. "We're from the Third District. This girl needs a place to stay for the night. I think Jennifer from HIPS might have called to talk with you about her."

"She did. What's her name and how old is she?" The woman asked, peering at Julie.

"She's…"

"I'm seventeen," Julie said cutting me off in mid-sentence. "And you can call me Julie." I gazed at her and smiled. She smiled back with a look that assured me she was going to be all right.

"Come on in, Julie. We'll get you a bed." The woman from the shelter said, waving her in.

"Good luck. I'm sure you'll do very well for yourself," I said as Julie walked past me.

"Thanks again, for everything," she answered, reaching up to place an innocent kiss on my cheek. "You two are the greatest!" With that, Julie walked into the shelter, her chin held up high. A second later, the door shut and she was gone.

"You should be really proud of yourself," I said to Gonzalez. "I think we did all right tonight." I turned and headed towards our car. I didn't want him to see my eyes reddening or the small tear sliding down my cheek.

"Yes, I think we really did," Gonzalez answered following a few steps behind. We got into our car and headed back to our little corner of the city, content that we had finally made a small difference.

The next day, thanks mostly to Jennifer and HIPS, Julie quietly escaped on a plane out of Washington, D.C. and headed for her new life. Jennifer clued me in on the details the following night. Everything that is, except for Julie's destination. Safety reasons required her to keep it confidential. I understood. I knew she would be OK and that was all that I needed to know.

That night, feeling a little overwhelmed, I left work and went home early. Sitting at my desk, I picked up the phone, dialing the number to my parent's house. It was early, nearly 6:00 a.m. After three rings, I hung up, tears swelling in my eyes. After six years as a police officer, I finally broke down and really cried. I wanted to tell my parents how much I loved them, because I knew how fortunate I was to have them. I wanted to tell them I had finally given something back, and that I was OK, because even though they never expressed it, I knew they really worried about me. Life had been hard since the death of my brother, and even though we had each taken on different paths of acceptance, I knew my mom always wondered if I was really doing all right. I wanted to tell them I finally understood what my life was really about, and that my life is a wonderful gift. Most of all, I wanted to tell them I finally understood I had no control over my brother's death, and the guilt was now finally gone. Instead, I sat at my desk for the rest of the night, content to let my tears ease me to sleep.

CONCLUSION

Several days later, I awoke one morning to the sounds of the television set I had left on from the night before. Showering and dressing quickly, I finally set out for the place I had avoided for so long.

Considering I hadn't been here for over twenty years, I was amazed how easily I managed to find my way back. Looking around, I slowly steered my car through the rolling green fields. It's amazing to realize that after the funeral, I had never been able to muster the courage to come back and visit my brother's grave. Maybe I was afraid of what I might see. Maybe I was afraid it was really me who died a long time ago and now I was somehow trapped in some imaginary world of confusion and despair.

I parked my car along the side of the road and exited into the cold, damp morning air. Several nights worth of showers had soaked the ground and left the air with an icy, musty chill that penetrated deep into my bones. A slight breeze gently caressed my face, carrying watery droplets from the distant trees. I quickly made my way across the soggy lawn, my shoes picking up blades of grass along the way. I was careful to keep my eyes focused on the ground, mindful not to step on any gravestones and glancing around for that of my brothers. It didn't take long before I located his grave, and for a brief moment, I was content to just close my eyes and conjure up memories of the funeral that seemed so long, long ago. But none would come. Back then, I was just a child, lost and unsure of what to do or feel. There seemed to be no reality attached to the event, like I had spent the past twenty years living in a dream world with no past. Now, I was an adult, and everything was so different. I was different. I was no longer so confused and the pain had escaped from my body. Although I don't think I'll ever really understand why certain things happen, why some people die so young while others live, I know I've finally found a sense of acceptance, a state of grace, so to speak, and an understanding that it's ok I survived. I no longer felt the agonizing need to live up to the expectations of both my brother and myself. Glancing around me, I realized I was the only soul here. I took comfort in this, as I wanted, needed this to be a uniquely personal time. I knew at any moment, tears would overwhelm my eyes, and a lifetime of holding back would rush to the surface. I glanced down at the stone resting on my brother's grave and carefully read the inscription aloud. It said Bruce Allen Archer. I read the name again, and then again, and again, until I could no longer form the words on my trembling lips. Quietly, I lowered myself to the ground and rested the side of my head against the cold, wet stone.

"It's OK, I'm here now," I whispered softly, knowing no one was around to hear but me. "I know I wasn't there for you, and I am so, so sorry. I know you worry about me, and I wanted to come and tell you I miss you, and I love you. And mostly, I wanted to tell you that I'm ok. I know it wasn't anyone's fault."

I'd like to think the soft chirping noise I heard in the distance was birds, but I know that couldn't be true, because this was winter, and everything was frozen and cold, and all the birds had since left for a much warmer place. But I know I heard something, and it was soothing, and it made me feel like nothing else really mattered right now, except I was here with my brother and I was very much alive and well.

"I'll be back to visit soon, bro," I said as I leaned forward to kiss the earth. I don't really know if it was the rain that suddenly opened up from the sky, or just the tears streaming from my eyes, but I was now completely soaked, and as I raised to my feet I raised my arms and let the cold rain fall against my body, blanketing me in its wet coldness. It felt so fresh and real and clean, and I felt so alive. As I made my way back to my car, I took one last glance across the grass at all the graves and felt, from the bottom of my soul; it's good to be alive. No, it's great to be alive!